Flyways

Flyways

DEVIN KRUKOFF

thistledown press

Thistledown Press Ltd.
633 Main Street
Saskatoon, Saskatchewan, S7H 0J8
www.thistledownpress.com

Library and Archives Canada Cataloguing in Publication

Krukoff, Devin, 1976-
Flyways / Devin Krukoff.

ISBN 978-1-897235-77-5

I. Title.

PS8621.R79F59 2010   C813'.6   C2010-905537-3

Cover artwork: Stevi Kittleson
Cover and book design by Jackie Forrie
Printed and bound in Canada

Mixed Sources
Cert no. SW-COC-001271
© 1996 FSC

FSC

Canada Council   Conseil des Arts
for the Arts   du Canada

SASKATCHEWAN
ARTS BOARD

Canadian   Patrimoine
Heritage   canadien

Thistledown Press gratefully acknowledges the financial assistance of the Canada
Council for the Arts, the Saskatchewan Arts Board, and the Government of
Canada through the Canada Book Fund for its publishing program.

For Kolya, my little bird.

House sparrow
(*Passer domesticus*)

Had the windows been open it might have passed straight through the house: into the living room, between the woman and the television, down the hall to the bedroom, between the girl and her reflection, and out — spiralling up to where the storm is building, though a single cloud has yet to form. This is the dream as the nut-shaped heart goes still and the body falls into the garden.

Samantha

HER MOTHER WAS IN THE NEXT room, tuned to the Weather Channel as usual. All day, every day, it seemed, she did nothing but sit on the sofa, watching a succession of anchors gesture at computer-generated maps. Her hands worked quilting needles, kept warm on cup after cup of strong, black tea, made restless forays across the cushions, as if straining to breathe the air beyond the front door, but the hands were captives of the head, and the head — cocked at a tilt of mild interest, mouth open, eyes seldom blinking — was captive of the weatherpeople.

As the weatherman of the hour droned on, Samantha closed her bedroom door and locked it, before stripping out of her clothes and returning her attention to the full-length mirror. Her bloated face. Her heavy breasts. Her grotesquely-distended stomach.

She applied a tentative pressure and considered the sweet pain of expulsion — how it would feel to pound at herself until her body rejected the foreign presence that had invaded it. For almost a year it had been growing inside of her, stealing her food, her air, her blood. Her prenatal instructor, a praying mantis of a woman named Carmen, had assured her that feelings of disconnection to the fetus were normal. "But when you're holding that baby in your arms," she'd said, making meaningful eye contact with each of the nine girls squatting on exercise mats before her, "when you're looking into its sweet, little eyes, all those negative thoughts will just go away. You'll know that this was *meant to be.*"

Participation in the class had been a condition of Samantha's temporary withdrawal from school. Wednesday afternoons they met in the lower gymnasium at the YMCA, slotted between twelve-and-under ballet and low impact aerobics for seniors. On the way in, small girls in leotards regarded them with fear and awe. On the way out, old women in Lycra shorts passed their judgment with tight, knowing mouths. Six of the girls had arrived at pregnancy through carelessness. The other two had, for reasons Samantha could not fathom, actively sought out motherhood. Dressed in chic maternity wear, these latter girls affected a worldly, philosophical air.

"It's a miracle," they assured one another. "I've never felt so beautiful."

Samantha wondered how they could be so blind.

In grade ten art, she'd seen a slide of a painting called *The Sabine Women*. At the time, she had doubted the impassive expressions of the women in question (each in the clutches of one or several naked Romans). Surely, she'd thought, they would have fought, screamed, wept, begged the men to spare them. Now she understood. You feel cold. You feel nothing.

One instant, it seemed, she was on her back in Karen Tasker's backyard, staring up at the few city-dimmed stars there were to see, the next she was standing in her own brightly-lit kitchen, her mother advancing on her in a rage.

"Where have you been?"

Samantha groped for the words to explain, but all that came to her were images, sensations. A face hovering over her. A searing rhythm between her legs. She gestured vaguely. "He — "

Her mother gripped her by both arms. "Do you know how long I've been sitting here? Three hours! *Three hours!* I've been thinking about calling hospitals!"

As Samantha swallowed the dark thing that had risen to catch in her throat, her father emerged from his bedroom, more hair than skin above his pyjama bottoms: swirling patterns on the back, denser patches on the chest and arms, thick shrubbery around the face and head. He shuffled past without a word and a moment later a forceful flow of urine resounded from the open bathroom door.

At any other time Samantha and her mother would have shared an ironic look and fallen over laughing, but the kitchen had become an interrogation room and her mother was taking her role as household disciplinarian seriously. She steered Samantha to a chair, put on a pot of coffee, and proceeded to lecture her until the first birds began calling outside. When she'd finally been released, Samantha went to bed without gratitude or relief — curled on top of her covers, hands locked between her thighs as she waited for sleep to claim her.

Seven months later, her eyes were ringed with fatigue, a vacant expression having taken permanent residence in her face. Nothing helped. She dragged pillows into her room and propped them under her head, her side, her belly. She'd tried heat packs, cold packs, and a variety of creams and oils. The rare moments when her body was at ease, her mind would not rest, the events of the last year tracking through her brain.

In the beginning, her friends had noted her listless behaviour and she'd blamed her mother. To her mother, she blamed her friends. The bruises on her arms first darkened, then lightened, then vanished altogether. Her torn centre healed. But soon she felt a new pain opening within. The drugstore test only confirmed what she already knew and she resolved to have the problem quietly dealt with. Every time she walked past the "women's clinic", however, (located across the street from a florist and a butcher) she could not bring herself to slow her pace, or even glance in that direction. There would be a receptionist. There would be a waiting room with husbands and boyfriends and stacks of magazines. It was too horrible to consider.

On the date that the organism mutated from flesh and bone into a legally-entitled human being, the decision was taken from her hands. It was going to happen, regardless of how she felt about it, and it would only be a matter of time before her body betrayed her.

She told her parents one evening in early May over dinner, a monotone statement of fact as she sliced open a bright wedge of salmon. They froze, watching her eat.

"Is that supposed to be funny?" her father finally said.

When she did not respond, her parents — first her father, then her mother (with a stifled, hiccupping sob) — set down their utensils and left the table without a word. Samantha finished her meal alone, listening to her mother grieve showily in the bathroom and her father consult his punching bag in the basement. An hour later, her mother sought her out in her bedroom. Her eyes were bloodshot, her hair wild. She wore a stubborn smile and had a manic gleam in her eye. "Okay then. So now that that's all done, let's just sit ourselves down and have a little talk about what we're going to do. Where did your father go?"

"How am I supposed to know?"

A dangerous look flashed across her mother's face. She leaned out into the hall. "Albert!"

His muffled reply came from the basement.

"Can you come upstairs, please?"

"What is there to talk about?" Samantha said.

"Don't you — ! Sammy, *please*." Samantha could hear her mother gearing herself up into a positive space, a Christian space. "I didn't ask to be in this position but we're going to have to deal with it. We're going to have to put our heads together and work this thing out. Have you been to see Doctor Wallace?"

"No."

"Well, then how can you be sure?"

She hiked up her sweater.

"Holy Jesus," her father said from the doorway. "I'll kill him."

Her mother reproved him with an upbeat, clucking sound. "All right now. Let's not get carried away. Sammie just went and made a little mistake. Kids made mistakes, don't they? Lord knows I made a few!" She located a pen and set about compiling a "to do" list, while her husband paced the room, picking up and putting down various objects, as if looking for something to break. He seemed to have only one thing on his mind.

"Who did it?"

She picked at the pimples on her arms.

"Sam."

"I heard you."

"Well?"

She looked away and he held his peace for a minute before exploding again. "Look. All I'm saying is he's got to have a name. I'm not going to . . . *hurt* him or anything, but if he thinks he's getting out of this, he's got another thing coming. If that little son of a bitch — "

His wife's head jerked up. "Albert! Language!"

"Okay, fine. But I'm just saying — and I know I've said this already — but he's got to have a name."

It was a common enough name, monosyllabic, the kind of name you'd expect from an all-star running back with good hands and straight white teeth. In her first trimester, Samantha had seen him most every day at school, shoulders squared away as he lounged in the hall with his teammates. Their barking laughter. A fist striking a locker for emphasis. He had told none of them, she was certain of that. They could never have contained themselves with such explosive information. There would have been knowing looks, snickering, high-fives all around. Which was how she knew that he knew precisely what he had done.

The bead of his cigarette pulsing in the darkness . . .

Out in the living room, the weatherman was making dire predictions. Samantha turned sideways in order to fully grasp her preposterous size in the mirror. She felt like picking up the phone and dialling random numbers. There was no one else to call. When the news of her pregnancy broke at school her friends had swarmed her in the washroom, wanting to touch her, to know what it *felt* like. She'd been buoyed by the attention at first, but then the inevitable questions came.

"It's Troy. Tell me it's Troy."

"Don't *push* her. She'll tell us when she's ready. Besides, Troy is a complete dick. Oh, *sorry*, Sam! It's not Troy, is it?"

"Two words. Brad. Miller. I've totally seen the way he looks at you. It's understandable. He looks at me and I get weak."

"Nicole!"

"What?"

"Do you or do you not have a boyfriend?"

"Oh, whatever."

. . . his voice speaking her name . . .

The fact was, all of them had boyfriends, none of whom could be sufficiently trusted, and her refusal to confide in them left them with no alternative but to align against her; whispering among themselves when they saw her, hissing at her when she passed, a sibilant word that stung like a whip.

Samantha wondered if there was not some truth to the designation. Her mother certainly seemed to think so, having long disapproved of her appearance — her neon-blue hair, the loop of metal she'd attached to her navel on her fifteenth birthday (an ornament her mother did not consent to, and threatened to remove with pliers while she slept). She remembered the "body artist" with revulsion now — forearms sleeved with tattoos, how he handled the skin down there, pinching it numb and swabbing it clean.

"Take a deep breath," he said, and punched the hole through.

. . . his hands . . .

At the time she'd believed his touch to be akin to that of a doctor. Now she knew that not even doctors could be trusted. Her family doctor, a grandfatherly man with tufts of hair in his nose and ears, had manipulated her growing body for sixteen years, but there was something predatory in his smile now, a glimmer of violation in his eyes. Behind the grey hair and medicinal breath, behind the armour of his white lab coat, he was, first and foremost, a man.

The afternoon that Samantha made her desire to change doctors known, her mother had been shopping for baby clothes on the Internet.

"Look at these jammies!" she said.

"Mom, you're not listening. I need a new doctor. A woman doctor."

"How do I do this? Do I click on the basket thingy?"

"Mom."

"Can we not discuss this? Let's not discuss this now."

"Mom!"

In the end, her mother allowed her this one small victory. The people at the Y referred her to a Jamaican-born female doctor, whose easy manner and musical voice Samantha found soothing.

Only one man remained in her life, and she saw him more rarely than usual. When not at work (leaving the house well before she woke, a cartoon elephant on the chest of his coveralls), her father would pound the heavy bag in the basement or play chess across the street with Mr. Gustin. At dinner he hardly spoke to Samantha, seemed to have trouble even looking at her. She didn't blame him. Had it merely been a question of the kind of concentrated weight gain she'd seen in some women — busts or behinds wholly out of proportion to the rest of their bodies — she might have accustomed herself to the change, but she was swelling to the point of breakage. Within her, *inside* her, among all the organs, a tiny skeleton was growing, an additional set of lungs, an additional fluttering heart. It kicked and the skin of her stomach visibly bulged.

. . . his eyes wide open . . .

The idea of adoption came to Samantha early in her third trimester.

"You would rather give him up to strangers," her mother said, needles clacking over a half-made bootie.

"I didn't say that."

"Strangers. Have I been such a horrible mother?"

"You don't understand."

In the next room, the Weather Channel was talking to itself like a mad, unreliable oracle. Her mother set her knitting aside. "What's to understand? You want to give him up for adoption, I'll adopt him. *We* will." She included Samantha's father — who had just come into the room — in an expansive gesture. "Isn't that right, Albert?"

He ducked and shrugged. "Sure."

"Dad! You don't even know what we're talking about."

He shrugged again, muttered something about craving oranges, and fled to the kitchen.

Samantha turned back to her mother. "All I have to do is fall down the stairs. Just let myself trip . . ."

"Sam!" Her mother's hands flew up to her mouth. "Don't say it! Don't you even *think* it."

Once articulated, the idea had taken root and grown quickly in the forcing bed of her imagination. It was not too late. Even now, as she gazed at her reflection, she knew that she had the power to end things. The overhead light lit her face unsparingly. The long escalators at the Valhalla Mall came into her head. A crowd of witnesses. An unfortunate accident. Her mother tapped at the door.

"Sammie?"

"Just a minute."

She rotated her body and saw the position of the fetus, as clearly as through an ultrasound: the head tilted down at forty degrees, the arms and hands precisely detailed, down to the creases in the fingers. Her body registered the seismic disturbance of a twitching limb. She felt nothing for it, less than she might feel for a kitten or puppy drunkenly weaving on unsteady legs.

Her mother tapped more insistently. "Sammie? Are you all right?"

"I said just a minute!"

She could be downtown and at the mall within an hour. The pain did not worry her. Pain was on the way regardless. She was more concerned with what would come after the pain if she failed to act. She had a Hollywood conception of the scenes: a blue-gowned doctor, a red-faced, squalling creature beating the air with its fists, a haggard mother overcome with maternal affection. She would have to take it into her arms and pretend not to see *him* in every feature: the selfish eyes, the hungry mouth, the thick, grasping fingers. She would have to change it, bathe it, feed it, act like she loved it. Surrounded by machines and well-intentioned strangers, she would have to look into its terribly familiar face and come up with a name.

Pulling on her robe, she unlocked the door and opened it halfway. Her mother peered past her, as if suspecting that she was hiding someone else in the room. "Everything all right?"

Samantha shrugged and grunted.

"There's going to be a storm tonight. A snowstorm, they're saying."

"So?"

"I just thought you ought to know."

"Why?"

"I don't know." Her mother hovered in the doorway. She seemed on the verge of saying something else, but nodded to herself instead and headed back down the hall. Samantha closed the door, put a disc in the stereo, and chose the repeat function.

She would wait until her mother was settled, then slip out the back door and take the bus to the mall. From the top of the escalator, she would watch the metal treads roll out flat and lock into place. She would close her eyes and step forward. Her foot would miss the stair. Her hand would miss the railing. When she opened her eyes, she would find herself in a hospital room, far from the maternity ward, and they would have nothing at all to bring her, nothing but relief.

Rock dove
(*Columba livia*)

Pigeon, skyrat, shithawk, gutterbird, ghetto chicken,
flying ashtray. As if in measured response, it jettisons its
payload — mid-flight, without hesitation, without regard for
tact or convention. One pearlescent globule falling. One of
millions. The point of impact left to chance: roofs, pavement,
the unlucky crown of human heads.

TOMMY

THE SONG HAD BEEN WITH HIM for days. A strong chord
progression. A thoughtful opening phrase. A bridge that wandered
off and became almost hopeful before tripping back into a sullen,
bluesy conclusion. Instrumentally, the thing was perfect. All he
needed now were the words. His right hand spanked the guitar.
His left hand tickled. The shadow of his Stetson went up and
down on the lawn. He hummed a slurry nonsense rhyme that
went nowhere. Wanda once told him about a Greek guy in hell,
starving, under a tree filled with fruit that he couldn't quite reach.
That sounded about right. "Wan-daaa," he sang. "I can't get me
no bananaaaas."

Tommy missed getting that kind of information from Wanda
when they were still together and she was in school; things he
could pull out and quote to people at parties. He'd never taken to

reading himself, preferring to have things told to him in stories or in songs. When working on his own music, he found the tune easily enough, but the words tended to straggle behind. Often he had to catch them off guard, snatch them up when they thought he'd lost interest. He tried this now, clearing his mind and meditating on his crop of dandelions.

Had he been inclined to cut the grass, he would have had to free the mower from piles of lumber in the shed, then yank the starter cord until his forearm was sore, then — assuming the engine actually caught — shove eighty pounds of smoking metal up and down the yard in the heat, when he could have been sitting right where he was, enjoying a well-earned day off. What some might call laziness, Tommy thought of as wisdom. He worked enough as it was. He'd been holding the same job for going on eight years, ever since Dalton was born. It was punishing work, but it suited him all right. With his earmuffs and hard hat on, he was free to work on his music, humming to himself as he chiselled a slow passage to hell. He liked the feel of the heavy bit driving through asphalt, the way his palms buzzed for an hour after putting the jackhammer down. His only real complaint was the way the suits looked at him when they passed in their flashy cars: like he was a cow grazing on the side of the road.

But today he was feeling generous towards even the suits. They had families. He had a family. They had kids. He had a kid. In another world they might have found themselves shoulder to shoulder on the bleachers of a football field, cheering on their boys and swearing at the referee. He tilted his face to the sky and summoned the floodlit field. Everything tinged an underwater blue: the crowd, the grass, his orange-and-yellow uniform, the few yards of turf between himself and his opponent. The quarterback scrambling. The target roped into his brain.

His big hands moved between chords. A cloud tracked over the sun and, for a second, he felt like hurling his guitar across the yard. Then he thought about his son and his grip relaxed. Whenever he talked about Dalton, he choked up — in a good way, in a proud way. Wanda had done all the right things, quit smoking, quit drinking, avoided certain foods. Tommy assumed that the problem came from his side of the family. People had always said there was something wrong with him. He laughed too much. He fought too much. His cousin, Gene, had once speculated that he was missing an important part of his brain, the part that told you not to punch the wall *before* your fist met the plaster. Maybe that was true.

His only real accomplishments in life had been graduating from high school and bringing his team to the city finals. His son, whose mind wasn't built for school any more than his body was built for sports, wouldn't have even that. Still, there was no space in Tommy's heart for regret. If someone came to him with a pill or procedure that would have made Dalton the same as other kids his age, he would have told them to go to hell.

The words were coming closer now, but something that sounded like geese honking cluttered his mind. Two white boys heading down the block, dressed like gangster rappers and talking loud. "Hey!" he called, and they started walking faster. "Hey, where you going Vanilla Ice?" They hurried past and he dismissed them, content to have taken out their swagger. Giving up on the new song altogether, he banged through a few heavy metal standards. They were going to rip it up at the Grinder tonight. It occurred to him to wear his old football helmet up on stage, and he chuckled at the idea. The chuckle turned into a deep belly laugh, which he made no effort to hold back. No one who knew Tommy would have been surprised to see him out there, alone on his porch, laughing to himself. He was cruising into a sunny, three-day weekend with money in his pocket. What more could he ask for?

A bird landed on his fence and he held out his hand, inviting it over. The bird flew away. He sighed and decided it was time for his cousin to wake up. Pain flared in his knee when he stood, and for a few seconds he resolved to get back into shape. He pictured the amazement on his neighbours' faces as they watched him stomp past in his jeans and cowboy hat, arms pumping, a lit cigarette in the corner of his mouth. Chuckling again, he headed back inside. The house was a disaster area: empty bottles and cans, improvised ashtrays, a bag of marijuana on the coffee table that had miraculously not been stolen the night before. Tommy propped his guitar on its stand and tried not to think about how he was going to have to clean the place for Dalton's Sunday visit. He banged open Gene's door. "Get up, you bum."

His cousin groaned and pulled the covers over his head. Tommy flicked the light up and down. "Get up! Get up! It's almost supper time!" Gene grabbed a shoe off the floor and threw it at Tommy, who ducked and laughed. He paused and looked at his cousin. "Hey, did I hit you last night?"

Gene burrowed back under the covers. "Yeah, you fucking hit me."

"Hard?"

"Hard enough."

Tommy vaguely remembered the argument, but not what it was about. It couldn't have been important. If it was important, Gene would be in the hospital and he'd be looking for a new roommate. By way of apology, he resisted the impulse to whip the blankets off his cousin and run off cackling. "All right," he said. "I'm going to take a walk. By the time I get back, your ass better be out of bed."

"Yeah, yeah."

"Don't 'yeah, yeah' me."

Back outside, Tommy slipped on his sunglasses and rolled up his sleeves, liking the feel of the sun on his arms. It was his kind of weather: hot with just enough wind to take off the edge; what they called an Indian summer. He wondered if there was such a thing as an Indian winter and, if so, what it felt like. Damn cold, he imagined. Leaning back to counterbalance forty pounds of stomach, he headed downtown. A dog chained in someone's backyard was barking steadily. The sky was pale blue and clear. A hot day on the prairies was often followed by an evening thunderstorm, but Tommy sensed that something more extreme than usual was on the way. Outside the Valhalla Mall, he stopped to listen to a homeless guy playing some complicated jazz on a red trumpet.

"Nice," he said, when the guy stopped.

"That's Miles Davis." The guy pushed his spit valve and blew.

"Yeah?"

"I saw him play once. Hardly moved at all. Bent over his horn like he was praying. And the sounds that came out of that instrument?"

Tommy looked up the street, to where they'd roped it off.

"They're putting on a parade," the guy said.

"What for?"

"Fucked if I know."

Tommy nodded at his case and asked if he had enough for a bottle yet. The guy looked offended. "This is my kid's college fund here."

Tommy laughed and gave him a dollar, before continuing on his way. The avenues between office buildings were crawling with white people on lunch break. Most of them looked down or stepped off to the side when they saw him coming, as if he were walking down the road with a rifle over his shoulder and an afternoon of killing planned. He should have been used to that kind of thing by now, but it never failed to put him on edge. He passed the usual crowd of snobby hipsters outside the Ground Zero café, then strode across the parade route and sent an ironic salute to a cop on a motorbike. He had no conscious destination, but kept going, into another residential area very much like his own, where the houses were small and close together and chain-link fences surrounded most every front yard.

Since he'd left the house, the tune had been on repeat in the back of his mind. It occurred to him now that it might not be a blues song after all. It might be a love song. He slowed it down and gave it a sweeter, less plaintive melody, bobbing his head as he worked it out. A rusty, old station wagon clattered past and honked at him. Tommy looked around. Wanda's place was only a block and a half away. It was not an official visiting day, but he saw no harm in stopping by. In fact, now that he was in the area, it would be rude *not* to stop by. He crossed the empty street slantwise, nervous in his belly but optimistic in his heart. If he just knew how to approach her, he was sure that the night ahead could unfold as it would have ten years ago: doing shots with Wanda and Gene after a legendary show, telling old stories, and feeling like family.

He turned the corner and saw Dalton crouched in the driveway outside Wanda's house, staring at something between his shoes. He could keep himself busy for hours that way, studying some small thing that had caught his attention. Tommy liked to think that he was seeing right into the essence of that thing, coming up with profound conclusions that he might one day put into words. He stopped before his boy and peered down at him. "Hey there, big man."

Dalton looked up and his slack face lifted into a smile that nearly broke Tommy in two. Tommy pocketed his sunglasses and squatted down. "What are you looking at there?" Dalton rocked back and pointed at the fissured cement.

Tommy looked closer. "Oh! Birdshit."

Dalton let out a honking laugh. He was no dummy.

"You tracking this bird?" Tommy swiped it with his finger and pretended to taste it. Dalton squealed and shook his head. "Hmm." Tommy nodded gravely. "About three hours old, I'd say. Heading south. All the way to Hawaii. Better hurry up if you want to catch him." Dalton rolled his eyes and smiled over his crooked teeth. Tommy got a hard lump in his throat. "Yeah, pretty silly. Your mom inside?"

Dalton nodded.

"All right, big man. See you in a bit." Tommy flexed out his bad knee, strode up to the house, and — feeling more like a door-to-door salesman every minute — gave his signature rat-a-tat-tat-tat knock and waited. After a few seconds, Wanda came to the screen door, dressed in her work clothes. Purple pants and vest. A white shirt with puffy sleeves. Tommy used to go to the Casino Dinero just to watch her work. She had hands like a gunfighter, keeping her eyes down and the cards flying, reserving her true self for Tommy and Dalton at home. But now there was no warmth in her eyes at all. She saw Tommy filtered through the past, old mistakes covering him like boils.

"It's Friday," she said.

He shuffled in place and looked at his feet. A foot shorter than him and a hundred pounds lighter, and still she could make him cower. "I was in the neighbourhood."

"You're always in the neighbourhood."

"Yeah . . ." He scratched his nose and jerked his thumb back at Dalton. "Big man's checking out some birdshit."

"What do you want, Tommy?"

"Nothing."

"It's Friday."

This happened every time. He had an idea that he could make things right, or better at least, but she had ideas of her own and was unwilling to bend them. He fumbled at his hands like a stupid, shy kid, suddenly very much wanting a drink. "Can I talk to you for a minute?"

"I'm getting ready for work."

"Just one minute."

Wanda sighed and looked at her watch, likely concluding that standing there arguing with him would burn more time than hearing him out. "All right. One minute."

Tommy let himself in and automatically did the first thing he always did at Wanda's place: looked for signs of another man — a shirt on the floor, a different brand of cigarettes, a handsomer and richer version of himself sitting on the couch watching TV. Nothing was out of the ordinary. He inhaled and detected only familiar smells. It smelled like home.

She disappeared into the bedroom and he called after her. "We're playing at the Grinder tonight. Should be a good time. Got some new tunes. I've been working on this one . . . "

She came out with her hair pulled back in a ponytail. "You came over here to tell me about a song?"

"No."

"Then what?"

"I don't know. I was over at my place, right? And then I was walking along and . . . now I'm here." He pinched his nose and shook his head. What the hell did that mean?

"Have you been drinking?"

"No. See, what I wanted to say was that I've been thinking about you. I mean, I've been thinking about us . . . "

Wanda hadn't moved, but she seemed to be retreating from him. "Are we going to get into this?"

"No."

"Because I'm late already."

Tommy nodded. The urge to drink grew more powerful the longer he stood there. He felt awkward and enormous, the ceiling somehow much closer than it should have been. He leaned against the wall. "So . . . how's work going?"

"Tommy."

"What?"

She folded her arms and looked at him. He coughed and muttered, "Yeah, well, I should probably get going anyway. I've got some stuff to do and — hey!" He made like this great idea had suddenly occurred to him. "Why don't you stop by the Grinder after work. Just for a bit. Leave Dalton with your folks."

"Tommy."

"I know, I know. I just wanted . . . " He laughed and shrugged. "I was just in the neighbourhood, you know?"

When she spoke again her voice was gentler. "We'll see you on Sunday."

"Yeah, okay." He headed for the door, his eyes stinging.

"Tommy?" she called after him. "Are you all right?"

He raised one hand over his shoulder and pushed out of the house. His hands were shaking. The new song was running through his head at twice its original tempo. He never learned. He'd break every finger in his hand and just keep right on punching that wall. Dalton was still hunkered over in the driveway, inspecting the birdshit. Tommy lit a cigarette and waited for him to look up. Everything seemed to depend on him looking up. He waited a full minute, then crossed the yard and headed back downtown. The first line of the song had finally come to him.

American crow
(*Corvus brachyrhynchos*)

Walking with one foot in front of the other, wings folded behind its back, it does not seem to know itself from other pedestrians. This is no idle pacing, but a pursuit of animate prey — a paper bag continually being trampled and kicked away. A hamburger bun skitters out into the street, smeared with bright red, bright yellow. Cars pass without slowing. It leaps out among them, like a diminutive matador in a stampede. Then a second drops from a power line, snatches the prize, and both take to the sky, jostling and tumbling over the café patios until the bun is knocked loose and taken by a third.

Jared

"I'm telling you, Jared, there's only one way to go with this. Immediate, decisive action. The problem is no one's prepared to actually *do* anything. They read the paper, they watch the news, they shake their heads and grumble a little, and then they head on down to McDonald's for a Big Mac and a ten-gallon Coke. They don't even think about where their money's going, or what they're supporting, which is the very status quo they were so concerned about five minutes ago. And even if they're willing to put their money where their mouths are and boycott the big franchises, what's it going to accomplish at the end of the day? It's like spitting on a bushfire. See what I mean?"

"Yeah."

"No, you don't. No offence, Jared, but you don't see, because you're not really looking. If you were really looking you'd be madder than hell. I'm talking rip snorting, flip-over-this-table mad. You'd want to run out and grab the nearest person and shake them and tell them to wake up! See? You jumped when I hit the table. That's good. That's what we need, a reaction. Raise your voice and people start to pay attention. See how quiet the room just got? I'm in their comfort zone and they don't like it. They just want to be left alone with their triple lattes, to, you know, give each other back rubs and talk all quiet and sensitive about the "big issues". Isn't it sad and isn't it this and isn't it that, but, hey, let's go play racquetball. I like Canada. You know why I like Canada? I've never been anywhere else where so many young people are happy to sit around smoking weed, talking big, and doing exactly nothing. Buy organic, recycle, maybe head on down to the protest. You've seen the kind of people that go to those things. They've got their signs and their slogans, their whistles and bongos and glow sticks. They come for the party. Because it's cool to be radical. It's cool to go to a sit-in, which is basically a circle jerk. You might have the odd rock thrower, the clowns at the front pushing at the barricades, but they're just pissing into the wind. Are you with me so far, Jared?"

"I think so."

"Good. Todd told me you're not a big talker. Nothing to be ashamed of. You've come to listen and learn. I respect that. Silence is just another form of argument. You know who said that?"

"Who?"

"Che Guevara. Which reminds me. The other day I'm walking by the Gap and what do I see? A rack of Che T-shirts. I shit you not. Have you read the man's diary?"

"No."

"I'll lend it to you sometime."

"All right. Thanks."

"No problems. We're on the same side here. We both know the stats. We know that forty thousand kids die of starvation every day. We know that half the world lives on less than two dollars a day. We know this. We see it every day on that big flashing box. Genocide. Wham! Torture. Wham! American soldiers in sand-coloured pyjamas. Wham! Wham! It keeps on hitting us, and we don't feel a thing. We're all sitting on our couches with our thumbs snug up our asses. How's the coffee, by the way?"

"All right."

"You want a cookie or something? Muffin? Don't worry, they bake them here. None of that pre-packaged crap. Buy one of those things, you might as well be putting a gun to the head of a Guatemalan orphan and pulling the trigger. I'm not kidding. Ripples spreading out. All right, so before I tell you a little about our organization, I want to stress the fact that nothing leaves this table. I'm only here because Todd says you're a stand-up guy, and so far I have no reason to doubt him. You're a university man, right?"

"Sort of. I'm taking some time off."

"Working?"

"Well . . . there's nothing out there for me right now."

"Over-educated and underqualified. The plight of your generation, buddy. So you're living at home?"

"Just for awhile."

"Hey, nothing to be embarrassed about. You know what the average age for leaving the home is these days? Twenty-eight. You're what, twenty-two?"

"Twenty-six."

"Anyways. You're not to blame. It's just one more symptom of this global crisis we're in. Not enough jobs to go around, unless you're prepared to work for slave wages with zip benefits, am I right? So what else can you tell me about yourself? Do you have a girlfriend?"

"Um . . . is that relevant?"

"Hey, we're just talking here."

"Well . . . it's complicated."

"And how long have things been complicated?"

"Four years."

"Jesus. Cut her loose, buddy. Best thing you'll ever do, I can promise you that. But, getting back to the subject at hand, would it be safe to say that you lean pretty far to the left, politically speaking?"

"Sure."

"And from a socialist point of view, do you think there's a single party out there worth voting for?"

"I guess not."

"What makes you say that?"

"Well, they're all politicians, right? No real change is going to happen no matter who gets in."

"What sort of change are we talking here?"

"You know. With the poor and the health care situation . . . "

"And that's just at home. Head overseas and the real fun starts."

"Yeah."

"I'm happy to hear you say that, Jared. Most middle-class folks don't see the big picture. They just go with the flow, keep to the status quo. They might seem political, but all they really care about is listening to the right music, wearing the right clothes, learning the secret handshakes. Think it's different in university crowds? Don't make me laugh. You were going for what? English Lit?"

"Psychology."

"All right. So let me see if I can guess how things went down for you. You're trucking along pretty good. Almost got your degree. Career's mapped out. School plus work equals mucho dinero. Wife, kids, the whole shebang. The thing is you're *tired* of listening to your profs go on about Freud and his cigar. And at the same time you're starting to catch a whiff of the kind of shit that's going down in the world. Everyone around you seems to think that everything's fine and groovy, but your common sense tells you that things are obviously not fine and groovy. So you drop out of school. Call it stress. Tell your dad, who is more than a little pissed. Say you'll go back next year. Meantime, you go to some meetings and rallies, and from the sidelines you can see how half-assed it all is. "Come on, Betty, let's hold ourselves a little candlelight vigil." It's like they *want* to fail. It's like you're the only one who sees that their tactics have to change if they want to get anything done. And then you meet Todd. You and Todd get to talking, and you start to realize that you're not as alone as you might think. Is that about right?"

"Yeah."

"Well I have to tell you, Jared, you've found us at an exciting time. It's been a long, hard struggle, but things are finally starting to come together for us. Pretty soon our organization is going to be on everyone's mind. But it's not about us, Jared. It's about *them*, all those poor, dark-skinned, non-Christian folks who've been getting the shaft since the Crusades. You're Lebanese, right?"

"On my dad's side."

"So here's a perfect example. Beirut in fucking ruins. Think the Americans had nothing to do with that? How about Rwanda, Indonesia, Iraq? The mind boggles. You want a refill? You're good? Okay, so I'm sure Todd told you this already, but just to recap, the focus of our organization is international. Yes, domestic issues are a problem. Yes, the environment's a problem. But what's more of a problem, an overlong wait for heart surgery, some missing trees that we're going to feel the hurt of in a hundred years, or the fact that twenty thousand people are going to starve to death? Today. And tomorrow, and the day after that. See, the problem with the mainstream left is that it tries to take on all the issues. Take on all the issues and you get bogged down, you get slow. Drop some of that baggage and you start to pick up speed. You just might pick up enough speed to plough through all the bullshit. So, we narrow our focus, that's the easy part. The tricky part is getting our message across. So, let's take a hot button issue as our model there. Israel and Palestine. You know the situation?"

"I think so."

"David and Goliath, right? Duking it out since before you were born. But it only starts to get attention around the world with . . . ?"

"Suicide bombers."

"Bingo. All of a sudden peace talks start happening, and the pressure's on to calm things the fuck down, because this looks bad. The problem is Israel's more or less in control. They tighten up the border, take a hit now and then, and hit back hard. Tanks, jets, the full meal deal. But let me ask you something. What do you think would happen if Israelis were the ones strapping explosives to their chests and hopping onto city buses? I mean, what if they started attacking *themselves*? Not because they felt threatened, but because they were moral people who disagreed with the way their country was handling things. And if it did go down that way, if the pressure was coming from *inside*, how long do you think it would take for a serious shake up? How long before Israel starts rethinking its policies in a big way? Which leads us to a sticky question. Would it be worth sacrificing a handful of your so-called countrymen to save hundreds, maybe thousands, on both sides in the long run? Well? What do you think?"

"I don't know."

"Let me put it another way. Take out the countrymen part. Would it be worth sacrificing a few dozen lives to save a few thousand?"

"In theory?"

"I'm not talking theory, Jared. I'm talking brass tacks. Is it worth it?"

"Could you be sure that less people were going to die?"

"There's no such thing as a sure thing. All you can do is play the odds. And in this case the odds, I'd say, would be overwhelmingly in your favour."

"Then, yes. It would be worth it."

"You see, this is why Todd sent you to me. You're a realist. Would it be nice to save the world by holding hands and singing happy songs? Sure it would. Is it going to happen? Not in this life. Listen, you want to move? Let's move. Let's sit outside. Take advantage of the sun while we can. They're forecasting snow tonight, did you hear that? Global warming. Things don't just get warmer, you know. Everything's out of whack. Over there, in the shade. I don't want to sound melodramatic, but you never know who's listening. Speech might be free, but you could end up paying for it down the line, if you know what I mean. Say the T-word out loud these days and people's ears tend to perk up."

"T-word?"

"Terrorism."

"Right."

"What are your personal feelings on the subject, Jared?"

"My feelings?"

"Are you inclined to see things in black and white? Cowboys and Indians? Or are you open to the complexities of the subject."

"I'd say I am. Or do. See it as complicated."

"Any intelligent person does, Jared. Evildoers versus Lovers of Freedom? Give me a break. The people we call terrorists aren't crazy. They're not killing for the sake of killing. They have reasons for doing what they're doing and, believe it or not, most of the time they're pretty good ones. It takes a strong person to commit to that level of action, a person with a broader moral vision. You look uncomfortable."

"I've just never heard anyone talk about it like that before."

"Of course you haven't. It isn't fashionable. But just because something isn't fashionable, does that make it wrong? Think about that. Think about what it's going to take to turn this world around. It's going to be hard. It's going to take sacrifice. And yeah, it's going to get ugly. But what are things now? Sunshine and roses? Look at all those people out there in the street. Everyone caught in their heads, worrying about their shitty, little problems. Is my wife cheating on me? Is my boss going to fire me? Is that homeless guy going to touch me? On they go. What do you think it would take to open their eyes?"

"I don't know."

"Nine-eleven didn't do it. Everyone just huddled together, not giving a thought to the why of it. Not for one second considering that we might have brought it on ourselves. What would it take? Ten more attacks? Twenty? Bodies everywhere, arms, legs, brains, people screaming, fucking chaos. Do you see it? Because it's happening all over the world, as we speak, as we sit here sipping our coffee, as they set up their fucking parade or whatever they're doing over there. I'm sure you saw the news last night. Guy walks into a mosque in Iraq and *blammo*. Twelve people dead. I don't know about you, but it makes me mad. And you know what makes me maddest? Not that twelve people — thirteen if you count the bomber — are dead, but that no one over here stops to wonder why, so it's just going to keep happening. It's easy to shrug off a threat when it comes from another country, another religion, another race. Fucking barbarians we say, and the wagons keep circling. But what if it came from one of their own? I know what you're thinking. McVeigh, right? Shit kicking, paranoid, gun freak. Kazinsky. Wild eyed mountain man hearing little voices in his head. What those guys lacked was some legitimacy. Now, I'm not saying there's nothing wrong with what they did. But what if they had an intelligent, clear-eyed agenda?

What if they had thousands of normal, taxpaying citizens behind them? What if they had political backing? Celebrity backing?"

"Do you?"

"This is just a theoretical, Jared. All you need to know is that we're a serious organization with a global agenda. But I'll tell you what. I trust those big boys making the hard decisions one hundred percent. I'm talking with my life."

"Can I ask you something?"

"Shoot."

"Where do you fit into things?"

"Strictly recruitment. There are six of us in total, always on the move, always looking for new talent. Ninety-nine percent of the candidates don't make it this far. That's something to be proud of, Jared. I look at you and you know what I see? A man I can trust. But trust works both ways. The organization trusts you with certain information, you trust the organization to make all the right moves. Nothing is done without the most careful consideration. They hash things, rehash them, look at them from a thousand angles. It can be frustrating how slow the process is, but, when we finally move, it's going to turn some heads and shake up all the right people."

"Sorry, but what's the agenda again?"

"That's all right. It's so simple you could miss it. Our agenda is to do whatever we can to help everyone in the world who's being harmed by the foreign policies of the United States and its allies."

"And what would I have to do?"

"I'm not going to lie to you, Jared. On the surface, it isn't going to look like much. Todd tells me you have a car?"

"Yeah."

"So, basically, you'll be a driver. Sometimes you'll deliver a package to a certain address. Sometimes just a message. We don't use the telephone or the postal service for obvious reasons."

"What kind of packages?"

"Oh, I know what you're thinking, but believe me, and no offence here, you wouldn't be trusted to transport anything major. No, you'll find the deliveries are pretty mundane. Groceries to a party engaged in surveillance. Books, personal items. You'll be one of the connecting points between people who, for security reasons, are never supposed to meet."

"Synapses."

"How's that?"

"Gaps in the brain. Information jumps between them."

"See, this is why we're interested in you. Do I know what a sin-axe is? I do not. But I've been doing most of the talking here. What do you think? Does this sound like something you'd be interested in being a part of?"

"I think so."

"Man of few words. But, seriously, you should think about this pretty carefully."

"You want me to think it over."

"Well, yeah. But I'll need to know pretty soon. I'll need to know pretty much now, actually. I've got to catch a flight to Montreal where I'm meeting another potential tomorrow. Sorry to rush you, that's just how it is."

"Well, it sounds . . ."

"Exciting?"

"Kind of."

"It isn't, really. But at least you'll be doing something worthwhile for a change. Not sitting on your ass moaning about how there's nothing to do. You'll be standing up to be counted."

"Would I have to meet anyone else?"

"Nope. I get the final say-so and I say you're the man for the job. You give me the thumbs up and things start moving. Your first delivery will happen tonight."

"Tonight?"

"Denny's. Midnight. Package is in the car."

"But, tonight?"

"Both feet, my friend. Only way to go. Listen, I've got to jet or I'm going to miss my flight. What's the verdict? Are you in or are you in?"

Loggerhead shrike
(*Lanius ludovicianus*)

Behind the strip mall, the two are briefly joined: the songbird
with the mind of a hawk, the field mouse merely terrified.
The release above the fence is deliberate and without malice.
A horseshoe toss. A precision bomb. The mouse writhes as
it falls, attempting to thrash out the mechanics of flight, but
the barbed wire rushes up to meet it, allowing the bird to
descend at its leisure.

Beth

"He's a sick man!"

The man in question loomed behind his daughter in thick
wraparound sunglasses, hands clamped to his walker. "I am a sick
man," he said.

Beth tried to maintain a neutral face. "I understand that,
but — "

"He's a dying man!" the woman said.

"I am a dying man!" the old man repeated, voice rising.

"I understand that, but unfortunately the procedure is — "

"How can you stand there?" the woman said.

"If you'll let me finish, ma'am. The procedure is that once a
delivery is attempted, the package comes to the nearest postal
outlet. Now the paperwork says that delivery *was* attempted on
the twentieth — "

"How's he supposed to answer the door? Look at him! He's half blind! He's ninety-two years old!"

"I am ninety-two years old," the old man proclaimed.

Beth wished he would just tip over and die, then.

They came in different guises (the fumers, the sarcastics, the explosives) and employed different moves (the sigh, the groan, the eye roll; hands splayed on the counter, pounding the counter, or spasming in the air like wounded birds) but they all had one objective: to seek blame. They had no idea what mailing a letter from one city to another entailed. They seemed to think that public mailboxes functioned like teleportation devices, instantly whisking their letters away. As if there were not dozens of hands for every piece of mail to pass through in the process: bags, trucks, and sorting machines. And when the occasional letter went astray or got the slightest bit delayed, what did they do? March right down to the post office to deliver the full responsibility to a single employee in a blue vest. As if by donning the uniform of the postal service, you *became* the postal service. Her persecutors were hateful caricatures of themselves, portraits of illogic that everyone in the room but themselves knew to be in the wrong. The accusations she was presently facing, for instance, were far too outrageous to be taken personally. Still, it felt awfully personal to have someone standing three feet away, hollering at you; a stranger who knew nothing about your life at all.

Her blood sugar seemed to have plummeted all at once. "It's regrettable," she said.

"That's it? That's all you have to say?"

Beth grew aware of a dim pulse, which she confused with her heartbeat for a moment, before realizing that she was hearing the drums from a marching band. As it did every year, the city was staging a parade in its own honour. The anticipation of the event, combined with the dire weather forecast for the day, had spawned a curious tension in the office. By giving voice to that tension, the old man's daughter was merely heightening it (as evidenced by the vigorous foot tapping and watch glancing going on behind her). Jackie and the new girl had gone on lunch break twenty minutes before, and the moment Beth found herself alone (*because* she was alone, it seemed) the place had filled up; customer after customer coming in to join the substantial queue that had formed behind the old man, who appeared now to have fallen asleep on his feet, a string of saliva hanging from his open mouth. Had his daughter been truly concerned about him she would have concluded her business by now, but she was leaving him where he was as a kind of object lesson.

Perhaps she thought Beth was so inordinately happy that she required an illustration of true misery. Beth required no such illustration. She had been working in a job she hated for twenty years. She injected insulin into her body three times a day to counteract the effects of a disease that was expected to kill her before she had a chance to retire. She had sworn off dating after a string of failed relationships and would likely die alone, with a drawer full of impersonal correspondences from her Indonesian sponsor child. But who was yelling at whom here? And how long could she be expected to maintain her composure, delivering these robotic platitudes?

Her glucose pills were close at hand but she did not reach for them yet.

"I understand your dilemma ma'am," she said. "Perhaps in the future you should secure a private courier and inform them of the precise nature of your situation." She could not prevent a note of irritation from entering her voice, which was, of course, just what the woman wanted.

"Oh, you are heartless," she hissed, quaking with rage. "Do you know what's in this package? His medicines!"

"My medicines," the old man moaned, not asleep after all — hunched there like a sick old bird. He put Beth in mind of her own grandfather, who had only recently, at her insistence, acquired electricity, running water, and telephone service. What he suffered, he suffered in silence. Not like this evil old man with his harridan daughter. They had to drag their troubles out and set them up on display for the world to admire.

With dwindling patience, Beth explained (for no less than the third time) that once she got the old man's signature they could take their package and be on their way.

"A signature!" The woman threw up her hands and delivered a broad look around the room, as if expecting all the other customers to rally behind her. "A signature, she says! You expect a blind old man to come all the way down here for a name on a piece of paper! How dare you!"

"How dare *you?*" Beth shot back.

The woman sucked in her breath, nostrils flaring. This was the reaction she had been waiting for. "So! You're going to get rude with me now. You all heard that, didn't you? You heard her curse me out?"

"Rude," the old man said.

"I've never been so offended. I might just have to file a complaint."

Beth had hardly raised her voice, let alone cursed her out. Now, however, she was having trouble refraining from striking the woman.

The old man had tilted his head up and seemed to be sniffing the air. His daughter turned and cooed to him. "We're just going to take a few steps now. There's some papers here. You need to make your mark. I'm putting a pen in your hand." The old man's head wobbled. He gripped the pen and made a slash across the page.

The woman glared at Beth. "Shame on you."

Beth managed a tight smile, her body screaming for glucose. "All right then. Have a nice day." She shoved the package across the counter and looked to the next person in line.

"Heartless," the woman whispered. For a moment it appeared that she was not going to leave. Then she turned and forced her father to match her pace in an attempt at a stormy exit, jostling a revolving rack of postcards that rocked and nearly fell over. "Heartless!" she shouted once more from the door.

Only after she'd gone was Beth aware of how hard her heart was pounding (much more rapidly than the drums from the parade), her hands trembling as she cleared away the old man's paperwork. She shook out two tablets from her pill bottle and took them without water. The instant Jackie and the new girl got back she intended to step out for a cigarette, never mind how many people were waiting in line. "Unbelievable," she said to the next customer, a young man with a detailed tattoo on his forearm: a bald eagle clutching a globe in its talons, an American flag rippling behind. "Have you ever seen anything like that?"

"Uh . . ." He looked over his shoulder, then back at her. "I need stamps."

Of course she would have no time to collect herself. Whatever happened in that room, barring police involvement, she was expected to remain in character, a friendly, efficient clerk. The tattooed man belonged to another category of customer altogether, for whom clerks were little more than automated tellers. They were almost worse than the aggressives, and certainly more common. The pulse and rattle of drums was growing louder. Through the plate glass window, Beth could see the old man's daughter haranguing a man in uniform over a parking ticket. Perhaps there was some justice in the world after all.

The young man's letter was bound for the United States. She held out her hand and asked if she could see it.

"Why?"

"So I can weigh it."

"All I need is stamps."

"I understand that sir. I have to weigh it first."

He gave the letter up, reluctantly, and she put it on the scale. Out on the street the woman was waving her parking ticket at anyone who happened to be passing by. The old man clung to his walker, his head bent to the ground.

"Military?" she asked the young man, determined to be friendly. Her composure was returning as the glucose did its work.

He looked up sharply, from a handful of quarters. "Excuse me?"

"Your tattoo. I was just wondering . . . " She trailed off and shook her head. This day was never going to end.

But of course it would end, that was one thing she could be sure of. The days were getting noticeably shorter as they moved into autumn, the tilt and spin of the world passing the sun through the sky in shrinking parabolas. After work she would go home and make a simple dinner for herself. She would eat in front of the television, tidy up the kitchen, water the plants, and read for an hour before bed, conscious of nothing but the lack of another human being in the house. Across the city, the strident woman would be in similar position (there was no question she was single). Perhaps she and Beth were perfect for one another. They could quit their jobs and move out to the country together, live on her grandfather's farm, all four of them — the women out strolling through the fields, learning the names of flowers and birds, while the old men played backgammon in the kitchen. Only a glimmer of this went through Beth's mind as she hunted for stamps in her drawer. Finding none, she turned to get some from the back.

"Where are you going?" the young man said.

"I beg your pardon?"

"I just wanted some stamps."

"I understand that, sir. I was about to get them."

"Can I have my letter back?" he stammered.

This was why postal employees went on rampages. Exactly this.

The strident woman and her father were gone. The parade had come closer. Beth could make out a simple, repetitive melody. "Of course," she said. But when she held it out, the man stepped back, eyeing the video camera in the corner of the room. The stasis among the other customers quivered and shook one voice loose.

"Guy," a beefy man said. "What's your problem?"

Beth closed her eyes. He had not said a word through the earlier confrontation but, now that she did not feel the least bit threatened, he evidently felt compelled to come to her defense. How heroic. Now the testosterone would flare. That was how these things happened, all the pent-up tension discovering an outlet, the volcano suddenly alive. It was the same with the blind old man's daughter. It was the same with Beth herself — compulsively shearing lovers from her life with rash words that could not be retracted.

"Sir?" she said. "Would you please step back in line?"

Her words were like pebbles off the windshield of an accelerating car. The man's course was set, his hands clenched at his sides. But just as they were about to meet, the young man did something surprising. He turned around and walked away, walked straight out of the building, leaving his letter behind with the postage unpaid. The beefy man returned to the line, obviously pleased with himself, and the conveyor belt jerked back into motion. The next customer, an obese woman with a limp, stepped up to the counter.

"My, my, my," she said. "It's a zoo in here today!"

Beth would not have qualified the observation with "today". She was still holding the young man's envelope. It had no return address and was addressed to one Olivia Nightingale in Gulf Breeze, Florida. For the first time in her career, Beth broke protocol. She secured a roll of sixty-five cent stamps from the back, affixed two to the young man's envelope, and placed it with the outgoing mail.

Blue peafowl
(*Pavo cristatus*)

An appreciative sound from the audience. Camera shutters open and close. The cumbersome tail rustles and quakes. Each feather holds an eye of Hera's watchman. The body is the mount for a Hindu god. Yet the object of its desire seems embarrassed, turned away as if from something ludicrous and naked.

James

Mrs. Ingram moved from window to window, fanning herself with a zoo leaflet and smiling at nothing at all. "Stay together now," she said, without much conviction. Since taking an unscheduled period of leave the year before, everything Mrs. Ingram said or did was without conviction, showing only the slightest awareness of the twenty-eight grade six and seven students in her charge. Today, for instance, she did not seem to realize that half the class had gone missing the moment they got off the bus.

A low-frequency warbling issued from her purse, and she fumbled for her cellular phone. "I can't talk . . . No . . . You *know* how I feel about it . . . I *do* care . . ." She turned away and James lost the thread of the conversation. His classmates were tapping at the floor-to-ceiling windows. The big cats did not respond — sprawled on the concrete as if they'd been drugged or shot. Lawrence Lutz came over and James willed him not say anything.

"Hey, James," Lawrence said.

James kept his eyes on the ground. One of the tigers seemed to raise its head slightly — tongue out, eyes in slits. Having put her phone away, Mrs. Ingram made a visible effort to compose herself before wandering out of the cat hut and back into the blinding sun. The temperature that week was hitting record highs, which was, she explained, why the cats had been so lethargic. She put her hands on her hips and looked around.

"Aren't they used to the jungle?" one of the girls asked. Mrs. Ingram looked at the girl and gave a single nod, as if merely to confirm that she was exactly where she should be.

"Why are the cages so small?" another girl asked.

A troubled groove appeared on Mrs. Ingram's forehead. "Well, I suppose they like it that way. It's nice and cozy. Like a den." She shaded her eyes and rotated her upper body. "We're looking for the desert dome." Panic crept into her voice. "Can anyone see the desert dome?"

One of the girls helpfully pointed out the only dome-shaped structure in the vicinity and Mrs. Ingram forged ahead. A dark bank of clouds was moving in from the north. Lawrence pulled up alongside James. "She's wrong, you know," he said. "They don't like to be penned up. No animal does. They might get used to being penned up, but that doesn't mean they like it."

A smell was coming from him — not unpleasant, but unusual. James stepped up his pace. An old security guard ushered them into the building, where the air was actually cooler; crags and foliage artfully arranged around a narrow walking trail to provide an illusion of distance, everything tan and washed out beneath octagons of tinted glass. At new bits of flora or fauna, Mrs. Ingram stopped to read the information plaques in a soft, halting voice.

The girls seemed to sense her vulnerability and clustered around her.

Lawrence rubbed the back of his neck and breathed through his mouth. His proximity inspired violent thoughts in James, who had begun to feel nauseous and lightheaded.

Mrs. Ingram squinted down at her feet. "Desert tortoises live in burrows in the ground."

When Lawrence moved up to the railing to have a closer look, James ducked into a door with a stick man in a safari hat on it. The bathroom was empty. He took refuge in one of the stalls, bolted the door, and sat on the toilet with his pants up. After a minute, the nausea began to pass. He studied the graffiti on the cubicle walls: names, jokes, improbable penises and triangles of hair. Layers of new paint concealed old acts of similar vandalism. Scraping it away, he thought, would have been like archaeology; new messages revealed at each layer, until you got down to the original "Fuck you".

The bathroom door swung open and hissed shut. James held his breath as a pair of adult-sized grey Reeboks crossed the room and took the stall next to his own. He listened to the unzipping of fly, the swish of pants coming down, and the toilet seat banging against the toilet bowl. The man sighed. Other than the white noise of the ventilation system and the trickle of water in the urinals, the room was quiet. James swallowed, certain the man could hear the click in his throat. After awhile, sounds began to come from next-door, sounds of effort. Then — *plip* — matter colliding with water. James sat utterly still. More grunting, followed by more collisions. Plips, plops, and the occasional more resonant *ploosh*. Abrupt *pfahhhs* of escaping air. The toilet seat creaked as the man leaned to improve his angle. Smells began to come to James, terrible smells. What kind of person, he wondered, could make such smells? The man hammered the toilet paper roll, and his imagination was forced to play with the prolonged, frictive sounds of wiping. Then he barked the phlegm from his throat, flushed with more violence than seemed necessary, and left the bathroom without washing his hands.

James counted to ten before emerging. The class had moved on. He backtracked towards the entrance, opposing the natural flow of foot traffic, but several wrong turns led him into unfamiliar territory. A black-lit corridor walled in by terrariums. Flying mammals, rattlesnakes, and scorpions. Walking quickly, his eyes still adjusting to the darkness, he ran into an employee in blue coveralls who steadied him with a hand on each arm.

James stared at the man's feet. Grey Reeboks laced up tight. In the nearest terrarium a beetle with the look of a polished shoe scuttled from one hole to another. The man released him and asked if he was okay. James nodded. "Are you lost?" James shook his head. He had yet to look the man in the face. "You've got to be careful in these tunnels," the man said. "Some kids have gotten hurt in them."

"Yes, sir."

"Are you here by yourself?"

James recalled a scene from a safety video he had been shown in early elementary school. The villain squats before a young girl opposite a chain-link fence to utter that exact phrase, in that exact way. The frame freezes and a caption appears over the scene: *Never say you're alone.*

He looked up at the man. Beige coveralls. A wild beard concealing the lower half of his face. "Yes," he said. "I'm alone."

The man appeared puzzled. Before he could say anything else, James turned and fled.

Gradually, things became familiar again. He made it to the building entrance and raced past the old security guard, who called after him, "Change your mind, son?"

The clouds that he'd glimpsed on the horizon minutes before had moved in to cover much of the sky. The boys from his class were roaming the grounds in small, hooting gangs. He looked at his watch. The bus would not be leaving for another hour at least. Colour-coded animal tracks on the pavement led him to a low building with a thatched roof. Inside, beyond a series of placards chronicling the life and work of Dian Fossey, two silverback gorillas stood in adjacent pens, glaring at one another through a cracked Plexiglas window. James was wondering about those cracks when the smaller male suddenly battered the glass with both fists. The larger male calmly watched him, then paced the circumference of his pen, and threw his shoulder against the adjoining wall. The impact boomed through the building. The assembled tourists jumped back. The large silverback stared out at them, at *him*, James felt, with intelligence and disdain, before joining a group of females who appeared bored with the whole affair.

James thought of his father. How that summer he had come home early on the worst possible day. How he had walked straight to his son's room and flung open the door, as if already knowing what he would find.

The drama between the silverbacks was over. The tourists laughed and spoke in loud voices to reassure one another. James went out a side door and followed a covered walkway to the aviary, where for the first time that afternoon he began to relax. He felt at home among the birds, sensing no judgment, or any real awareness of him in their fierce, dispassionate eyes. If it was true, he thought, that they had evolved from reptiles, there must once have been a creature that was exactly half-bird, half-reptile. He wondered why such an animal had not survived, why it seemed they had to be one or the other — warm or cold blooded; flying or crawling; feathers or scales.

He lingered in the aviary as long as he could, before reluctantly going back outside. The wind was still blowing hard and the sky had grown very dark. Employees were battening up the pens of the more vulnerable animals, and many of the visitors were hurrying towards the parking lot. James stopped beside the elephant walk, where a male and two females had clustered together like cows in a storm.

"It's unnatural. Keeping them together like that."

Lawrence had come up behind James and was standing with his arms crossed, shivering in his T-shirt. James looked at him. "In the wild," Lawrence explained, "the males only stay with the herd during mating. The rest of the time they go off on their own." Over his shoulder, James could see Mrs. Ingram heading for the school bus, her hair loose and blowing, four girls from class trailing behind. Lawrence stepped up to the fence and gripped the high, iron bars. James stared at the back of his head: the feathered hair, the groove running down his neck.

Lawrence turned around. "Are you mad at me?"

James flushed and looked away.

"Is it about this summer? Because — "

"Shut up."

Cold rain angled down, striking transparent spots into Lawrence's shirt. "It's not a big deal, you know."

"I said shut up."

"My dad says it's normal."

"Your dad?"

"It doesn't mean — "

"You told your *dad*?"

The fact that Lawrence's father not only knew what he'd done, but *approved* of it, was more than he could take. He lashed out, caught Lawrence in the face with his open hand, and sprinted away. The wind carried him to the far end of the grounds, where he stopped, drawing in painful, sobbing breaths. Wadded paper and plastic cups skittered past. The desert dome gleamed in the strange light. In the doorway of one of the service entrances, the man with the grey Reeboks was smoking a cigarette and watching the sky. He spotted James and raised a hand in greeting.

James backed up against a chest-high concrete wall. The man started walking towards him, smiling, sending his cigarette spinning off into the rain. Without thinking, James hoisted himself up onto the wall. On the opposite side, a drop of fifteen feet led to the sunken floor of the bear den. The silhouettes of people were visible in the windows of the underground viewing area, though the den itself appeared to be empty. James dangled his feet over the edge and looked over his shoulder. The man was running now, eyes wide, one arm extended as if to shove him or to pull him back.

FRANKLIN'S GULL
(*Larus pipixcan*)

Wheeling above the landfill, as if above the ocean. As if rats and flies were crabs and sea lice. As if dirt and mould were sand and kelp. As if the dozer shaping drifts was the moon forcing the tides. The buildings of the city are not distant, metal bins behind each like fetid ponds.

MIGUEL

THE FIRST THING THAT HE NOTICED was the smell. The second thing was Cadenza, propped in her armchair with her head tipped back and her mouth agape. The apartment lights were off, the curtains drawn. He closed the door, crossed himself, and approached his aunt's lifeless body, feeling no sadness, merely relief. In the five years since his mother's death, he had considered it his duty to pay weekly visits to Cadenza, in a neighbourhood he visited far too often in the course of his work — collecting people who had been done physical damaged (most often by other people) for transportation to the emergency ward at the General Hospital. For Miguel, these visits with his aunt had always been trying. She'd delighted in antagonizing him, gleefully mocking his faith at every opportunity. Moreover, she had been mad, retreating into a world of elaborate delusions after the death of her son a decade before.

Standing over her body now, Miguel allowed a charitable notion to enter his heart. Perhaps, he thought, her madness would be the source of her salvation. Perhaps the Lord tailored His judgment to circumstance, made exceptions for the unbaptized children, the insane, the animals. He did not believe this but hoped it, briefly, for her sake, as he reached out to press a forgiving hand to her brow.

The instant he touched her, she groaned and opened her eyes. "Miguel? Is that you?"

Miguel recoiled as if burned. "Of course it's me," he snapped. "The door was unlocked. Are you trying to get robbed?"

Cadenza yawned and stretched out her legs. "Nothing here worth taking. What time is it?"

"I don't know. Around three o'clock. Why is it so dark in here?"

To his shame, Miguel was growing increasingly irritated to be in his aunt's living presence. He crossed the room to jerk the curtains open and Cadenza's doughy features sharpened. She flicked her hand at him.

"Took my juice last week."

"Your what?"

"My electrical."

"Haven't you been paying your bills?"

Cadenza laughed. "I don't need their juice. I've been getting along just fine, thank you very much." Miguel noticed several tin cans around the room with utensils jutting out of them and realized that the smell that he'd taken for his aunt's corpse when he came in was likely emanating from her refrigerator. She rubbed her eyes and glowered at him. "What day is it?"

"What day do you think it is?"

"Don't test me, boy."

"It's Friday. The twenty-second of September. Two thousand and — "

"All right, all right." She sat quietly for a moment, apparently lost in thought.

Miguel looked out the window. On the sheltered porch of the building across the way, a man with a trumpet case and a man in a cowboy hat were passing a bottle back and forth and watching the rain. The city was afflicted with a wasting disease, and Miguel felt that he was standing very close to the source of the infection. No one came downtown anymore unless they lived or worked there, and when a city has a sinkhole at its centre everything negative tends to drift towards it.

"I was having this dream," Cadenza said, "of a bird on fire. A huge, fiery bird, screaming through the sky."

Miguel sighed and passed a hand through his damp hair. "Are you having money problems?"

Cadenza gave him a scornful look. "Money *is* the problem, don't you know that? The slave and the master. Makes you feel all powerful when it's got you in chains. *They* know it. But they don't know how stubborn one old lady can be. I've been through hellfire twenty times over. What's a little bit of darkness?"

"And your telephone?"

Cadenza ignored him and jabbed an accusatory finger at a week-old newspaper on the coffee table. "See what your man's been up to? Dropping bombs on churches. Killing babies. What do you think about that?"

Miguel was familiar with the story — an errant American bomb destroying a mosque somewhere in Iraq. He did not know if by "your man" Cadenza was referring to George W. Bush (whom Miguel supported, inasmuch as a Canadian citizen can support an American president) or to God, and nor did he care. He settled in the furthest chair in the room from hers. "It's sad," he offered. She could not have shown him anything that he didn't see on a daily basis at work, first hand.

"Nothing sad about it. It's plain ugly. Your man's having himself a grand old time. Got his magnifying glass out just to watch the ants burn. It's nothing new. It's been going on since forever." Miguel took off his glasses and rubbed his eyes, sensing the approach of a history lesson narrated by the vampiric Cadenza, who, in addition to certain healing powers, claimed to have direct recollections of her many past lives (in each of which she had been conveniently persecuted by servants of God). Having managed only four hours sleep the night before, his irritation was quickly turning into something like hatred. Violent images flashed through his head and he willed them away.

I must not think of murdering my aunt.

He knew that he should eat something before his shift started, but his stomach churned at the thought. Eating had become a chore to him, one more task to accomplish, grimly, without pleasure. Dead things went in the mouth. Calories flooded the body and kept his feet moving through the day.

Cadenza was making spells with her hands and muttering. She broke off and observed, "Stomach bothering you, huh?"

A chill went through him. For a moment he wondered if she were not, in fact, tapping into dark, pagan forces. "I don't know what you're talking about."

"I could fix that up for you, if you'd let me. Get some blue fire into your belly."

Miguel laughed without humour, appalled at the thought of her laying hands on him. "I don't think so."

They lapsed into silence and he looked around the room for something to comment on. New age books, crystals, and amulets. A macabre shrine to her son in a nook by the kitchen door. In his youth, Miguel had believed that he and his cousin had been fathered by the same man, a man who passed through town at fourteen-year intervals like a comet. He had few memories of

Carlos; most prominently, a Thanksgiving dinner in that very apartment. Too much food to fit on the table. His mother drunk and laughing at everything. Cadenza bent over the turkey with an electric knife, breasts heavy from nursing. Miguel watched her, his hand under the table, gripping the swell, unconsciously squeezing. She looked up at him. His eyes lost focus and he gasped, feeling the pool begin to gather and leak onto his good pants. His face was on fire. Something tugged at his leg. Carlos crawling under the table, wanting a hand up. Miguel kicked. The boy began to wail.

Five years later he would be dead, struck down in the street by an inattentive driver. This was the kind of death that most frightened Miguel, the one that took you unawares, that could come at the most inopportune moment imaginable. The narrow stairs were climbed among fields of fire, temptation everywhere. At thirty-two he had retained his virginity, but was plagued by lustful thoughts. They came upon him most urgently at night: women he had seen throughout the day with naked breasts and hooded eyes, luring him into their beds. He wondered if Cadenza remembered that old Thanksgiving day. His shame. The lust that still resided in his heart.

I must not think of killing my aunt.

She appeared innocuous, half dozing in her armchair, but he knew how quickly her moods could shift. As if inhabited by a demon, she would suddenly jump out of her chair and pace like a caged animal, sermoning him about the power of the blue fire. She sat up to regard him more closely. "Course if I healed you," she finally said, "it would just come back tomorrow. Your stomach's just a symptom. You've got to tackle the real problem."

"And what might that be?"

"You know what I'm talking about. It's all over your face. You need to get yourself a woman. Or, you know, a man if that's how it is for you. I don't judge."

"I should go," he said, intending to do just that, but Cadenza seemed to be holding him in place with her eyes. He sighed and folded his arms.

"How come you always come here on Fridays?" she asked. "You ought to be going out on dates, having fun. Not wasting your time talking to some crazy old lady."

"I don't mind," he said, automatically.

"Of course you do. A boy your age has needs."

He groaned. His aunt might as well have passed her tongue over her upper lip, or made a ring of her thumb and forefinger and penetrated it with the finger of her opposite hand. Did she have no shame?

Cadenza sighed. "Why don't you take up the priesthood, then? Get yourself one of them fancy collars. One of them monk robes."

"Not everyone is called."

"*Called?*" His aunt snorted and slapped her leg. "That's good. You're expecting him to ring you up on the telephone?"

"Of course not."

But in a way, that was exactly what he expected: a simple, unambiguous sign. He wanted the birds to speak to him as they spoke to Francis. He wanted the clouds to part and a thick shaft of light to send a voice resounding within him, telling him what to do. His aunt watched him, smugly. He felt compelled to explain himself.

"You know what I do for a living," he said.

"Of course I do."

"But do you know *why* I do what I do? Because God *wants* me to help people. He didn't tell me that on the telephone, but I know it in my heart." He claimed the lie, willing it to be true. "That's what it means to be called. That's — "

"Shhhh!" She raised a hand and took on an abstracted, stealthy look.

"What?"

"That noise!" she hissed.

"Are you hearing voices?"

"Shut up and listen."

He listened more closely and picked up the faint sound of drums. "It must be the parade."

"What damn parade?" She looked suspicious.

"The city . . . Never mind."

"I don't know what to do with you," she said. "You're not stupid. Just stubborn. Got that from your momma, I expect. Stubbornest woman I ever knew." She yawned, then sat back and closed her eyes. A long minute passed. It occurred to Miguel that she might have been dead when he arrived, after all, and that he'd been talking all this time with her ghost. Either way, he was leaving. He'd made it halfway to the door when the telephone rang. Cadenza jumped and fumbled for the receiver. "Hello? A blizzard! Hang on a second . . . " She furiously waved Miguel back to his chair. "No, no. I haven't been watching the TV. Listen, hon, I'm going to have to call you back. That's right. I've got company."

She hung up and regarded Miguel sternly.

"What?" he said.

"Trying to sneak out on me?"

"You were sleeping."

"I was resting my eyes."

He looked at his watch. "Anyway. I think I'd better — "

"Hold your damn horses. I've got something I want to say to you."

"All right."

"You going to listen?"

"I'm listening."

"Okay. Now, I know you don't want to hear this, least of all from me, but I'm telling you for your own good. You've got to give this church business a rest. It's not healthy. You spend more time on your knees than them girls who wander up and down State Street all night long, looking to get picked up."

"My god. Cadenza, I realize you're sick — "

"Sick nothing. Listen to me now. This is no joke. Your man's not home. There's no such thing as hell. There's no such thing as heaven. There's just this cycle of souls jumping from body to body, and you've got to accept that. You've got to try and be happy in this world, because it's the only one you're gonna get."

"Thank you for the advice."

"Don't sass me. I'm telling you, you've got a mind like a one-way road and it's time to do some construction on it. There's lots of space in there. Enough space for an eight-lane freeway with traffic going both ways. "

"Construction. All right." He was through arguing with her, there was no sense in it.

"If your momma could see you now," she said. "It would break her heart. To see you so closed, so serious."

"Me? What about you?"

"What about me?"

"What would Carlos say if he saw how you were living?"

"It's not the same."

"No, it isn't. Because if you continue to shun God's mercy and love, you'll never see him again." He intended these to be cutting words, but to his surprise, Cadenza laughed so hard that she began to choke.

"And what," she said when she'd recovered, "do you figure I ought to do about that?"

"Repent," he said.

She raised her quavering arms. "Praise Jesus!"

I must not think of murdering my aunt.

"I'm serious, Cadenza. This could be your last chance. Look at it this way. If I'm wrong, you won't have lost a thing. But if I'm right, you'll live with Carlos for eternity in Paradise."

She stared at him in disbelief. "Is that what you think? That it's all one big crapshoot and you're just playing the odds? What would your man have to say about that? Shoot. You don't even believe in what you believe in."

Miguel's stomach contracted. He stood up. "I don't know why I come here."

"Go on, then, I'm not keeping you."

"Should I come next week?"

"Do what you like."

"But do you want me to come?"

"I want you to do what you like."

Miguel sighed and headed for the door. Shielded from his aunt by a partition, he sifted through a pile of unopened mail on the floor and slipped her latest power bill into his pocket. He would pay it on his way to work, give her light for the days remaining prior to her eviction, which he assumed were numbered. After that, he would consider his duty to her accomplished. Family or not, she was on her own.

Zebra finch
(Taeniopygia guttata)

Six cubic feet of space. Glass to the front and back. A span of parallel rods. Flitting from one rod to the other, interminably. Next door the canaries peck at each other. Above, the cockatiels rage in distorted human voices. Not so much a cage, then, as a cell in an avian madhouse.

Doug

THE LAST CHERRY TOMATO WENT INTO his mouth. He applied pressure. The eruption happened. Pulp and skin mingled together. Across the food court, the girl at the Orange Julius stand was wiping down the counter. He swallowed and watched her breasts jog out a vigorous lateral rhythm. Doug did not know when exactly he had become invisible to girls of that age, but it had certainly happened. They deflected his speculative glances without hesitation or mercy. On the wrong side of forty, he could no longer present himself as an older model of the boys they went to school with, tricked out with an apartment and a fridge full of legally-acquired alcohol. To them he was not "older" at all. He was simply old.

He finished his taco salad and wiped his mouth, entirely focused on the Orange Julius girl. Invisibility had its advantages. Every day he rode the elevator down from Contrail to the food court, to grab a late lunch and watch the girls on parade: high school girls who had yet to suffer the effects of gravity and age, all zippered and strapped into bits of outrageously-priced fabric that he'd had a hand in selling them. He studied them as he would have studied an enemy, for their vulnerable spots, their insecurities and vanities.

In Doug's mind, a good advertisement was like an accusation, shaming the consumer into reaching for their wallet. Everyone was beautiful. Everyone was having sex with beautiful people. So why weren't *they*? Sex was the instrument, but it had to be used properly. His company favoured a "suggestive" approach, which meant imbedding an ad with innuendo that was not always meant to be consciously detected, but Doug knew that to tap the money vein you had to be blatant and crude. You had to slam through the radar of propriety with a phallus-shaped plane. The Europeans had been doing it for decades and, in his opinion, North America was primed and waiting, her legs spread-eagled. If management took his advice more often, business could triple overnight, along with his salary. Until then he would remain stranded in cubicle land, cobbling other people's lukewarm visions together on a computer screen.

Not that his job was without benefits. He was well-liked in the office. He could surf the internet all day long, he imagined, and his position would have still been more secure than some of the executives'. But, at times, he could not help craving more. He wanted to spearhead a winning campaign, to not only be liked but respected by his colleagues, to see his framed portrait hanging outside the boardroom above the Employee of the Month placard.

And of course there was the money.

As he sucked his diet cola down to the ice, his gaze drifted over to a wall-sized ad for Serendipity, a perfume with a five-hundred-percent markup — the model's hair in windy disarray, her lips making a neat little blowjob circle. The image did what it was designed to do, triggered minor explosions of desire in Doug's brain. He glanced at his watch. It was almost four o'clock. No one would miss him for the extra hour. He would linger in the mall awhile longer, filing choice specimens into his mental database, then head home, shower, and pick up a box of condoms on the way to Kathleen's. He opened his laptop and fired an email upstairs, passing on a cut-and-paste job that had come his way that morning. Let squirrelly Martin deal with the *Woebegone!* snafu. The weekend had arrived.

He loosened his Fred Flintstone tie and watched the girls pass, details from his youth returning in a visceral, jumbled rush. Strawberry lip gloss. The eager spring of an unclasped brassiere. A body on top of his own that he hardly knew was there but for the slick and narrow friction. The bittersweet feeling that came to him at moments like this was similar to a feeling inspired by the more artful ads, a feeling that made rational people vulnerable to all kinds of wild ideas, that marriage, for instance, was a good idea. To surrender the boundless sense of sexual possibility that he carried around with him — the prospect of guilt-free congress with strangers, the half-dozen women he could call on short notice, who, like him, *preferred* not to spend the night — to exchange all that for a life of bondage was beyond irrational, it was insane. And yet, one by one, his friends had donned the manacles and leg-irons, the loop of metal around the finger, conditioned to marry by the media, who, for reasons he had yet to divine, insisted on idealizing the custom.

He popped the lid off his cup, jerked an ice cube into his mouth, and tongued the hollow before pulverizing it between his molars. A girl with glasses and neatly plaited hair passed his table and he admired her denim behind, idly working out the logistics of seduction. The quiet ones tended to respond to an aggressive approach: hyperbolic praise followed by an abject declaration of need. He would bring her back to his apartment, lead her up the fire stairs where the neighbours wouldn't —

"What time is it?"

Doug ripped his gaze off the nerdy girl's jeans to find another girl standing before him, a girl with no makeup and bright-blue hair, who was very young and very pregnant. The Serendipity sign loomed behind her. He swallowed and checked his watch.

"Coming up on four o'clock."

The girl sat down at the next table without thanking him. Doug jiggled the ice in his cup, and regarded her out of the corner of his eye. She was attractive enough, in spite of her condition (or because of it, pregnancy being one of his pet fetishes), and he wanted to talk to her. Never one for timidity, he collected his laptop bag and shuttled over to her table.

"Hi there! I just gave you the time a second ago. Hope you don't mind me inviting myself over." He slid his business card across the table, calling her attention to the deeply embossed font. "That's me. Doug Foster." She stared at him. He smiled, cheery and harmless. "And you are?"

"Samantha." She said, in a flat monotone.

"Samantha. That's one of my all time favourite names. No kidding. So here's the situation, Samantha. I'm here on a kind of assignment. I work for a marketing firm in this very building and my boss sent me down here to do a survey on the spending habits of fourteen- to eighteen-year-old girls. Now — is everything all right?"

The girl was regarding him with a disquieting intensity. "You look like him."

"Who's that?"

"Someone I know."

He grinned. "Must be a hell of a good-looking guy."

"No," she said. "He isn't."

Doug laughed, deciding to translate this as an attempt at playful flirtation. "Well, about this survey. I'd really appreciate it if you could answer just a couple of questions. It'll hardly take any time at all. You're not waiting for someone, are you?"

She shook her head.

"Great! So, like I say, fourteen- to eighteen-year-olds. And you're . . . ?" His mouth was suddenly dry.

"Sixteen."

"Perfect."

"But I'm not average."

"No, you're not. You're above average, if you don't mind me saying. Very fashion conscious. You've got this kind of hippie-Goth thing going on. I dig it, I really do. But anyways. You've caught me — or I've caught you, I guess you could say — on kind of a weird day. See, every week my boss gives me a new focus area, and sends me out in the world to talk to people about their shopping habits. Statistical analysis, we call it. One day it's diapers, the next it's computers. This week, it's . . . well, underwear." He laughed and shook his head. "Can you believe that?"

The girl was no longer looking at him.

Doug held up his hands to reassure her. "I know it sounds creepy. I don't want to be asking you about your underwear anymore than you want to be telling me about your underwear, but if I don't come back with some answers today, my boss is not going to be a happy camper. Five minutes and I'll be out of your life. What do you say? Help a guy out?" She appeared to give a slight shrug, which was all the consent he needed. "Wonderful. You're saving my life here." He pulled a pad of paper and a pen from his laptop bag and made a show of marking down some preliminary notes, wondering what the hell he was doing. "All right. So . . . " He sat back and regarded her with contrived detachment, trying to keep his eyes off her stomach. "First question. Where do you generally do your undergarment shopping?"

The girl had begun absently tearing his card into strips.

"I know, I know. You shop in a million stores. How are you supposed to remember just one? Try to think about the last time you bought something. Do you remember where it was? La Senza? The Bay? The Gap? You know what, skip it, we'll just move on to question two. Frequency of shopping. How often would you say that you shop for undergarments? Annually? Monthly?"

She frowned and made a humming sound.

"Monthly?" He scribbled it down, wanting to stop, but feeling compelled to finish what he'd started. "That's great. Our clients will be happy to hear that. They're looking for serious shoppers. People who know how to spend. Okay, so question number three. Now I know this is kind of personal, but they're also concerned with style, what the kids are wearing these days. You know, bikini, boyshorts, um," — he cleared his throat — "thongs. Do you have a personal preference?" One of his legs set to bouncing as he waited for her answer. "Not sure? That's okay. I'll just write that down. *Not sure.* Which brings us to question number four. Colour. Do you prefer plain old white? Solid colours? Something with patterns?"

The girl looked at him. "Will you help me?"

"Yeah, it's — what's that?"

The girl had tears in her eyes. Doug's card sat in a little shredded pile before her. "I didn't think it would be this hard," she said. "I thought I could just come here and do it. But I couldn't. I need someone's help."

"Hang on now. Are you asking me for money? Because I make a habit of not carrying any cash on me."

"I don't need money. I need a push."

She said it like she was a little girl on a swing who couldn't touch her feet to the ground. Doug gripped his pen. "A push?"

She nodded. "From behind."

Cold runnels of sweat slid down either side of his torso. Was that what the kids were calling it these days? A push? "I don't — I'm not sure that I know what you're asking right now, but I don't think I can do that."

"You can do it when no one's looking. I won't tell anyone it was you, I promise."

Doug wondered if her nipples had darkened like the other pregnant women he'd seen, if she had that weird seam running down the middle of her belly, if she still trimmed or let the hair grow wild down there.

"I can't do it myself," she went on. "I thought I could but I can't, and you look so much like him. I think maybe you were sent here."

"Sent here?"

"*Please.*"

Doug shook his head and put the pen and paper away. This was not supposed to happen. The fantasy was not designed to be realized. That was the whole point of the fantasy. "Look, I don't know how you got the idea that — okay, maybe I do know how you got the idea, but . . . " — he lowered his voice — "are you sure you know what you're doing? I mean, you don't even know me."

Samantha lowered her head and began to cry.

"Oh, fuck. Hey, don't . . . " He stood up to go, then, realizing how suspicious it would look, sat back down on her side of the table. "Look, I'm sorry if — " She listed towards him, forcing him to catch her. He glanced around the food court. No one seemed to notice. They probably assumed he was the girl's father, which (he had not done the math until just now) would actually be a reasonable assumption. He touched her head and tried to think of something fatherly to say. "It's okay." He stroked her hair. "Shhh. It's okay."

A pregnant girl sobbing in the arms of her father. It was a strong image. He could do something with that image.

COMMON GRACKLE
(Quiscalus quiscula)

From the pavement the trees are cathedrals, the buildings monolithic, too huge to be realized. A bicycle whirs past, scaring it up, and the world telescopes back. Within seconds the trees have become smudges, the buildings two dimensional and miniaturized — parts on a circuit board, pedestrians like specks of information, inconsequential to the elevated body pulsing with the wind.

DARBY

To a casual observer, the gathering might have appeared to consist of environmentalists and left-wing activists, but Darby knew that the fifth annual Western Canadian Alternative Medicine Conference and Trade Show was a fundamentally corporate event. Stacked on abutting plywood tables in the spacious main hall were a vast array of balms, powders, lotions, aphrodisiacs, digestives, SAD lamps, acupressure masks, and something called a healing wand, which looked and functioned exactly like a vibrator. Everything had a price tag, and everything was branded with an appropriative logo, from the stylized slashes of Chinese iconography, to the silhouette of a Native American elder in full headdress, to the black, red, and yellow of the pan-African flag.

Darby navigated the maze of exhibits with her hands in her pockets and her backpack on. It had rained heavily on her bike ride from the university to the conference centre and she felt like a wet cat, skulking underfoot at a crowded dinner party. The air was dense with sandalwood and potpourri, everyone raising their voices to be heard over the general din. "It's called Vitamin Q," someone nearby said. "It's like a superdose of complex B, Omega 3s, and ginseng."

Joe would lose his mind when he found out what she'd done. What she intended to do. He would never understand. He had no idea how lucky he was to own that thing called ethnicity. When she first saw him at the community theatre, she'd been taken with his soft eyes, his angular features, and his post-performance exuberance (which she would later discover to be on the manic side of bipolar), but when she fell in love with him, she did so in relation to his family. She loved everything about them, their swerving vowels and dropped consonants, their spicy cuisine and tragic history. Her own family tree sprawled across Western Europe, spanning the Atlantic to flower and die for three generations in the bland Canadian air. She could never understand Joe's apparent desire to detach from his family and merge with the uninspired monoculture to which she was a reluctant heir — vaguely apologetic and wholly uncertain of who she was. He had always been showily apathetic towards issues that she considered vital, as if cynicism were the worldlier, more mature response.

Of course, she had no idea how he really felt about anything. When they argued he changed his positions frequently, without seeming to realize it, more concerned with the performance (loud, theatrical, the windows thrown open for the benefit of the neighbours) than with what he was actually saying. Darby had found these fights strangely exhilarating, screaming terrible things at the man she loved, secure in the knowledge that they were acting. But in recent weeks, the shouting matches had tapered off and a quieter, more ominous tension had begun to reign in the apartment. The previous weekend, she'd tried to break that tension by joking that, when she attended his film debut (in a poorly conceived, morally offensive, blatantly propagandistic Hollywood production about the Vietnam War) she was going to feel like Eva Braun on Hitler's arm.

"Well, you won't have to put up with it for long," he said, flatly.

Darby laughed — a bright, false laugh — and came up behind him. "We're not in the bunker yet, darling." She passed an affectionate hand through his hair and he recoiled, not deliberately, but involuntarily, as if physically repelled by her. Darby was shocked. "What's wrong?"

"Nothing. I'm just saying. It's not like it's going to last forever."

With those words, she understood why the fighting had stopped. Some relationships ended in escalation, others in gradual withdrawal. If she was to retain any dignity in the situation, she was going to have to act fast and act first. The next day she saw an advertisement for the naturopathy conference and an idea came to her that had since acquired an almost talismanic force: activism would be her infidelity. Her preemptive strike would be preceded by a show of defiance against his values, his lack of values. That was why she had come here, why she was just now focusing on, and heading towards, a banner displaying a single La Koi leaf against a pale blue backdrop.

There was only one *Woebegone!* representative at that stretch of table, a bald, weary-looking man with crooked eyeglasses, a brown sport coat, and a paper sticker on his yellow shirt that read:

Hello, I'm
FRANK GARNETT

To Garnett's left, a woman with mannish features and silver hair was selling tubs of beeswax moisturizing cream. To his right, a man was sitting cross-legged on his chair, with an energy-channelling pyramid on his head, and a dozen or so paperbacks (also arranged into a pyramid) before him.

Garnett looked up with a hopeful smile. "Interested?"

Darby inhaled. "A natural resource of a community is a sacred thing, not a commodity to be exploited for the benefit of the wealthy and the privileged in the so-called first world."

"Excuse me?"

She hesitated. What had been so cutting in her head sounded vague and pedantic out loud. Still, she repeated herself and waited for the counterattack.

Garnett looked pained. "Are you sure you have the right table? This is *Woebegone!* The mood improvement supplement?" He launched into his sales pitch. "You see, by genetically modifying the La Koi plant, our scientists have created a product that clinical trials have determined uplift a person's mood. Originally, the pollen and branches of the La Koi were — "

"I know what it does," she snapped. "It's only been used by the people of Northern Vietnam for hundreds of years."

"That's right." Garnett seemed pleased that they were on the same wavelength. "The hill people would dry it out and grind it up into a powder."

"Hill people?" Darby said.

"People who live in the hills."

"*Hill people?*"

Garnett coughed. "The, um, villagers? Look I'm just going by what I've been told. I've never actually been to Vietnam."

"Oh, I have." The man with the pyramid on his head had leaned over to insert himself into the conversation. "Lovely country. Lovely people. Did you know that the collective energy gathered by headwear was a decisive factor in the Vietnam War?"

"Is that right?" Garnett said.

Darby glared at the pyramid man before returning her attention to Garnett. "Aren't you ashamed?"

"Excuse me?"

"Don't you know what those people have been through?"

"Who?"

"The Vietnamese! Decades of war. Genocide. A population decimated."

"I'm sorry." Garnett was squinting at her mouth. "Are you saying that *Woebegone!* was somehow involved?"

"No, you're not . . . The La Koi isn't ours. It's theirs. It's one of the last things they had that was truly theirs and you had to go and steal it from them."

"I did?"

"You know what I mean. Don't you care? Doesn't it bother you?"

Garnett seemed genuinely bemused. "As far as I know, *Woebegone!* is an all-natural, organic, environmentally-friendly product — "

"That's not the point." He was being far too agreeable. She should have been striding out the front entrance by now, with security on her heels. They needed some escalation in volume. "You people," she said. "You people use words like 'natural' and 'organic' as if that's all that matters. They're just *words*. The same old corporations are driving the train, and that train is fuelled by nothing but profit and greed." She was gratified at having found the opportunity to use the train metaphor, but Garnett seemed to be barely following her.

"Look," he said, "I'm really not the one to talk to about all this. Our parent company?"

"Blueskies Incorporated. Oh, I know all about you guys. But I don't exactly have the time or the money to go all the way down to Tampa Bay to talk to Chris Fields in person, do I? Assuming he would agree to talk to me, which he wouldn't. So, I'm here talking to you. You're just as responsible as he is."

Garnett looked at her like she was speaking another language. She wondered if it was all an elaborate act. It did not seem possible that a *Woebegone!* foot soldier could be so staggeringly ignorant of the war. "If you have a complaint or something," he said, "I could pass it along."

Darby shook her head. She was going to have to spell out his crimes. "Chris Fields, your boss, has patented the La Koi hybrid. A living organism. Which means that no one but Blueskies can legally grow the plant, or have in their possession a single seed. Don't you see a problem with that?"

Garnett raised his hands in surrender. "I don't know anything about any of this. I just sell the stuff."

"So, you're not responsible."

"If I thought it was hurting anyone — "

"But it is hurting people. It perpetuates the colonial mindset that everything in the natural world is ours. Not just ours to manipulate and change, but to patent and own. And don't tell me," she went on, "that the Vietnamese can still use the original La Koi, because they can't. The hybrid has infected their crops. And you have the gall — *the gall* — to demand that they cull it out and destroy it." To Darby, the process couldn't have been more deliberate or insidious. The La Koi was one small instance of a vast cultural hemorrhage: fast food chains, American movies, and handguns bleeding into defenseless nations across the globe.

"That doesn't sound right to me . . . " Garnett said.

"You don't know this? How can you not know this?"

Garnett opened a glossy *Woebegone!* pamphlet and ran his finger down the slickly presented factoids. "Okay. It says right here that five percent of the profit goes back to the villages around where the plant was discovered. Now that doesn't sound like much, but in Vietnamese dollars . . . "

"Propaganda." She unshouldered her backpack. She couldn't wait to tell Joe. He would never forgive her. He would storm through the apartment, claiming that she was vying for attention with her newly famous boyfriend, on the night of his premiere no less, and it would all be very convincing, but in reality he would be ashamed. He would be ashamed that he hadn't done it himself. This thought, along with the convincing heft of the Mason jar in her bag, dispelled all of her previous doubts. She was ready to pronounce her sentence. She reached into her bag.

"This is for — "

"Excuse me," the bee woman on Garnett's left said, sternly interjecting. "May I ask who you're representing here?"

Darby continued to hold the Mason jar, but did not remove it from her bag. "What do you mean?"

"Well, from what I couldn't help overhearing I gather that you've come on behalf of the peasantry of Vietnam."

"That's right."

The bee woman gave her a sardonic smile. "You're an official envoy, then. They've given you a mandate, so to speak"

"I don't think this is any of your business."

"Oh, I disagree. As long as you're standing there projecting hostility, people are avoiding this entire section of the table. Simply put, your business is affecting my business, so your business *is* my business. Now, these Vietnamese peasants. They sent you here?"

"I'm following my conscience."

"How very noble of you. You've taken it upon yourself to defend their interests."

"Yes, I have."

"And you're quite certain that you're representing those interests."

Garnett was sitting very quietly, attempting to hide behind his *Woebegone!* pamphlet.

"They're being exploited," Darby said.

"Do they feel they're being exploited?"

"Of course they feel they're being exploited."

"You've spoken to them about this."

"When the injustice is clear . . ." Darby trailed off. The woman was snaring her in semantics, the impotent jargon of the United Nations. She might as well have been wearing a teal-blue helmet, standing between armed troops and an impending genocide.

"Have you allowed for the possibility," the woman said, "that this gentleman might be correct in his assessment of the situation? Or are you simply expecting him to take your word for it? What, exactly, are you trying to accomplish here? What is it that you expect him to do?"

Darby knew what she wanted Blueskies to do, that was easy: surrender the rights to the La Koi hybrid. Pay the Northern Vietnamese damages. As for what she expected Frank Garnett to do, she was less certain. She had come here for a public shaming, to stain the *Woebegone!* rep's expensive suit (which, in reality, did not look expensive at all) with vermilion paint, symbolizing the cultural massacre that his company was wreaking in the forests of Vietnam. As far as she was concerned, Frank Garnett didn't have to do anything but sit there.

"You have a right to your opinion," the woman continued. "But this is hardly the time or place to air your grievances. Look around you. We're all on the same side here."

Darby released her grip on the Mason jar. The woman was wrong. They were on opposite sides, all of them — Garnett, the bee woman, the pyramid man, Joe, herself. They were selfish creatures making occasional selfless gestures to ease their consciences, every last one of them a hypocrite. Standing awkwardly in front of these strangers, Darby suddenly felt very much alone.

"Cultural piracy is wrong," she said in a voice stripped of all conviction.

A voice came over the PA system, announcing the beginning of a lecture on iridology in the main hall. As Darby backed away from the table, the pyramid man held out a small, plastic pyramid.

"Please," he said. "Take this. It will help."

Horned lark
(*Eremophila alpestris*)

Compelled by a kind of madness, it flies straight up into the sky, perpendicular to the contrail of a graceless, stiff-winged airplane. At 500 feet it circles, singing to itself. Then it banks and free-falls, a streamlined projectile, the ground rushing in until, at the last conceivable moment, it snaps out its wings and skims the ground, two feet from its own darting shadow.

Roger

"Are we nearly there?" he shouted.

His therapist grinned and held both thumbs up. Roger did not return the gesture. Soon he would be launching his small human self out into the troposphere with nothing more than a dwindling amount of faith in the thin material compacted into the bag on his back. The odds of disaster might have been low, but he was due for a spell of bad luck. He visualized the jump and saw only bad things: the chute failing, the lines twisting, the earth rapidly taking on definition as he hurtled towards it. Would he think of his wife? His job? Would he open his mouth and scream? Would he shut his eyes and pray? He saw his body face down in the mud, obliterated. His cellphone ringing with no one to answer it. The voice of a dead man calmly assuring people he would call them back shortly.

His ears popped as the plane shed altitude. The windows were streaked with rain, the sky beyond an ominous blue-gray.

"Hey!" He waved to get Decker's attention. "This weather! Is it going to be a problem?"

Decker tapped the side of his head, indicating that he couldn't hear. Roger repeated himself, his voice cracking on "problem." Decker smiled and hoisted both thumbs again. This, Roger thought, was what happened when you found your therapist in the classified section.

Fred Decker's office was located in the industrial part of town, above an auto parts dealer and a carpet outlet. The afternoon of Roger's first visit, he'd circled the building three times before discovering the side entrance, which led to a narrow staircase, which led to a series of numbered doors. Roger had looked at the number written on his hand and opened door number twenty-two. The walls of the waiting area were bare, folding chairs arranged around low tables, the smell of new paint in the air. At the sound of the bell striking the door, an overweight woman with tall hair and a wad of gum lodged in her cheek emerged from the back room (Decker's office proper, Roger would soon learn). Easing herself into the receptionist's desk, she took his name and gave him a lengthy, and, as far as he could tell, irrelevant questionnaire.

Ten minutes later, Decker strode out to greet him, his large, chapped hand outstretched to grip Roger's smaller, smoother counterpart. He had the look of a rancher about him — string tie, blue jeans, tinted glasses, and cowboy boots. He was clean-shaven and jowly, his hair combed back into a ducktail and sculpted at the front into a frozen wave.

"So, you're the famous Roger Ingram!" he said. "Your reputation precedes you."

"It does?"

"In a manner of speaking. I've been going over your information here. Very interesting. Ve-ry interesting." He ushered Roger into a windowless office furnished with little more than folding chairs and an overlarge desk on which four items sat: a scratchpad, a cup of pencils, a half-finished crossword puzzle, and an imposing stuffed owl on a stand. Roger sat on the client side, while Decker perched on the edge of his desk and passed an eye over his questionnaire, making noises that seemed first judgmental then confirmatory. "Hmm," went the first noise. "M-*hm*," went the second. "So!" He slapped the paper down on his desk. "What brings you to my office today?"

Roger laughed. "My wife." Decker pursed his lips and Roger coughed into his hand. "She — uh, she saw your ad in the *Globe*. That long list of symptoms or whatever. She's gotten it into her head that there's some kind of an overlap with my behaviour."

"Do you have somewhere to be, Mr. Ingram?"

"I'm sorry?"

"You were consulting your watch."

"I was?"

Decker chuckled and moved his bulk into a leather swivel chair. "I suppose you're thinking this is all a bit silly."

"To be honest?"

"Of course."

"Look, I'm sure that whatever you do here works for some people. I just don't happen to need any help."

Decker indulged him with a puzzled frown. "That's strange. How did you find yourself in this office?"

"Like I said. My wife." He glanced at his watch again. Decker scribbled something in margin of the questionnaire.

"Well, as long as you're here why don't we go ahead with the preliminary interview?" He peered at Roger over his glasses. "For your wife's sake. Now. Do you have a cellphone on you?"

"I'm sorry?"

"A cellular telephone. If you do — and frankly, I know that you do — I'm afraid I'm going to have to hold onto it for the duration of the session, along with any paging device you might happen to have. Your wristwatch, as well."

"Are you serious?"

"I realize this is difficult for you, Mr. Ingram. Don't you see that that's exactly why you're here? Telephones and timepieces are just cattle prods in disguise. We have to liberate ourselves from them. Use them only when absolutely necessary. And, when you think about it, they're hardly necessary at all, are they? I mean, really necessary. I myself have not owned a wristwatch for nearly ten years."

Decker seemed to expect a response to this declaration so Roger tried to look impressed. "Wow."

"Look around you. Not a clock in the room."

Roger made a show of looking around. "Wow," he said again. "But is that practical? How do you know when a session's over?"

"A session takes as long as it needs to. We could be here five minutes or five hours. My rate's the same either way. That's my commitment to you. In any case, if we're going to start, I'll need your cell phone, your pager, and your watch." Decker smiled, his eyes vague behind their amber lenses.

"Why don't I just turn them off?"

"Well, that's sort of a given. But physically entrusting them to me is a symbolic gesture as much as anything. It's the first step towards breaking your psychological dependence."

A brief standoff followed, in which Decker watched him with folded arms while Roger smiled and shook his head. Finally — still shaking his head, still smiling — he took his pager and cellphone from their respective holsters, undid his watch, and placed all three items on the centre of the desk. Decker swept them into a drawer and put on a sympathetic expression. "I can see this distresses you, Mr. Ingram. Can I ask who you were expecting to call?"

Roger shrugged, unnerved by the thought that he was officially, for the first time in recent memory, unreachable. "Clients. Employees."

Decker peered down at the questionnaire. "You work in a managerial capacity at Sears."

"That's right."

"Do your employees call you often at home?"

"Sometimes."

"And do you encourage them? Tell them to call you night or day, no matter how small the problem? Berate them if they don't?"

"Now, why would I do that?"

"Defensive," Decker muttered and jotted something on his scratch pad (presumably "defensive"). He tapped his pen against his front teeth. The stuffed owl stared at Roger. "All right. I want to do a mental exercise here. I'd like you to ask yourself a question. If something, god forbid, were to happen to you tomorrow, do you think operations over at Sears would cease entirely? I mean, would they even close up shop for a day?" Roger thought about this. It did not seem inconceivable. "Of course they wouldn't," Decker said. "And I don't say that to belittle you or your occupation. I'd say the very same thing about myself. We're not presidents of nations, Mr. Ingram. We're not surgeons or soldiers or firefighters. We're just average, unimportant individuals. And let me tell you," — he wagged his finger at Roger — "we should take a great deal of comfort from that fact. But for you there's no respite. You go from one crisis to another, exaggerating the pressures around you. I would almost say you thrive on that pressure, if it weren't for the fact that it was hurting your marriage."

Roger laughed. "Who said anything about my marriage?"

"I don't like to waste my clients' time, Mr. Ingram. Bear in mind that I am not a psychiatrist, and this is not a medical diagnosis, but from what I've observed of your behaviour so far, and from your responses to our questionnaire, I can say with some confidence that you are an adrenaline compulsive of the lowest grade. That's actually good news. I've seen far more acute cases, with much more severe manifest symptoms. Train dodging, for instance."

"*Train dodging?* I hardly think — "

"Let me finish. Your own behaviour, while unhealthy, is not nearly as extreme, and, I'm happy to tell you, entirely treatable."

Roger could not seem to stop fidgeting. "You say unhealthy. Isn't that kind of subjective?"

"When no pleasure or reward is derived from an activity, and that activity is actively and repeatedly sought out, the activity is, by definition, compulsive. Unhealthy. It's nothing to be ashamed of. We just need to find a more constructive outlet for these impulses. Which brings me to the crux of our therapy." He leaned forward and regarded Roger seriously. "Have you ever jumped out of an airplane, Mr. Ingram?"

For a moment, Roger suspected himself the victim of an elaborate practical joke. "An airplane?"

"That's right."

"No, I can't say that I have."

"Did you know that jumping out of an airplane is no more dangerous than taking an anti-compulsive medication? It's actually safer. Granted, there haven't been any" — he made disdainful air quotes — "*official studies* in the area, but when you look at the mortality rates, there's really no comparison. Why am I telling you this? Well, in addition to a small amount of cognitive behavioural work, your therapy will consist of periodic exposure to massive doses of adrenaline. We overload the circuit. An analogy I like to make with my male clients is the sex addict. The sex addict constantly craves sex, but derives no pleasure from the act. For the sex addict, our therapy would be like spending a night with a harem of beautiful, aggressive women. Afterwards, he will not only stop craving sex for some time, he will be physically incapable of it."

"And this involves jumping out of airplanes."

"I know that it sounds strange, but I've seen it borne out time and again. My success rate is over eighty-two percent. Completely cured."

A light sweat had broken out on Roger's forehead. He was experiencing something like physical withdrawal at the prolonged absence of his personal effects. "I'm sorry," he said. "I don't think I can do this."

"Problems with heights? Because there are alternatives. Swimming with sharks. Whitewater rafting. Of course, for most people, the experience of falling is recommended. It seems to trigger something primordial in the brain, allowing for a more even distribution of the endorphins."

"It isn't that. I just don't have the time."

"Say that again."

"What?"

"*You don't have the time.* That's like the alcoholic telling the counsellor he's too drunk for rehab. You're here for a reason, Mr. Ingram. Besides, it won't take up that much of your time. After your first jump we'll tailor the dosage to the frequency and intensity of your cravings. For some, once a month is sufficient. For others, once a year. I've had clients walk away completely cured after a single jump."

"I don't know . . ."

"I'll admit, it isn't for everyone. But many have come to appreciate jump therapy as a holistic alternative to conventional medication. Without side effects."

"Besides possible death."

"Again, with the standard therapeutic jump, the risk is quite low."

In retrospect, the words, "low risk" were absurd. An investment was low risk. Skydiving was a *foolish* risk. And if his therapist was a reliable mirror, he looked the part. In his helmet and goggles and baggy orange jumpsuit, he was not going to make a dignified corpse. A broken clown was what they would find down there, alone, his wife having not even come to support him.

He couldn't understand why she had suddenly lost interest after prodding him the entire way. After that first meeting, he'd left the office intending to never go back, but as he related the story to his wife over dinner (chuckling and broadly caricaturing Decker), she had remained humourless. It did not, she said, seem unreasonable to her.

"Are you serious? Skydiving? Purging the adrenaline?"

She kept her eyes on her plate, fork and knife moving with savage little strokes.

"Come on. You know how I feel about alternative medicine. Anyway this is the worst time, the absolute worst time, to be taking on something new. Two shipments didn't come through this week, did I tell you that? If they're not here by Tuesday, we're going to miss the flyer sale."

Gayle looked at him.

"What?" he said. "You're not actually mad about this."

She stood up and began to clear the table.

"Gayle?"

"Why would I be mad? You obviously don't have a problem. Your job *doesn't* dictate what you do every minute. You're home *all* the time. You're *never* on the phone." Roger stole a look at his watch. The interview with Decker had put a serious dent in his day. He had allotted forty-five minutes for dinner. If they opened up this argument now, he'd never get to his paperwork, let alone the new time chart he'd been working up for the temps.

"And what about babies?" Gayle was saying. "I have *lots* of time for babies. After all, I'm only thirty-eight years old. Why *not* wait another year — "

"Okay," Roger said.

"What? Okay what?"

"Okay, I'll do the therapy thing. I'll just have to make time for it."

Gayle dabbed at her eyes, the torrent of sarcasm trickling away. "Really?"

"Really. Now, can we change the subject?"

She came up from behind and put her arms around him. "You know I'm just worried about you, right?"

"Hmm," Roger said, and patted her hand.

The next day he phoned Decker, who talked at length about scheduling difficulties before deciding all at once, in dramatic fashion, that his other clients would just have to wait. They would start his therapy immediately.

There was surprisingly little probing of the psyche involved in the sessions preceding the jump. For a hundred dollars a week, Roger essentially got a motivational speech. My job is unimportant. My life is unimportant. These were the phrases Decker encouraged him to punish himself with as he winnowed away his overtime hours and engaged in more idle pursuits with his wife. The subsequent time spent watching television, making love, and playing inane board games weighed heavily on him. He sensed a tsunami of work gathering, which, while not immediately visible, would inevitably overtake both him and his wife as they paddled about in the shallows. He began to actually look forward to the jump, if only to have it over with. It would take him months to catch up on all the unfinished work, all the side projects stewing in his mind.

He peered out the airplane window and tried to remember everything Decker had taught him. *Keep your legs under you. Monitor your altimeter. Remember to pull your ripcord.* It didn't seem like nearly enough. They'd prepared for the jump in the YMCA gymnasium, dropping from moderate heights onto exercise mats like commandoes, allowing their knees to buckle and their bodies to roll with the impact, calling out their mantras as they fell.

"I'm an ant!" Decker bellowed. "A gnat! A dust mite!"

A Lamaze class had been in session beyond a heavy vinyl curtain that divided the gym in two. From time to time, Roger could hear a woman's calm voice saying, "Breathe. Breathe. Breathe."

The jump had been purposely slated for a weekday, forcing Roger to take his first unscheduled day off in ten years. That morning, Gayle had taken briefly and violently ill. She said she was nervous about having to supervise a field trip to the zoo later in the day. Roger reminded her that he would be jumping at more or less that exact time. He looked up from his BlackBerry. "You *are* coming, aren't you?"

"How can I?"

"What do you mean? Get a substitute!"

"Don't yell at me."

"I'm not yelling. But you *have* to come. I'm committed to this thing. I've already paid for it!"

"Well, maybe it isn't the best idea after all."

"What? It was *your* idea. And on today of all days — "

The look in her eye (and the way she was holding her butter knife) gave him pause. But he'd be damned if he was going to back out at the last minute, and told her as much. She took a Zantac and two valium with her coffee and went off to work without a word of support.

Roger spent the rest of his morning poring over requisition forms, the phone at arm's-length. No emergencies arose at work to force him to cancel. Around noon, a weather bulletin gave him hope, and he called Decker, who scoffed at the forecast of snow and said that he and his secretary would be there shortly to pick him up in the company car. Roger hung up and called Gayle, intending to guilt her into leaving work early, but she'd said they were at the zoo already and, in any case, she could never have made it in time. She sounded different, more remote than usual.

On the hour-long drive to the airstrip, Roger tried to remember the last time his wife had menstruated. Given her recent fixation on children, he suddenly felt very foolish for leaving the contraception to her. It wasn't that he didn't want children, he simply couldn't accommodate them. And he frankly doubted that they would make very good parents. As they bounced along the highway, Roger watched Decker's sleeping head loll back and forth on the seat rest in front of him and decided that whatever happened — whether his wife was pregnant or not, whether the jump failed or succeeded — he was looking at the responsible party.

The airplane bucked through a patch of turbulence. The view out Roger's window was bleak and forbidding. Decker unbelted and patted him on the shoulder before going up front to confer with the pilot and the outfitter. After a moment, he began shouting and gesticulating angrily. The pilot shouted and gesticulated back. The outfitter took the role of mediator, speaking calmly to each man in turn. Roger strained to hear what was being said. Decker glanced back at him and indicated that everything was fine. He looked like an overgrown child in an orange snowsuit. Finally, an agreement seemed to have been reached. The pilot turned back to his instruments. Decker hollered at Roger and jabbed his finger at the floor. It was time.

Ten seconds of freefall. Adrenaline flooding his body. The ripcord. The chute. Decker's secretary waiting in the designated landing area — one microscopic speck on the pale fields below.

Calmer than he'd expected, Roger unbuckled and had begun to stand when he felt a familiar vibration against his thigh. He clawed at his leg. Against Decker's explicit instructions he had smuggled his cellphone in, set on vibrate. His suit prevented him from getting at the phone, which stopped buzzing after four rings and started again almost immediately. He closed his eyes, every nerve in his body focused on the device in his pocket. He was no longer afraid of the jump. He was afraid of the jump *working*; that the moment his feet hit the ground, his life would appear as meaningless as Decker would have him believe it was. He saw what his wife's meds did to her, how they left her with a vacant quality — a steady, untroubled wind blowing through her head. Was that really what he wanted?

He opened his eyes. The outfitter and Decker were having a conference by the door. The plane banked left, shedding altitude. Decker shouted to him over the roar of the engines. Did he still want to jump? Roger remained where he was, his hand on his leg. The phone rang and rang.

KILLDEER
(Charadrius vociferous)

An instant before contact, it jigs up into the air only to immediately hurl itself back down on the lawn, luring the cat further and further from its nest. With each strike, the distance between flight and capture narrows. Physics are gauged: angles, mass, velocity. The stakes are clear, the risks measured. Again and again they explode off the ground, as if compelled by the same thought, committed to what hangs between them.

CAMERON

"CAMERON? IS THAT YOU?"

"Hi, Mom."

"Oh, my god! Where are you?"

"I'm all right. How are you?"

"*Where* are you? What's that noise?"

"Oh. Cars and things. I'm on a pay phone. It's strange being out again. Everyone running around, bumping into each other. You forget what it's like."

"What do you mean, out again? Where have you been?"

"Inside, obviously. Connecting. That's the irony, isn't it? How the most social and democratic forum ever devised is primarily accessed in physical isolation. You know, people say "the web" these days without even thinking of it as a metaphor, but it's the best word for it, really. The symmetry. All the points of convergence."

"I don't understand."

"Well you *can't* understand, can you? That's the problem. Things are *designed* so you don't understand. One day you think you understand and the next day everything's changed. Built-in obsolescence."

"Cameron, you're not making any sense."

"I guess that's what happens when you learn a new language. Everything gets muddled. So, how are things with you? How is Marionette?"

"I'm...she's fine. She's outside somewhere, I think. Cameron—"

"Cats. There's a funny one. I wonder if they could make the transition. You wouldn't think so, with them being so much more physical than we are. Even if they made it through, their poor, little, cat consciousness wouldn't understand. They'd just be sort of *drifting*. That's the problem with evolution. Someone's always being left behind. Cats. Birds. Mastodons."

"Cameron, I'm just going to put the phone down for a second. I'm going to call your father. Will you stay on the line?"

"Well, I'm not online yet. That's what I'm calling to chat with you about. How did you — Oh! The *telephone* line! LOL! That's priceless. The whole language thing."

"El oh ...? Just a second, don't hang up. George! Cameron's on the phone! Cameron! On the phone!"

"Mom, I can't — "

"He's coming."

"I really can't chat long. Things are going to start moving along quite soon. I'm not even supposed to be — "

"Hello?"

"Hello, George."

"Hello?"

"I'm here, George."

"No. All I'm getting is static. It's this damn portable. I'm coming down there."

"He's coming down here. I'm by the computer."

"I heard. Listen, Mom, I really don't have much time. Forum rules. Silly, but you've got to have them. Rules are important. That's something I've learned in the last little while."

"Ten months. You've been gone for ten months, Cameron."

"Rules are a function of discipline. And discipline is how we hack into our latent potential. But you already know that, don't you?"

"Cameron, I honestly don't know what you're saying right now. Where have you been? Why haven't you called?"

"It doesn't matter. None of it matters. This whole plane. What does it have to do with objective reality? Nothing. But it's hard to let it go. To surrender the comfortable, the familiar. The Buddhists were close, but they didn't quite get it. It wasn't their fault. They didn't have the technology."

"Cameron? Your father's here. I'm going to pass the phone."

"It's too late. There isn't enough time."

"He says there isn't enough time . . . I don't know. Cameron? Your father wants to know where you are."

"It's not important. What I wanted — "

"He says it's not important . . . Your father says of course it's important."

"Tell him — "

"Your father wants the phone."

"I really don't — "

"I'm passing you over."

"Cameron?"

"Hello, George."

"What's going on? Where are you?"

"Why are we so *obsessed* with triangulating our position in three dimensional space?"

"Where *are* you?"

"I'm in the city, George. I never left."

"Where in the city? What's with this George talk?"

"It's your name, isn't it? Don't worry, I forgive you."

"You — Do you know how worried your mother's been? We filed a missing persons report with the police. Did she tell you that?"

"Some very important changes have been happening in my life."

"More important than your family."

"Some things are more important than what you would call family, yes."

"Such as?"

"You wouldn't understand."

"Try me."

"Well, such as your webmaster."

" . . . Cameron. Where are you?"

"Put Mom back on the telephone."

"Tell me where you are."

"Put Mom back on."

"Cameron — "

"Goodbye, George."

"Okay, okay. He wants to talk to you . . . I don't know."

"Hello?"

"You didn't have to call the police, Mom. I'm thirty-two years old."

"I know that, sweetie. We missed you on your birthday."

"I need to refresh."

"Cameron?"

"Refreshing."

"Talk to me, Cameron."

"They say it's going to snow tonight. Do you know how rare that is? Can you remember a single time that it's snowed this early in the year? What do you think it means?"

"Please stop this. You're scaring me."

"It's okay. Everything will be explained in the mass email. How we're going to do it, get rid of these bodies. See, right now you're my mother, but when you think about it, I'm *your* mother and you're *my* son and we're both someone else. You just have to plug in and — "

"Cameron?"

"Dad!"

"Your mother is crying. She's sitting right here beside me crying. What did you say to her?"

"They told me this would happen. They told me I'd regress."

"They who?"

"Firewall. IP 657.493.442.8. I'm going online, George. Wireless. Beyond DSL, beyond the speed of light. I'm leaving tonight. Are you still there, George? Put Mom back on."

"I will not."

"It's all right, George, I forgive you. That's something I've learned how to do since I've been gone, but it hasn't been easy. I stream things. I've been streaming so many things. Nothing is ever deleted, you know. Once something's on the system it's always on the system. It's always *right there*. What is consciousness? Software. What is body? Hardware. What if you could upload your software into a newer, better piece of hardware? You see, the consciousness is perfect. It's the body that's flawed. The body can be infected. The body can be corrupted. The body can be abused. Because the body can't always defend itself, can it, George?"

" . . . "

"George? Put Mom back on."

"What are you going to do?"

"Goodbye, George."

"Wait. Just . . . wait a second. I'll ask her . . . He says he wants to talk to you . . . I don't know."

"Cameron?"

"Don't cry, Mom. There's nothing sad about what we're doing. You'll see for yourself soon enough with the resurrection and the digital harrowing. All will be forgiven."

"Stop this! Stop it!

"I'm sorry, I shouldn't have called. I didn't want to upset you. I wanted to reassure you. All this pain you've been carrying around with you will disappear in an instant, and you'll wonder how you could have ever lived any other way. You're the sleeping fish, and one day soon you're going to wake up and find that you've become the ocean. But you have to be patient."

"Cameron — "

"I have to go now. Watch your inbox for new messages."

"Cameron!"

"I forgive you, Mom. Stay online."

NORTHERN PINTAIL
(Anas acuta)

Regular wingbeats close to the ground. Rain above, an enormous force behind, driving it over fields and sloughs. Below, the water is occupied by familiar shapes, familiar cries beckoning. It swerves and comes around for a second pass. The reports are not so much heard as felt, tearing holes in the flock, which — immense, unbreakable — sews itself together and continues on.

LEAH

AN AFTERNOON SHOOTING CLAY TARGETS HAD not prepared her for this. There were more birds than sky up there: ducks and geese, honking and whipping about in the rain. Beside her, her brothers were already breaking their stocks open and reloading, all the more like soldiers in their camouflage gear. Their efficiency was almost frightening. She could not imagine the collision of their world with her world. Or rather, she could imagine it all too well: her friends casting ironic looks at one another as her brothers clanked long necks and made broadly homophobic remarks.

Ian smiled over at her, his face wet and happy. He was half drunk, she could tell by the laziness in his eyes. She was fairly sure that neither of her brothers should have been handling firearms at this point, but it seemed part of the routine. Everything about the trip had a feeling of ritual about it, a ritual from which she had been excluded for the last twenty years, and to which she was only now, in the wake of her father's death, being granted reluctant access.

At the end of each trip, her father had mounted the camera on a tripod to catch them posing together by the kill in the open flatbed. This year, there would be a new camera, a new threesome. She'd been grateful for the invitation, but hoped her brothers understood that she was making a sacrifice of her own in being there, that she was no more comfortable holding a gun than they would have been discussing Wittgenstein over cappuccinos in the Ground Zero coffee bar.

Rain cascaded over the brims of their hats as they swivelled their guns and shot at the sky. Leah wondered if this form of camaraderie held an intrinsic value that she was incapable of appreciating. She raised her own gun and sighted the birds. All the tension in her body caught in her wrist, unwilling to proceed up her hand to her finger. It should not have been this difficult. She had killed things before. Countless insects. Once, a family of mice, when the live traps failed to work. As an omnivore, she had been indirectly responsible for hundreds, if not thousands of deaths. If she was going to eat an animal that someone else had killed, it only made sense that she should be prepared to kill that animal herself. But now that she was standing inside the classic hypothetical, logic did not carry her far. Only the thought that both of her brothers — Bill especially — expected her to back down was enough in the end to nudge her out of paralysis. She loosened her wrist and squeezed the trigger. The gun bucked her shoulder. A goose separated from the flock and dropped out in the marsh. Leah shrieked in surprise.

"Atta girl!" Ian hollered.

Leah gasped and laughed wildly. The weapon's manifest power sent an unexpected, reckless charge through her, and the awareness of transgression only enhanced the thrill. Her next shot was more purposeful. She squinted up along the barrel, isolating and tracking a single goose.

This one dies.

As if bound to her finger by an invisible string, it dropped from the sky.

"I meant that!" she said.

Her brothers might as well have been in a different time zone, speaking to one another in clipped voices:

"Got her."

"See that?"

"Dirty bugger."

Leah felt as if she was eight years old, trying to get their attention as they worked on the car in the driveway — lost in that drawling man-speak — until Ian took pity on her and galloped her around the yard on his back. He had made that effort, at least. He had always been the gregarious, democratic one. On her twelfth birthday, he invited half a dozen friends of his own (each with liquor in tow) and seemed to genuinely think this would improve the atmosphere for everyone. Bill, however, had not even come.

The birds continued to flood the sky from the north. Leah watched them with increasing shame. It did not take a philosophy major to read the symbolic implications of their actions: white North Americans with guns, waging war on nature. Ian finally noticed that she was holding an empty gun and helped her reload.

"Is this normal?" she said.

He bent closer. "What?"

"All these birds! Is it normal?"

He shook his head and grinned.

Bill was giving them an amused, sidelong look.

The night before, they'd arrived at the campsite just before sundown. Her brothers quickly set up camp, while she hovered about, trying to make herself useful. When the stars began to come out and they sat down by the fire to drink, she saw that they had constructed an environment where there would be nothing to do but speak. The conversation was strained at first but, with each warm beer, Leah grew bolder and more talkative, barraging Ian with questions and feigning absorption in his answers until Bill lobbed an empty bottle into the bushes and went to bed muttering. She felt as if she had been winning an argument only to be silenced by a single, contemptuous blow.

"Why does Bill hate me?" she'd asked Ian.

He jabbed a stick into the campfire and stirred up the embers. "Bill doesn't hate you."

"Okay, maybe hate's too strong of a word. How about dislike? Why does Bill dislike me?"

Ian shrugged and offered a neutral smile. The charred log sent wisps of smoke into the sky. Leah drew her knees to her chest and looked up. The stars seemed to have density and weight, like sand scattered across black paper, arbitrary and meaningless. "I just don't understand," she'd said, "why he has to be such an asshole."

Now, as Ian passed her the newly loaded weapon, it occurred to her that Bill might have been awake in the tent and listening the whole time. Well, what did it matter? He *was* an asshole. She watched him take down bird after bird — unwavering and, it seemed to her, unfeeling. Flecks of sleet had begun to bite into her face and hands. The clouds were moving quickly, wrestling with each another in aggressive formations. It seemed unwise to be out in the open with metallic implements raised, but she said nothing and waited for her brothers to finish.

After some time, Bill lowered his gun and turned to Ian, yelling to be heard over the wind. "That's me! What're you at?"

"All my dark, all my pins!" He took lazy aim and brought down two birds in one shot. "All my light!"

Bill laughed and jerked his head at Leah. "How many'd she get?"

Leah was coming very close to hating them both, but when Ian looked at her again, she immediately felt embraced. "What are you up to, Lee?" he said.

"Four," she lied. "Four geese."

"Dark or light?"

"Dark?"

Ian nodded and squinted up at the sky. "Well, I guess that's it."

Without even looking at Leah, Bill suggested that they split her remaining limit. Boyish excitement came into Ian's face. He turned to her. "You don't mind, do you?" Leah gave her brother a look that was supposed to communicate everything she was feeling: that she was cold and wet and a little afraid, and that however irrational it might seem, those birds were *hers* and she wanted to spare them. But Ian just smiled expectantly and, when she shook her head, her brothers whooped and took up their guns again.

The killing had become a massacre. And the birds kept coming. She wouldn't have thought there could be so much waterfowl in the province. It was no migration. They were fleeing from something. There was little cover around, and the truck was parked on the shoulder of a grid road, some twenty minutes away. Staying out there was sheer, dumb machismo. Yet she remained quiet, hunched in the pummelling sleet, her jacket soaked through and weighing her down. After a few minutes the shooting stopped and her brothers looked at one another.

"That's it," Bill said.

Ian nodded and again seemed to remember that Leah was there. "Are you all right, Lee?"

"I'm fine."

"Want to head back?"

Bill had begun to wade into the marsh. He stopped and looked back at them, his expression flat and unreadable. Leah shook her head and headed out after him in her oversized hip waders. She had feared that she would find the birds wounded and thrashing but all that she came upon seemed dead. She hefted two geese into her bag and began to slog back towards the shore. A sudden dimming made her stop, knee-deep in water. The decoys swayed around her. She scanned the horizon. The sleet had given way to snow. Her brothers were yelling to one another. A dark shape tumbled past along the water. Bill's hat. Then, all at once, the storm hit. The wind came roaring down, parallel to the water. She covered her head, fighting to remain on her feet. Her brothers seemed incredibly far away. The wind turned her around and they blurred out entirely. She froze, arms outstretched, blinded by the snow and flying grit. Dimly, above the wind, she could hear the frantic cries of birds, and what sounded like helicopter blades. Huge projectiles tore past her head. She was in the middle of the flock. Birds crashed into the marsh all around her. One struck her full in the face and she found herself horizontal and half-submerged, anchored in mud up to her wrists.

She kept her head above the water and instinctively prayed to a god in whom she had never believed for deliverance. Gradually the impacts around her stopped. After several failed attempts at standing, she managed to remain on her feet. The water was thick with bodies. She had lost her gun. The snow erased everything, like some terrible lesson at the end of a morality tale. Every way she turned seemed to lead her into deeper water. Her face was burning. She whirled and clawed at the air, as if wind was an element that could be swum through. She did not deserve this death, and yet it had come for her, and it would not be moved by pity or reason. A dark veil descended over her eyes. She reached out, found her bag of geese, and held onto it. Then someone — whether it was Ian or Bill she couldn't tell — was gripping her by the arm and leading her away.

Brown-headed Cowbird
(*Molothrus ater*)

Deep in the ribs of the spruce, it opens its mouth and cries out
for more, a giant among its siblings, ravenous and implacable.
First fed, last fed, while the other fledglings starve. The
surrogate parents come in from the rain, seem to marvel at
their prodigious heir, accepting what has appeared in their
nest against all logic. A changeling.

Wade

It wasn't that he wanted to hurt his boy. He just knew from
experience that corporal punishment worked. If they'd made
James sweat it out a little in his room first, then called him out
and, calmly but firmly, introduced him to a belt or hairbrush, the
only thing on his mind would have been how not to find himself
in that position again. But the nature of his punishment was not
up for debate. Charlene had set the terms without consulting him:
two weeks grounding, which, to Wade's mind, was like confining
a fish to its bowl.

"He never leaves the house," he said.

Charlene gave him a look that said, *and how would you know
when you only see him an hour every day?*

They were having this discussion in the master bedroom, as
Charlene changed out of her work clothes and he changed into his.

She traded her slacks for a pair of stylish jeans and walked by him in her brassiere. "I told him no television."

"What about the computer?"

"I restricted his computer time."

"Restricted?"

"He needs it for school."

A gust of wind peppered the window with what sounded like sleet. Wade buttoned his shirt and frowned down at the creases he'd ironed into it (Charlene left the chore to him, claiming that they were equally capable of doing it, which was simply not true).

"Was that Larry character there?" he said. He wasn't entirely clear on what James had done that afternoon, but assumed the Lutz boy had put him up to it. Until recently he hadn't given Larry Lutz (Wade refused to call him Lawrence, thinking it a ridiculous name for a twelve-year-old to go by) much thought. He'd been more concerned with the boy's parents, whom Charlene had aggressively courted, organizing gatherings that were, for Wade, always uncomfortable. But when he stumbled on the boys in James' room that summer doing something that would have been perfectly normal for boys their age to be doing had they not been doing it together — *to one another* — he concluded that Larry was a decidedly bad influence on his son.

"Lawrence?" Charlene said. "I really don't know. Oh, that reminds me, we're doing dinner with the Lutzes on Sunday."

Wade looked at her.

"What?" she said.

He sighed and shook his head. The last thing he wanted to be doing on one of his rare days off was sitting in some overpriced restaurant, making strained conversation with Oscar and Gloria Lutz — the women talking about whatever they talked about, while Oscar made patronizing attempts to engage Wade in conversations about football or home renovations; the diagonal shifts where Oscar engaged Charlene on something and Wade and Gloria sat back, thinking (he assumed the doctor's wife shared this thought) that their spouses would have made a very good couple.

"Do you want me to cancel?" Charlene said.

"No. Forget it."

"Okay," she said, brightly.

"Okay?"

"I'm sorry. Was I supposed to argue with you?"

Wade's arms tensed. For an instant, he imagined throwing his wife across the room. As usual, she had steered him into a situation he could not win. Had he insisted they cancel, she would have sulked about it for days. But his angry silences — this angry silence — had no effect on her. She would cheerfully wait him out until he forgot what he was mad about in the first place.

He stood up to tuck in his shirt and Charlene's eyes went down to the service revolver on his hip, her mouth bunched in disapproval.

"Do you have to wear that in the house?"

"Am I supposed to hide it?"

"You could put it on later. You could wait until you get outside at least."

The suggestion was ridiculous, but she hadn't intended to make a fair or valid point, just shift the focus of the conversation, negatively, onto him. This accomplished, she went into the bathroom and closed the door.

"You might have asked me," Wade called after her.

"About what?" she called back.

"About James. You can't just do this stuff, what, unilaterally."

Charlene laughed. "Where did you get that?"

"What?"

"Unilaterally."

"It's a word."

"It's not one of your words."

Wade did not know what galled him more, that she presumed to know the extent of "his words", or that she was right about him having recently picked it up (on the CBC, in reference to the American war effort in Iraq). As he combed out his moustache in front of the vanity mirror, his wife pointed out through the closed bathroom door that he had been sleeping when she picked James up from the zoo, and that she had tried to do him a favour by not waking him. Wade smiled bitterly. Since starting the night shift, he had taken to sleeping in the basement, it being darker and quieter during the day. In his absence, Charlene had claimed the master bedroom as her own, redecorating so gradually that he hardly knew it was happening. First she changed the bedding, then feng shui-ed the furniture all around, then shuttled most of his clothes to the spare room (for his convenience, she claimed). Now, as he scanned the dresser below the mirror, he noticed that one more thing had been changed.

"Where's my horse?" he said.

Charlene flushed the toilet, and he waited for the water to stop running before calling out again.

"Your what?" she said.

"My horse! My bronze horse." The statuette had no particular significance or value that he could think of (he could not even remember where it came from), but it had been with him since his bachelorhood and he liked knowing where it was, reared up on its hind legs beside their wedding photo on the dresser.

"Isn't it on the counter?" Charlene said.

"No, it's not on the counter."

"I might have put it away."

"Away?"

"My horse, my horse," she called to herself in a plaintive voice.

"Away where?"

"I don't know, Wade. The attic?" She came out of the bathroom, her face washed, her hair brushed out. Even without makeup, she could have passed for thirty — a streak of grey in her hair the only thing to betray the extra decade.

Wade sat down on the bed and she inserted herself between his parted knees. "Aw." She looked down at him with a mocking pout. "What's the matter?"

He kept his eyes on the floor. "Nothing."

"Come on. Give."

"I don't know. First you're painting, then you're moving the bed, and now . . ."

"Your horse," she said in a solemn voice. "Do you want me to put it back?"

"Forget it."

"No, no. I'll go and find it right now. I'll get your big, muscular horse and put it back in its special place."

"Forget the fucking horse."

Now they were fighting. Charlene's face had shut down, as if he'd suddenly hauled off and slapped her. She went over to the closet and began flitting through blouses. As usual, she had managed to twist everything around so he was the one at fault, he was the one who was being unreasonable.

"Two weeks isn't long enough," he said to her back.

She pulled on a white shirt with a severe collar. "For goofing around on a school field trip?"

"It isn't just that."

"No?"

"We have to put our foot down."

She laughed. "What are you talking about?"

Wade had hit his son only once, out of fear, when he was still in diapers and had gotten into the cleaning products under the sink. At the time, Charlene had assured him that, if it ever happened again, he would come home from work to find them both gone. Why couldn't she see what to him was so obvious? James acted up because they let him act up. And if they didn't intervene soon, with *conviction*, he was going to wind up in serious trouble.

"Four weeks," he said, looking down at his feet.

She had buttoned up her shirt and was fixated on the mirror, sliding bobby pins into her hair. "Two weeks is a long time for a kid."

"Three weeks." His voice was getting smaller, his toes fisted into the carpet.

Charlene moved closer to the mirror and touched her face. Her eyes shifted to his reflection and she sighed. "I've told him already. It wouldn't be fair to change our minds now. Two weeks grounding. That's the sentence." She opened the bedroom door and looked back at him. "Okay?"

BARN SWALLOW
(*Hirundo rustica*)

The nest, fastened high on a wall above the hayloft, is composed of mud, leaves, tarp, twine, saliva, grass, wire, hair, and cigarette paper. The barn is built of iron and wood. Outside, the wind gropes and pries at the boards. But, in the nest, it remains untroubled, as if the building was constructed generations ago for its protection alone.

FRED

HE HAD BEEN WATCHING HIS REFLECTION in the television for the better part of an hour. Although the curved glass was blank, he knew that it contained the power to transmit sound and images to him in his chair. He understood that the machine functioned on scientific principles, not magic. He was not stupid. Still, he experienced a great deal of unease with the remote control in his hand, as if holding the stick with which he was about to prod a sleeping bear.

He had never understood the appeal of those sinister-looking boxes. Even through the long, prairie winters there was no lack of things to do. What free time he had was amply filled reading month-old newspapers and recording pertinent information in his ledgers. The entries were literal and spare. He made note of crop yields, animal illnesses, and weather conditions, all in the precise block lettering of a ten-year-old. He never recorded his personal thoughts, because he did not require the comfort of talking to himself. He did not require the comfort of talking to anyone, he had found, so long as he was occupied, and he had always been occupied.

But, in recent months, his body had begun to oppose his will, and the language of its protest was pain. It required tremendous effort at that moment to simply lean back and look out the window. Had he been deaf and blind with the house on fire around him he would have known the dramatic shift in weather by the ache in his bones. He reached for his pencil, paged that year's ledger open and wrote: SEPT 22 — SNOW. In any other year such an early snowfall would have been very bad news, but all three hundred acres lay fallow, and would remain so, he guessed, until he could find someone to rent them in a manner he approved of.

He picked up the remote control again and returned his attention to the television. For most of his adult life, he had remained untouched by the trappings of modern civilization. But all that changed when his granddaughter began to visit.

"You need a phone, Fred," she would say, blowing a tight stream of smoke out the corner of her mouth and tapping the ash from her cigarette into a glass of water. "It's time you moved out of the dark ages."

Beth had sought him out after her mother passed away in the summer of 1995, a death Fred had not learned of — the death of his own daughter — until the day she arrived at his front gate in her small, yellow car. He had known Cecilia only as a stunned and hungry fish, gaping in her mother's arms in the window of an idling truck. Less than a hundred kilometres from his front porch, she had lived and died, raised by a man he had never met, married in time to a man who would give her a daughter of her own.

To Fred, Beth's existence was both impossible and utterly usual, the way a seed contains a pumpkin, a sunflower, a crabapple tree; the way they repeat themselves, season after season. By the same principle, though he had not invited it, or even hoped for it, blood of his blood had returned to him. Her visits became a regular occurrence on the farm, as inevitable and unpredictable as hailstones or drought. At least once every summer, she arrived without forewarning: sunglasses on, cigarette in her mouth. Alerted by the barking of the half-wild dogs that roamed his property, Fred would leave off his work and show her inside with the courtesy of a well-bred child. Together they would sit in the main room on chairs that he had built, and she would talk about her life — her health issues, her work in the post office — while he sat with his hands clasped between his knees, erect and attentive.

When the conversation occasionally turned to him (or when she turned it to him — he was entirely passive in the process) she would gently berate him for what she considered to be his backward way of living. "You need electricity," she would say, to which he would shrug and nod as if fully sympathizing with her position. "I'm serious, Fred. How can you be comfortable here in the winter? Look at that gap under the door. Isn't it freezing?"

He would shrug again, amiably, and wait for her to lose interest in the subject. The old wood stove had always suited him fine. Even now, it was keeping him (and the two cats currently nestled under it) warm, and would continue to do so until he lost the ability to properly stoke it. Cats and dogs came and went on his property as they pleased. Some stayed. Some left. All died, eventually, and every time he came upon one of their stiffened bodies in the grass or was forced to help one along, he experienced a vague, but tangible, sense of loss. This feeling was one of his most valued possessions. That it had dimmed over the years but not guttered, was how he knew that he was still human, still decent in his core.

Time might have blanched his hair, rotted his teeth, and whittled the very meat from his bones, but he still shaved daily, scrubbed his clothes weekly, and always made a point to change his hat when sweat ruined the bands. These rituals of hygiene recalled him to the man he once was (before his parents and brothers were caught in a vehicle that misjudged the road and rolled down into the Pelican River; before, in the aftermath of grief and confusion, he fathered a child with his cousin; before that child was taken away). For nearly three-quarters of a century, he had lived alone, worked alone, and would have died alone had it not been for Beth.

Why she continued to visit him each summer, he couldn't say. He didn't mind her company, though she made him aware of his hands and seemed anxious to leave from the moment she sat down. He was not unaware of her unconventional lifestyle and neither approved nor disapproved of it. When at first she referred to another woman as her "girlfriend", he'd simply nodded, processing perhaps half of what she was saying at the best of times. But when she arrived one summer with a tall, handsome woman in the passenger seat of her car, he gathered the nature of their relationship quickly enough; not from any show of intimacy or affection, but from the quality of the discord that lay between them. This revelation would have shocked even his younger neighbours, but Fred had cultivated a rare tolerance in isolation — so removed from the machinations of the world that nothing his granddaughter said or did could have offended him.

The tall woman seemed to take an instant liking to him, or at least to find everything he said or did hysterically funny. "You're telling me that you don't have a bathroom?" she'd said. He shrugged and covered his mouth, assuring her that she was welcome to use the outhouse around back. The tall woman shrieked with laughter, then sat back and regarded him as if he were an impressive sight, indeed. "That's wonderful, Fred. No, really. I mean it. One of these days I'm going to do it myself. Just chuck it all. Move out into the woods, build a house, grow my own food."

Beth was giving her an incredulous look.

"What?" the tall woman said.

"Life without Starbucks?"

"Yes?"

"Life without Blockbuster?"

"You think I couldn't do it?"

Beth shook her head. "It's not a challenge, dear. I just don't see the appeal."

The women fell silent, gazing off in separate directions. The significance of this exchange was clear, even to Fred. The following spring, Beth came without the tall woman and he did not ask after her. This was the year that she began to express more fervent opinions about his mode of living, telling him what modern conveniences he needed — absolutely *needed*. When she saw the sum in his Credit Union passbook she feigned a heart attack. "Oh, my lord, Fred! I'm calling the phone company!"

He did not know why Beth was so intent on him having a telephone, but it seemed a small enough concession at the time. She made the arrangements and soon a line was strung from the road to the house, linked by a row of wooden crosses. For months after the installation, he would stop in the middle of the yard and look up, caught by the sight of the heavy wire bisecting the sky. After the telephone came electricity. After electricity came heat and running water. Workmen gutted one room of the house and filled it with tiles, pipes and gleaming fixtures (not liking the idea of squatting so close to where he slept, he decided to use this room as a walk-in pantry). Movers brought a refrigerator and an oven, which he quietly accepted and paid for, though he continued to make use of the wood stove and cold storage. Still unsatisfied, Beth tried to convince him to move into town, telling him that he could afford to buy an air-conditioned house with six bedrooms and a swimming pool out back. What she did not understand was that trips into town were the most stressful events of Fred's life.

Every second Friday he drove in to visit the bank, the grocer, and the hardware store. Sitting high in the cab of his truck, in a freshly ironed shirt, he would make his way down a series of gravel roads to the main highway (driving at least ten kilometres per hour below the speed limit, never once using his turning signal). When he hit the town limits, he would keep his face forward and his hands on the wheel, tension coiled in his stomach. Feeling himself a spectacle among the townspeople, he would avoid all eyes on the street, and respond to any questions put to him in the shops with a philosophical shrug and a soft, lilting moan. Then, with the strength of a man half his age, he would load up the bed of the truck and drive slowly from town.

Back home, he tried to ignore the modern implements steadily encroaching upon his living space: the sleek appliances, the cold heaters along the baseboards. Until his injury, only the telephone had seen any use (Beth calling once a month to ensure that he was making use of her gift, along with fast-talking strangers who wanted to sell him more conveniences he had no use for). The single outgoing call he had ever made had been accidental. Reaching for a jar of preserves in a cupboard above the sink, he slipped from a footstool and upset the cradle on his way down. Beth had programmed one number into the phone, emergency services, which the impact dialled. The receiver skittered out of his reach but they heard him cursing well enough and sent an ambulance out to fetch him.

Nothing in his experience had prepared him for the indignities of the hospital. He shared a room with two other residents, his only privacy being a vinyl curtain around the bed that was rarely drawn. Nurses were present to witness his most private acts, feed him, bathe him, deal with his waste, and it seemed that they intended to keep him there indefinitely. But when Beth came to visit and saw how they'd swaddled him in diapers and left him in his own filth, she stormed through the hospital, holding everyone who worked there accountable. Even the doctors were cowed by this bossy woman from the city and, as Fred watched her lecture them, his body hummed with embarrassment and pride. After that, they were eager to discharge him. Beth attended to the details of the move, hiring an ambulance to bring him back to the house and arranging for the necessaries to be delivered to his door.

All but incapacitated, Fred was forced to make use of the refrigerator, the sink, and the indoor toilet. His waking hours consisted of periods of agonized activity followed by much longer periods of recovery, but at least he was home. In the following weeks, Beth began to travel out to see him more frequently. On her latest visit, she brought along a 14" colour television and a small satellite dish, which she bolted to the house as he protested through the open window. For all his noises to the contrary, he was secretly pleased by her ministrations and, as she gave him a tutorial on how to operate the machine, he experienced a fondness that he had no way of communicating.

"You don't have to watch it if you don't want to," she said, after going through her instructions three times, "but I'll feel a whole lot better knowing you have some distraction."

"If it's so important," he said, with a martyred shrug.

Before he could process what was happening, she stood up and kissed him on top of the head. He reached for her hand too late. She was already striding to the door and wiping her eyes. It took him three weeks to sit down and seriously think about using her gift — a gift that would be passing back into her hands soon enough. Although she did not know this, he had seen to it that she would inherit everything. What she did with the house and land when he was gone did not concern him. He only hoped that the figure in his bank account that had so impressed her, and that he'd never had any use for himself, would make her happy.

Outside his window, the wind kicked up wraiths of snow and swept them away. A high whistling sounded through a hole in the eaves. The remote control in his hand was covered in a daunting number of buttons, each marked with an enigmatic letter, number or symbol. He aimed it at the television, as Beth had instructed, and boldly pressed the largest button. Nothing happened. He pressed another button, then another, moving methodically from top to bottom until a dull tone sounded in the television and blue light swelled in the screen. He sat back and waited for a program to begin. The cats watched him from under the stove. The solid blue did not change. He aimed the remote once more and resumed pressing buttons.

Finally, an image appeared on the screen: a man and a woman sitting behind a desk, looking into the camera and talking, their faces bright and glossy. Fred grunted and gestured at the television, indicating to the cats what he'd done. He sat back and watched for some time before realizing that although the mouths of the people were moving, he could hear no voices.

"Arrow for sound," he remembered aloud, and pushed one of many arrows on the device. Another program appeared: three young people standing in the middle of a room, waving their hands and talking to one another. Still there was no volume. He strayed to the smaller, round buttons and a row of blue text overlaid the image. Slightly alarmed, he returned to the familiar arrows, but this time they caused the picture to take on a greenish cast. He pressed more buttons and the text disappeared. The arrows now functioned as they had previously, though the colour remained distorted. The picture changed to a giraffe running across a field. As he continued to press the arrow, random imagery passed across the screen: exotic landscapes, massive buildings, real and animated animals, people doing obscure things or speaking out at him as if they could see him. He watched each channel, dutifully, for a short period of time, before pressing the arrow again. Without volume, the images were more bizarre than they might have otherwise been, and he did not try to interpret them. He felt as if he was peering into a box at another species of being, the way conquistadors must have felt as they watched the doomed tribes of Mesoamerica. He was looking at the empire beyond his land. This, evidently, was the world.

GREY PARTRIDGE
(Perdix perdix)

Nothing will move her. Not the wind or the snow. Not the erratic human footsteps labouring past the hollow she has made in the earth. Her late brood. Beneath her, fourteen embryos yawn and swell inside brittle ovate pods. Her stillness is meditative, guided by an instinct that is not unlike love, and a patience that is not unlike faith.

DAWN

LAID OUT IN THE BACKSEAT, HOWLING away, you'd think he was the only person on the planet to ever break something. In her life, Dawn had broken her arm, her nose, her collarbone, and two fingers. She'd had her tonsils, her appendix, and her uterus removed. She'd been attacked by dogs, wasps, and an abusive ex-husband. She'd been to the emergency room so many times that some of the nurses knew her by name. So she was something of an expert on the subject of pain. And she had no doubt that Roger Ingram was being a baby.

People that paid to jump out of airplanes, people with the money to blow on that kind of thing, didn't know pain. They didn't know what it was like to live on rice noodles and white bread for a month. They didn't know what it was like to flinch every time the telephone rang because the collection agencies were hounding you. They didn't know what it was like to come home from work, aching and numb, day after day, for little more than welfare. And when the least bit of pain finally hit them, you'd think that someone was shoving strips of bamboo under their fingernails. Well, welcome to the real world. Now, for the love of Christ, suck it up and shut your mouth.

"Can't you go any faster?" Ingram moaned.

Dawn ignored him and concentrated on the road, gauging her distance from the ditch by the intensity of the gravel juddering beneath them. With all that snow rushing the windshield, they might as well have been in a submarine, navigating on sonar. Decker was quiet in the passenger seat, likely thinking about lawsuits. He'd be right to worry. Dawn had seen his business for what it was the minute she walked through the door. He didn't need a secretary. He needed the appearance of needing a secretary; someone to field the odd telephone call, greet clients in the office, and collect them in the station wagon following jumps.

With little actual work to do, she'd made herself useful in other ways. At first it had almost seemed a fringe benefit of the job, like a complimentary membership to the gym, but lately he'd been using the words "we" and "us" far too often. Since her hysterectomy, she'd had little use for men outside of the bedroom. She had plenty of friends to drink with and confide in, and could always stay with her sister and nephew in times of crisis. She was a good aunt, doting on Wanda's son, but with no kids of her own, commitment was the last thing that she wanted, least of all from a man like Decker.

His scheme had been doomed from the beginning, not because of any shortage of rich idiots in the city, but because he was overconfident. Wanda called it his "tragic flaw". Well, today it had finally caught up with him. When Dawn saw the storm moving in from the ground, she'd assumed that they would abandon the jump, but the pilot stayed right on course and soon two parachutes were flowering open in the blustery, overcast sky. Right away she could see that something was wrong. The chutes were diverging fast, Decker fighting his way to the drop zone while Ingram drifted off, seesawing crazily in the wind. Decker landed first, and as she drove out to collect him, hailstones started popping off the hood of the station wagon. By the time they loaded up his gear (he insisted on gathering his chute before going after his client), the storm was nearly upon them. They found Ingram writhing in a bright mustard field three kilometres away. He blinked up at Dawn like a shot and terrified deer, and for a moment she almost felt bad for him — a sympathy that vanished when, after she'd disentangled him from his chute, he screeched and swore and forced her to all but carry him to the car. As she slammed his door and glanced up at the darkening sky, snow had begun to mingle with the sleet. Now it looked like it was going to keep falling until Christmas.

Hunched over the wheel, working at a walnut of tasteless chewing gum, Dawn tried to maintain an equilibrium between caution and haste. She had to make it to the highway. The thought of being stranded out there with those two (Ingram yowling in the backseat, while Decker stared though the windshield at looming criminal charges) was not pleasant.

"This," Decker said, "is why we do what we do." Dawn glanced over and saw that he was regarding her with a manic, almost deranged smile. "Can you feel it? How close we are to the edge? We're *beyond* the edge now. We're *in* it."

"We're in it all right," she said, grimly.

"I'm serious, Dawn. Some people live their entire lives without experiencing a fraction of this. True danger. Mortal danger."

"Oh, shut up!" Ingram said.

Decker ignored him. "Flight and pursuit," he went on. "The animal racing towards you. The spear in your hand. Your senses blazing. I'm telling you, Dawn, this is what we were *made* for."

It looked like she'd misread his silence. He wasn't worrying. He was getting off on this. She'd often wondered why he risked operating an unlicensed business when it was obviously so unprofitable (for proof of this she had to look no further than the car she was driving). Now it all made sense. He wasn't motivated by profit at all. He was piggybacking on his clients' expensive "therapies". He did whatever they did, and they paid his way. It was as simple as that. He was as crazy as they were, if not crazier.

The back of the car began to drift out and Dawn wrenched the wheel in the same direction, fighting to keep it centred. What she felt in that moment — working furiously at her gum — was not pleasant. She regained control and eased her foot off the accelerator. Neither of her passengers seemed to realize how close they'd just come to slamming into the ditch. She glanced at the rear view to find Ingram talking into his hand. Decker spun around.

"Mr. Ingram!"

"Hello? Hello? It's me. I've had an accident. Can you hear me?"

Before Dawn could stop him, Decker had unbuckled, climbed onto his knees, and lunged into the backseat. "Give me that thing! Give it to me!"

"Ow! Are you insane?"

Decker's wide behind kept nudging Dawn, and it gave her some satisfaction to elbow him and sit him back down. He had won the wrestling match and was brandishing the cell phone. "This is — "

"Strap in," she said.

For a second it looked like he was going to argue with her, but he sat back and buckled in, before twisting around to look at Ingram. "This is *extremely* disappointing, Mr. Ingram. We'd been making so much progress. And now it's all been undone."

"You bastard," Ingram moaned.

As tense as she was, Dawn began to laugh. If she didn't make it home, the real tragedy would be that she'd never get to tell the story. Decker's ridiculous speech. Two grown men, about to die and squabbling like kids.

"Do you see this?" Decker said. "Look at me. *Look at me.* This is for your own good." He cranked his window down and let the wind tear the phone from his hand. Ingram howled and kicked at the seat. Dawn shook her head, laughing uncontrollably.

"That's right," she sputtered, wiping her eyes. "That was real smart. What do we need a cellphone for?"

Decker looked at her warily. "Jesus, Dawn. Get ahold of yourself."

She roared and pounded the steering wheel.

"Watch it!" Decker said.

A man was standing in the middle of the road. She gripped the wheel and pumped the brake.

"What are you doing?" Decker shouted. "Drive!"

"Am I supposed to drive right through him?"

"Go around him!"

The car came to a stop two feet from the man. He went for the rear passenger door, and Decker reached back to lock it.

"Let him in," Dawn said.

"He has a gun, Dawn."

"I can see that. Let him in."

"There's no room," Ingram said.

"Make room," she snapped.

The man tapped at the window, almost politely, and Decker relented. Once the door had opened a crack, the wind tore it open all the way. The hunter manoeuvred in with his gun and fought the door shut. His face was raw, his eyes wide.

"Are you alone?" Beth asked him.

"Yeah . . . No . . . My brother and sister . . . " He had dark patches on his face. His fingers were discoloured and swollen. Dawn could see that they needed to get him to a hospital. Ever since her sister's ex came banging on her door after the cops dropped him ten kilometres from town in the dead of winter, she'd known what frostbite looked like. The car rocked in the wind. The hunter was shuddering uncontrollably. She wanted to ask Decker if he thought he'd been having fun out there.

"Do you have a phone?" the hunter asked.

Dawn gave Decker a pointed look that he did not return. She could see that the hunter was noticing the men's orange jumpsuits and wondering what they were doing out there. "It's a long story," she said, and put the car in drive. The tires spun and failed to catch. She put it into reverse and they continued to spin.

"I told you not to stop," Decker said, quietly.

Dawn put the car into park and looked at him. "Well, I guess you'll just have to get out and push."

Black-and-white warbler
(*Mniotilta varia*)

In the shadow of the apartment complex, it creeps up the throat of a willow, talons fastened against the wind and the sleet. The head probes deep crevices in the bark — methodically, compulsively — until a soft clutch of grubs is located, writhing against the beak's point. Drawn out one at a time, they slide down the dark, acidic passage, unassembled and absorbed.

Adams

THE DUCK WAS DEEPLY BRONZED, THE steamed vegetables tender and bright. The salad had been oiled and dusted with hand-shaved parmesan. The skins of the baby potatoes would slide free at the slightest pressure of the fork. Altogether, the meal said everything Adams wanted it to say. Simple. Elegant. Masculine.

He poured himself a glass of moderately expensive Beaujolais and toured the apartment one last time. The cleaning woman had done a fine job, but a bit of chaos was needed, some evidence of life. He deposited a few choice books in every room but the bathroom, made a small display on the coffee table in the den (a leather-bound notebook cracked open to a page of uncorrected verse, a pencil imprinted with his canines, an enigmatic score of music), narrowed the seating space on the sofa with additional throw pillows, then stepped back to survey the scene through female eyes. Rugged ocean vistas on the walls, erotic Chinese figurines on the mantle, custom-made bookshelves brimming with titles, including his own modest contribution to literature: twelve volumes of poetry, his memoir, and one failed novel. This last venture, he was convinced, was directly responsible for the stomach difficulties plaguing him in his seventh decade of life. Five years, four hundred pages of bone-bright prose, every word in place, every comma, every fucking semi-colon, for what? A single press run and a smattering of reviews written by pissants (graduate students and failed writers all) who saw fit to chide him for the "difficulty" of a book it was doubtful they had even read.

Just the other day he had come upon a dozen hardback copies in the discount bin of a major bookstore, tagged at $3.99 apiece. If that weren't indignity enough, a man with the face of an anteater had picked up a volume, skimmed the first paragraph (as he stood not five paces off, looking at the photograph of himself on the dust jacket — a black and white of him reclining on the porch of a rented cabin, staring darkly out at the water), chuckled and tossed the book back down. The man glanced over and, though he shrank from the fury of Adams' gaze, there was no apparent recognition of the cause.

If only he had been born in another era, when poets attained the status of Gods! He saw himself strolling along the icy banks of the Volga with a brass-handled walking stick and a gloriously ostentatious mink hat, delivering grave nods to passers-by, each of whom knew him by name. But this was no time for self-doubt. *She* would be there at any moment. Since she'd appeared in his second-year poetry workshop, Adams had developed a pleasant fixation on the girl. She possessed a form in which imperfections became attributes: jade-green eyes angled gently towards one another in the manner of roofs, a slight underbite shelving the thin upper lip on its swollen partner, an uncommonly high forehead framed by short, boyish hair. Moving down: the long neck, the sharp clavicles, the small breasts, the exposed midriff (that plane of impossibly taut flesh), the intimate jut of pubic bone. Her slim hips and thighs, her muscled calves, her naked, sandalled feet. Lambda. He wanted to kiss the parents who had given her such a bizarrely fitting name. She had the long body of the Greek letter, an absence of curvature that made him ache to explore the understatements of her body.

She was young enough to be his daughter, his granddaughter, but he had no doubt that he could have her. In the weeks preceding this evening, he had not profaned that fact with bestial imaginings, but rather took her abstractly — their coupling refracted in a series of prismatic moments, some visual (a hand sliding up her calf), some sensual (the warm give of his reception).

Although he felt it his duty to adopt a critical stance towards the university as an institution, he knew that he owed them a great deal. So many young and lovely girls prancing about — backs arched, rumps raised as if presenting. True, there were just as many young bucks that he could never have competed with physically, not even in his prime, but fame was his advantage, and few could outpace him in the art of verbal seduction (a talent he had increasing opportunities to exercise in the wake of his third wife's passing).

Back in the kitchen, he covered the vegetables and checked on the duck in the warmer. One of Mozart's less ruminative sonatas was playing on the stereo. The music called to mind rolling Scottish fields: a peasant girl humming a folk tune as she strides out to the well with a wooden bucket, starlings pulsing from tree to tree in the midsummer sky.

The prosaic clanking of the door chime shook him from his reverie. He looked at his watch, smoothed back his hair and carried his glass to the door.

He found the girl looking over her shoulder, as if wary of an attack from the rear. "You're late," he said, extending one arm across the doorjamb to bar her entry. Most of his students would have been cowed by this manoeuvre, but she merely rolled her eyes. The shoulders of her denim jacket were dusted with white.

"My god," he said. "Is it snowing?"

"Started on my way over." She gave him her jacket and went straight for the bookshelves — hands in her back pockets, head tilted to read the titles. Adams put her jacket away and looked out the window, stunned at the volume of falling snow. He turned to her with a tutting noise.

"You might have to wait this out."

Lambda seemed unconcerned. He was charmed by her casual attire: scuffed tennis shoes, a form-fitting beige sweater, blue jeans frayed at the cuffs and fading at the knees. "So this is where the great poet lives," she said.

"You were expecting something more opulent?" He dipped into the kitchen and returned with the bottle of red and a second glass, pleased to find that she had fixated on the score of music on the table.

"What do you play?"

"Nothing," he said. "I read them for pleasure."

She laughed. "Are you serious?"

"Always." He filled the second glass and gave it to her.

She handed him the score. "Show me."

Adams peered down at the sheet, elaborately cleared his throat, and made some experimental noises. He hummed a series of quarter notes, slipped down an octave and sang his way back up through a stumbling arpeggio. Then he found the melody and picked up the tempo, hand sawing out beats of four. The piece allowed him to exploit his range, gravelly below the staff, falsetto above. Not reading at all, he finished with a flourish and tossed the sheet aside (it seesawed through the air and scudded to a perfect landing on the table).

"Ravel," he said. "Nice bit of fluff." He turned and headed for the dining area, where he removed the cover from the vegetables, fluffed up the salad, and set the duck on an artistic little trivet in the centre of the table. The girl followed behind, trying very hard to appear as if this were all commonplace. He wondered what her usual dates consisted of. Pizza in greasy cardboard. Thoughtful discussions of silly art movies. Boys in black turtlenecks and expensive eyewear playing at grown up. Before he could protest, she'd taken the seat he had reserved for himself with his glass, where the light came from above and behind to paint blocks of mysterious shadow on his face. He hesitated before the other seat. The girl was looking at the duck as if it were a dear relative, glazed and braised.

"I thought I mentioned," she said. "I'm a vegetarian."

"Oh? No, I don't think you did mention that. How interesting." Why hadn't he been prepared for that possibility? Something of the farm girl in her. He'd assumed that her childhood would have been informed by the routine slaughter of beasts, that she would have been the kind of person a vegetarian meal actually offends.

"Birds don't count, you know," he quipped. "They're a species of vegetable."

"Sorry," the girl said, not looking the least bit sorry. "It looks like you put a lot of effort into this."

"Not at all. Entirely my fault." Determined to remain cheerful, he peered into the fridge, the freezer, and the pantry. "Ah. Here we are." He weighed a bag of pasta shells and whistled a snatch from *La traviata*. "I'll just whip up some pasta."

"Eggs."

"Of course." Damn these fundamentalists!

"I'll get by on vegetables."

"You'll starve," he said, trying not to pout.

"I don't take much filling. Wow, is it dark in here. Could you turn on another light?"

Adams sighed and turned up the faux chandelier a notch. Direct attack was not going to work. He was going to have to flank her. "I have to tell you," he said, "it is nice to have company. I have so few opportunities to cook for someone else these days." He allowed his widowhood to settle into the girl's mind as they dished up. Pity was a powerful weapon in his arsenal, and one that he was not above using. He took a few bites of duck, washed it down, then clapped his hands together. "All right. Let's get down to business. Did you bring work?"

Unexpectedly flustered, Lambda extracted a folded sheet of paper from her back pocket. "I've been working on this one for awhile. It still has some real problems, but — "

"Don't prevaricate." Adams snatched the paper from her. This was the part he enjoyed. "Go on, eat. I can't concentrate with you watching me."

The poem was better than most of the trash that came his way in workshop, competently written, clearly addressed to a lover (ex-lover?). He wondered how it must feel to have such a girl directing such passion at you.

"What?" she said.

"Hmm?"

"You sighed."

"Did I?"

"Is it bad?"

"No, not at all." He returned the poem and skewered a potato. "How are the vegetables?"

"You're not going to comment?"

Adams chewed for a while, then shook his head. "I don't think so. Are you sure you don't want to try the duck? Brave little flier." Her body stiffened. He had to be careful. Praise would have been the safest, most profitable course at this juncture, but the merits of her work made him uneasy. He felt compelled to remind her of her place. "Tell me about the boy," he said.

"What boy?"

"The boy you wrote it for."

"Why?"

"Because I'll bet that when you were making love you didn't feel like . . . what was it? His 'hands were the true measure of your body'. Fine words. Fine sentiment even, for a love note, not a poem. Help yourself to more potatoes. They're no good the next day. What was it Plath said about potatoes? *Unpoemed, unpictured* — "

"You can't do that," Lambda said. "You can't just dismiss it without some helpful comments."

Adams suppressed a smile. "Can't I?"

"No, you can't. You're a teacher. If you weren't going to help, you shouldn't have read it in the first place." There it was, that passion he had seen surface at moments in class: her chin tilted up, the long throat exposed.

"My dear," he said, adopting a British accent. "I believe that the host reserves the right to direct the conversation in whatever direction he sees fit. Furthermore, over the dinner hour, it is generally understood that serious topics are to be avoided. Frivolities are placed at a premium. A little airy talk to help with the digestion. Do I take it you're asking me to break this rule?"

She remained serious. "Yes."

He refilled both their glasses, then leaned back and crossed his legs. "I'll be frank with you. Personally, I find this line of conversation . . . unilluminating. Come see me during office hours and we can talk about your poetry, my poetry, any poetry you like."

"You're the one who brought it up."

"So I did. I apologize."

She stared at him with folded arms.

"Well, if you simply can't wait ..." He injected an ironic huffiness into his voice. "I'll break my rule here. Provided that you respond in kind."

"Meaning?"

"Meaning you step out of your role as student and address me as an equal. We become a man and a woman passing a pleasant evening together."

She regarded him analytically. "All right."

"Good. Give it to me."

He skimmed the poem once more, confirmed what he had sensed on the first read, and handed it back. "You can keep the last line. The rest has to go." That registered. Not in her face, but in the sharp intake of breath, the sudden swell of her breast. "Don't look so shocked. As a poet you're going to have to learn to be ruthless. The last line would be a fine first line for a poem."

"You're saying I should cut the whole poem."

"I'm saying that you have your beginning." Her eyes went cold. Adams sighed. "There's nothing wrong with the writing. It's polished and technically fine. You have a good instinct for rhythm and a knack for metaphor. But you talk about love with such authority. What can you possibly know about love at your age?" She began to protest, but he talked over her. "I'm not saying don't write about love. I'm saying don't write about love in *this* way. Infuse the love with passion. Infuse the passion with loss. Do you understand?"

She remained silent.

"Now. Tell me about the boy."

Something like disdain flashed across her face (for the boy? for himself?). "Nothing to tell. You know him."

"Oh?" Someone from the program, then. He was offended by the thought of her yielding to their clumsy, pubescent advances.

The girl laughed, unexpectedly. "Start with the first line. Okay." She emptied her glass and looked around the room with evident amusement. His judgment of her work seemed to have an emboldening effect on her. Or was it the wine?

"Is something funny?"

"I'm just noticing how much work you put into all this. Got the Mozart going and everything." Adams struggled to hold onto his smile. "It's all right," she said. "I was pretty much expecting this."

"Expecting what, exactly?"

"Seduction." She angled her head down and turned her eyes up, emphasizing the "duck" of the word.

Adams spread his hands. "Just a meal between friends."

"You have a reputation for friendliness." She emptied her glass and refilled it before he could think to take the bottle away. "You know what they call your apartment at school? The lair. They say it's funny that no male students are ever invited back to the lair." Adams shifted to conceal his excitement. Even as she mocked him — *especially* as she mocked him — the blood rushed to do its work below.

"I think it's time we talked about something else," he said.

"All right. How about Eliot? Can you explain Eliot to me?"

"Oh, I doubt it." He had to rein the girl in. She was working herself into a frenzy. "Let's talk about fear," he said, cryptically. "And desire."

"Oh, my god." She covered her mouth. "That's what it always comes down to for men, isn't it? De*sire*." She pronounced the word theatrically, pushing her lower lip out further than usual. In that instant, she looked no older than twelve.

"I'm not talking about sexual desire. I'm talking about a desire for love, for God, of which sex is just one manifestation. I'm talking about desire compelled and compounded by fear." She had left off her wine, and he continued, believing he had her attention. "When you look up at the stars, how do you feel? Terrified and small. You want God to reveal himself. You want the universe to explain itself. You want everything that you can never have. So what do you do? Out of desperation, you turn to the act of physical love. Because however insufficient that union might be, however messy and difficult, it's the nearest you will ever come to a union with God. Or with yourself." He was using his lecture voice now, liking the soft rumble in his throat.

"He," the girl said.

"I'm sorry?"

"You just said God was a he."

"He, she. The point is — "

"It's important. It's important that you used "he". Or that you're talking about, like, one god singular."

"I say "he" instead of "she" or "it" because that's the convention. I say "God" instead of "gods" or "pervasive life force" or "nonexistent being" because that's the convention. Metaphysics and gender politics are not the current topic."

"But it's *important*," she said. "And it relates to a question I have about your work."

Adams shook his head and began ferrying dishes over to the sink. "I think we've had enough work talk for one night, don't you?" He raised his hand. "Please don't argue. Now, I sometimes like to have a joint after dinner. Tonight happens to feel like one of those nights. Since you appear to be stranded here by the elements, I have no choice but to invite you to join me."

"Are you serious?"

"The young haven't cornered the market on recreational drug use, you know. Don't worry, it's one hundred percent vegetarian. If you'll wait for me in the other room, I'll be out in just a minute."

This time his assumption about her lifestyle proved accurate. She liked the idea so much that she gave a small cheer before leaving him alone in the kitchen. He took his time with the dishes, located a Ziploc bag at the back of the freezer, then peered around the corner into the den. She was on the sofa, leaning forward to read the journal he had left open on the coffee table.

"Shame on you," he said, causing her to jump.

"I wasn't — "

"Of course you were." He came over and sat beside her. "It's all right. I would do the same thing in your position. When I was a boy, I read all of my sister's diary entries. Every tedious page." He rolled a thin joint, put it in his mouth, and patted at his pockets.

"Here," Lambda said. She opened a flip-top lighter and made him bend for the flame. The end caught and Adams inhaled deeply. He passed the joint to the girl, and a casual shift resulted in their knees pressing together. She drew in the smoke and held it.

"You know," she croaked, "it's kind of reassuring."

"What's that?" Already the drug had begun to massage his anterior lobe.

"To see your work in such a rough state."

Rough? As far as he was concerned, the poem was finished. It had gone through no fewer than eight drafts before he printed it in that notebook.

"I mean," she continued, "so much work is going to have to go into that poem before it's, like, publishable." Adams searched her face for signs of irony and found none. The joint was back in his hand, puckered and wet. "You can tell you're just, you know, blah! Getting it out there. Leaving the clichés, the clunkiness, the melodrama."

Adams was slow to respond. His face had begun to slacken. "Everyone's process is different."

"Totally." Lambda seemed unaffected by the pot. "Like it just doesn't *come* for anyone." She touched his leg for emphasis and when she drew away, the nerves continued to tingle. "This is so cool, Trevor.

That we can just talk like this. Two artists. There was something else I was going to say. Oh, yeah!" Whatever it was, Adams was sure he did not want to hear it. "So, I was wondering. And I don't mean this as a personal attack or anything. But I was wondering about the presentation of women in your poems. It seems that they're always, you know, over there. Up there. Totally idealized."

His head moved up and down, slowly, as if underwater. "We all see what we want to see."

"Okay, but aren't you kind of objectifying women when you praise them the way that you do? Isn't it kind of degrading?"

Adams was accustomed to this particular criticism, and gave one of his usual replies. "There's no degradation in adoration. No harm in simple, reverent . . . " — he placed his hand on her thigh — "contact." She covered his hand with her own and looked at him seriously.

"No, Trevor. It's degrading to *you.*"

Adams shuddered. Suddenly, she appeared alien to him: her cheekbones shunting up and rounding off, her upslanted eyes catching light from various parts of the room. She saw his fear and smiled. Then she grabbed him by the lapels and drew him towards her. He tried to claim the momentum as his own, to become the instigator, but she easily wrestled him back and straddled his body. She seemed to have become possessed by a cool, malicious spirit. As she studied his face, he grew conscious of his thinning hair, the extra weight around his middle, the seared animal flesh on his breath. She rotated her hips. "I know what you want," she said. "And you can have it. But first you have to promise me something." He turned his face away, but she gripped his hair and forced him to meet her eyes. He saw his bent, terrified reflection in the curve of her pupil. She lowered her mouth to his ear. "You have to promise me that you'll never write a poem about this."

Blue Jay
(*Cyanocitta cristata*)

Circling the floodlit building, it sends its voice out through the snow, the shape of the other imbedded in its mind. A spasm in the nest, a cloacal kiss. Fluid passing from body to body without the invasive stab. With this gentle coupling the bond was forged, their future mapped. They were to remain faithful to one another for the whole of their lives.

Rose

HER DISPLAY PRESENTED TWO TREASURE CHESTS and a pirate. Her plastic bucket was empty. Without hesitation, Rose stood up and headed for the cash machine. The floor seemed to tilt beneath her, vines writhing in the darkly patterned carpet. Employees passed in burgundy vests and blazers, their features queerly arranged. She stopped at the ATM by the tinted front doors, withdrew her limit for a single transaction — $200 — and exchanged it for dollar tokens from the dispassionate teller at the cash window.

She had forgotten how the casino was like a parallel universe, where time moved incredibly quickly (there were no clocks in the building and no natural source of light) and money had no absolute value. She hadn't intended to end up there that afternoon. She had simply been out shopping when a sudden downpour drove her to seek shelter, and the nearest building happened to be the

Casino Dinero. She'd ordered a sandwich and coffee in the lounge, intending to do nothing but eat and ring up a cab to take her home, but the merry, repetitive tunes from the casino floor tugged at her. She felt like doing something mildly irresponsible for a change. She had twenty dollars in her purse. Leah was out of town with the boys on their annual hunting trip. The house was empty. No one would miss her. When the twenty was gone she would leave.

Had she lost her money immediately she very likely would have left, but she quickly doubled it on the slots, then doubled it again. She exchanged her tokens for chips and moved to the blackjack tables, where, within minutes, the dealer — an aboriginal woman with a complicated brooch at her throat — took back her sixty dollar surplus, along with the initial twenty. She had the dealer reserve her spot at the table and made her first withdrawal at the cash machine without even thinking about it.

Decades before, on holiday with her husband in Las Vegas, she'd won two thousand dollars on a quarter machine. Back home there had been limits to how much she could lose on bingo and the lotto, but when they legalized VLTs, she'd begun to visit the casino regularly, stopping only when her husband sat her down and explained that if she did not stop they would have to mortgage the house.

She'd read that in any game of chance, the odds of winning or losing were identical on every play, regardless of prior outcome. Flip ten heads in a row and the odds of the eleventh flip coming up tails will be no greater or less than on the first flip. The contrary belief (that the odds of flipping tails increased as one flipped a succession of heads) was so common it had a name: The Gambler's Fallacy. Whatever the mathematicians might say, her intuition told her that a run of bad luck was a windfall waiting to happen. With this in mind, Rose had joked with her fellow gamers throughout the day, making light of her losses and celebrating her small victories, never once believing that the damage she was inflicting on her bank account was permanent, that her streak of misfortune could continue for so long.

Now, as she carried her newly filled bucket of tokens down the main aisle, the turn was as near and elusive as ever. She tried to open her mind and intuit which machines were impregnable, which were friendly and loose. Altogether uncertain of herself, she sat down at a bank of cheery progressives across from the bar.

"Mrs. Cartwright?"

Rose froze with her hand in the bucket, praying that she had misheard, or that there was another Mrs. Cartwright in the vicinity, or that, by remaining still, she would somehow be camouflaged by her surroundings. "Mrs. Cartwright? It is you!"

The woman sitting down at the next machine was, at a glance, a stranger. Judging by her age and the formality of her address, however, Rose guessed her to be a former student. After thirty years of teaching, she was accustomed to a certain amount of celebrity. What they never seemed to realize was that, for her, they were one among thousands. Her machine flashed impatiently. She attempted a smile, feeling as her overweight friends must have felt when she met them in Safeway, browsing among the cakes. Teachers were not supposed to have vices. They were paragons of virtue, like parents, like the clergy.

"Lucy Bennett," the woman said, touching her chest. Her fingernails were hot-pink slivers, her mouth a dark, glossy shade of red. A cheap, blue bracelet dangled around her wrist.

Rose shook her head. "I'm sorry . . . "

"Grade six? Pemberton elementary?"

This was not exactly helpful. Her entire career had been spent teaching grade six at Pemberton. Still, she transformed her shaking head into a nodding one. "Yes, of course! Lucy Bennet! How are you, dear?"

Lucy laughed. It sounded as if she were trying to force something out of her throat. "Not so good," she said. "My date just ran out on me, if you can believe that. Fucking men."

"Oh, dear," Rose said. An aura of mental instability was radiating off the girl, an aggressive, feral quality.

Lucy shook her head in wonder. "Fifteen years. Can you believe it? I bet you're still married to that good-looking dude, kids all grown up, working cushy jobs, grandkids on the way. Yada yada yada." She lit a cigarette (having evidently not heeded the stark warnings from Rose's health unit). Rose waved her hand in front of her face, but the girl seemed oblivious to her discomfort. "Hey," she said, "remember those silhouettes you had us make out of black construction paper and tape all over the classroom walls?"

Rose remembered. It was one of her staple projects.

"And the Christmas pageant? Remember how you had us stand in rows at the front of the gym? You always wanted me to sing louder. You kept pointing at me in the back row, doing this." She held her hand out palm up and made a sweeping motion. "I could never sing worth shit. And then on Valentine's Day? You had us bring those books filled with cheap cards and made us fill one out for every single person in the class and think of something nice to say. Christ, I hated that."

"Yes," Rose said, "that does bring back memories. You know, I've been retired for five years now."

Lucy regarded her coolly. Rose cleared her throat and asked what the girl was doing those days. Was she working? Did she have a family?

"Oh, I'm working." That barking laugh again. "Work, work, work." A woman in a short dress and far too much makeup passed by. Lucy flipped a hand at her. "Co-worker," she explained. "God. Mrs. fucking Cartwright. This is so trippy."

"Yes." Rose gave a conclusive smile. "Well . . ."

"So, where's Mr. Cartwright? Is he around here plugging the slots somewhere?"

"Oh, no. My husband passed away last year."

The girl did not acknowledge this revelation, but merely looked around the room, apparently searching for someone. Her cigarette-free hand worked the blue bracelet around and around. She turned back to Rose, her smile falsely bright. "So, are you up tonight?"

"Excuse me?"

Lucy gestured at the bucket.

"Oh, I just play for fun."

"Uh-huh." Lucy crushed her cigarette in the ashtray between their machines and stood up. "Well, I'd better get back to work. But from me to you? Get out while you can. There's no winning on those things. See you around, Mrs. Cartwright."

Lucy wandered over to the bar, where she sat down beside a balding man in a yellow shirt. The bartender brought her a bright-green drink with a straw. She turned to the bald man and began chatting with him. Rose watched them until the man glanced over and caught her staring. She looked away, confused by the hostility in his face, and played her machine for awhile. When she looked again, they were up and walking, Lucy with her arm snugged in the older man's elbow. Only then, as she watched them pass out of sight, did she understand what Lucy was doing in the casino. *Working* in the casino. She snatched up her bucket of coins and hurried after them.

"Lucy? Lucy!"

She went up and down the rows. She had no idea what she would say or do when she found her — give her money? take her home? — but if she failed to intervene, she felt that she would have failed the girl twice over. After two full passes of the building, she locked herself into a stall in the ladies room and wept as quietly as she could. The washroom had the feel of a boardroom:

oak-panelled walls, muted light, peaceful music on the sound system. She listened to other women come and go; all there for the same reason, in defiance of the odds, all believing that they were somehow different. That Rose's children had not ended up like Lucy was a matter of luck. That she had been recognized by her old student that evening was also a matter of luck. Had things gone differently, had she only *seen* the girl, she might have transformed that meeting into a stroke of good luck for them both. It was all so unspeakably random.

Once her emotions had settled, she washed her face and returned to the casino floor. The rhythm was easy to find. She moved from machine to machine, her mind empty, her arm rising and falling, her fingertips blackened by the tokens. After twelve trips to the ATM, she felt as if she might pass out. Finally, the machine informed her that only one hundred and forty dollars remained in her account. She withdrew the entire sum and brought it to the cash window. Her bills were taken. Tokens flowed down a plastic ramp into her bucket. The cashier wished her luck.

As she bore the last of her savings away, Rose considered, with something like pride, what she had managed to accomplish. In a matter of hours, her chequing account had been wiped out. She would not have enough for groceries. She would have to pawn the television. Beg for change. Walk the streets. Her body shook with giddy laughter at the thought. Then she remembered the girl, and feared she might break down weeping all over again.

A squat machine in the corner of the room beckoned to her — an old-fashioned contraption with a lever on the side and ill-lit reels; crystal balls and tarot cards taking the place of the traditional cherries and bars. She sat down, inserted three tokens, and pulled the handle. Twenty-five spins later, she had yet to win back a single dollar. She might as well have been pouring her money into a hole in the ground. The experience was brutally cathartic, like striking someone over and over again who keeps asking to be hit. She was playing to lose now, to escape the grip of the machines. Her growing sense of relief was marred by the presence of a vulture pacing behind her: a fat man with tinted sunglasses who jiggled his bucket of coins whenever he passed.

The bowl-shaped cameras in the ceiling kept their impassive vigil. The vulture turned tighter and tighter circles around her.

Rose spun on him. "Do you mind?" The man appeared shocked, perhaps believing he was invisible. He made a gobbling noise and took two steps back, not embarrassed enough to fully yield the opportunity. She turned back to her machine. Her fingers scraped the bottom of the bucket. She dropped the coins into the slot. The wheels turned. Three identical symbols slid into place in the display window. An alarm sounded. A light flashed on top of the machine. The payout icon blinked, but nothing fell out into the tray.

"That's a good one!" her neighbour said, a woman with frizzed hair and eyes made huge by powerful lenses.

"I think it's broken," Rose said.

"Oh, no, they'll come around and pay you. The machines don't hold that much." The brief moment of fellowship passed, and the woman narrowed her eyes before returning to her own machine with increased vigour. The vulture uttered a defeated squawk and sidled away.

Rose looked up at the list of combinations and prizes. Three Seeing Eyes was the top payout, at five thousand dollars. She did not even smile. All the tension drained from her body, leaving her limp and quaking. A minute passed and a vested employee came up to her, brandishing a set of keys on a string.

"So, you're the lucky lady! We've been waiting for this one to hit." He opened the machine and turned off the alarm. Rose held onto her seat, suddenly quite dizzy. "I just have a bit of paperwork for you here, ma'am. To make it all official." Rose took his pen and made the necessary notations. Her fellow gamers cast envious looks at her, clearly deeming her unworthy of the windfall. "So, what's going to happen now," the employee said, "is you're going to take these forms to the cashier and they'll pay you over there. All right? Mrs. Cartwright?" He was peering into her face as one peers into a muddied window.

Rose carried the papers to the cashier, who made a phone call before counting out fifty one-hundred dollar bills. She swept them into a thick stack, then paused, remembering something. "Do you want any of this in chips or tokens?"

Rose was having trouble focusing on her. Only her eyes remained clear. Jade-green wheels, pitted with black.

"Ma'am?" the cashier said. "Do you plan to continue gaming this evening?"

PURPLE MARTIN
(*Progne subis*)

Order has returned to the house in the courtyard. The sparrows have been evicted. The vacancy in unit 22 was quickly filled. The newcomer sits watching the snow fall outside its entrance. A more desirable tenant, it has nothing to fear.

CHRIS

SHE STRODE THROUGH THE KITCHEN, DID a sultry catwalk spin, and cast a coquettish look over her shoulder. "What do you think?"

"Please!" Mr. Bojangles said.

"Who's that sexy lady? That's what you're thinking, right?"

"Please!"

"What did that foxy mama do with Chris?"

"Pleeease!"

"All right, Jangles, settle down." She pushed a sunflower seed through the bars and he snatched it away. Anyone who thought that birds had no feelings had never owned a parrot. Mr. Bojangles not only employed the word "please" in the right context, but added to it a wheedling tone that was all his own. At different moments, he could be fearful, despondent, wrathful, manipulative, playful, and loving. His emotions were so humanlike that Chris had taken the unusual step of removing poultry from her diet while continuing to eat red meat (her sympathies did not extend to pigs and cows simply because she had never befriended one, or even seen one up close; she'd always felt threatened by the emptiness that lay beyond the city, the uniform land with its insular, narrow-minded garrisons).

She gauged her appearance in the kitchen mirror: black skirt, burgundy coat with a ruff of false fur, purse snugged up against her body. She looked good, there was no question about it. She *felt* good, her stride coming easy and natural. Humming to herself, she topped up Mr. Bojangles' feeder, made sure his water was full, and propped open the kitchen window with a thick book. It was snowing outside, but the radiator had kicked in and she wanted to make sure that he had fresh air for the night. He took another seed from his dish and fixed her with a haughty look of reproach.

"Jangles . . . " She wedged her hand through the bars and tried to stroke his tail. "Don't be jealous, honey. You're still my number one man." He ruffled out his feathers, apparently unconvinced. "I'm *sorry*. I have to go. I'll see you tomorrow, okay?"

Before she could change her mind, she turned off the light, grabbed her keys, and slipped out of the apartment.

Her plan was to catch the number 22 and be well on her way to Farley's before anyone from the neighbourhood saw her. He hadn't wanted her to take the bus alone. He could be sweetly protective in a way that she was not entirely sure was good for her.

She hadn't thought much of him at first — his big hands, his unruly hair and shabby suit; more of a welder than an artist. She'd been too busy resenting her friends for bringing her to an art gallery on a Saturday night to appreciate his work. But, when she stepped out for air later that evening and found him having a cigarette on the sidewalk, he displayed an appealing combination of confidence, self-effacement, and sexual directness. Later still, on the bed in her apartment, he told her he wanted to photograph her. She nuzzled up against him. "Kinky. You want to tie me up first?"

"Not now. Formally. I want to do a series. To document the changes."

"Document the changes."

"That's right."

"That's the nicest euphemism for "exploit" that I've ever heard."

"It wouldn't be like that at all."

Eventually, she agreed to sit for him, clothed and in the nude, in the controlled environment of his studio. She'd never thought that she would end up with an older man, let alone an artist with the build of an aging professional wrestler, but his rumbling bulk beside her in bed had come to ease her own passage into unmedicated sleep. She had trouble imagining her life without him, and that scared her.

Mr. Bojangles' angry vocalizations faded as she hurried down the hall, away from her apartment. The floorboards creaked in other units, and she pictured her neighbours at their peepholes, watching her pass. She knew that no one cared. But knowledge and belief were two very different things.

She made it to the stairwell and descended three flights to a heavy metal door. Outside, the street was empty. As she waited for her bus, involuntary tremors radiated from her core to her extremities. A short, balding man shuffled down the sidewalk and stopped beside her. Chris knotted her hands at her waist. Her shadow leaned strangely on the pavement. Sirens swelled in the distance and stopped somewhere nearby. She was about to abandon the enterprise altogether when the 22 materialized from the snow down the street like a ghost bus. It pulled up at her stop and the driver peered down from his seat. The bald man stepped back, indicating that she should board first, and it was this gesture (which she interpreted as not merely polite, but *chivalric*) that decided things for her.

The driver did not return her greeting when she climbed on the bus, but that was not unusual. Nor was it unusual to have the seated passengers stare at her coldly, as if blaming her for forcing the bus to stop. She'd intended to make a point of sitting beside someone, perhaps even striking up a conversation, but headed for the empty back instead, taking a seat against one of the walls. The bald man sat up front, and the bus started moving again.

Chris studied her reflection in the opposite window. She looked like what she was: a young woman heading across town to meet her lover.

The bus crawled south, gradually filling up. Every time a new passenger got on (appearing battered and disoriented as they hauled themselves out of the snow), Chris held her breath, but they seemed unaware of her; so much so that she began to wonder if she was being pointedly ignored. Normally she would have said something lighthearted and random to shake people out of themselves, but tonight she feared that the silence had spawned around her.

Halfway to Farley's, a pair of teenaged boys climbed on, their clothing overlarge and sagging, their ball caps intentionally askew. All but shouting at each other, they swaggered to the back of the bus.

"Yo, I don't even care."

"Forget about it, dog."

"Don't take my fucking transfer. I got that transfer, like, five minutes ago!"

"I know. I saw you, dog."

Chris smiled to herself. White boys from the suburbs, playing at being gangsters. At their age she had been just as loud, just as coarse, only she had dressed in military fatigues and sported a mohawk and a safety pin in her ear. As they sat down across from her, a banner from the City Day parade, torn loose from wherever it had been draped, swept past her window. She wondered what the protocol would be when the streets finally became impassable, if the driver would simply abandon the bus and leave them to find their own way home. Her eyes settled on the advertisements above the boys' heads. The Poetry in Motion for the month read:

> *Autumn Haiku*
>
> Naked limbs outstretched
> The last plum of the season
> A bird with no mate.
>
> T.E. Adams

In the next panel, an advertisement for the Kids Help Phone presented a grubby-faced boy on a street corner. Farley had done a series on the homeless a few years back and could have provided them with dozens of more convincing photographs. He had an eerie ability to insinuate himself into the personal space of his subjects without calling attention to himself. In the studio, he was firmer with his models. When Chris sat for him, his requests took an imperative form. *Tilt your head. Lean forward. Lift your arm. Like this.* Wading into the frame, he would shape the pose with his hands, force her body where he wanted it, then step gingerly away and command her not to move. She wondered what it said about her that she was most attracted to him when he was holding her head this way, in the vice of his hands.

At a certain point, Chris realized that the boys' banter had ceased. She glanced over to find them openly watching her, their expressions cool and predatory. She smoothed out her skirt and sighed. She was not experienced enough to know what the look meant, whether it was cruel or merely lascivious. Well, let them look. In fifteen minutes she would be sitting in Farley's living room with Mingus on the stereo, a glass of wine in her hand, and her feet in his lap. As his rough hands worked the tension from her feet, she would tease him about the boys that had checked her out on the way over.

But it was impossible to ignore them. They had become the one still point on the bus, talking now, in low voices. She leaned back and watched for landmarks.

"Hey," one of the boys said.

She ignored him, her head twisted away at an unnatural angle.

"Hey," the boy repeated. "You a chick or a dude?"

The wipers at the front of the bus banged back and forth. The surrounding passengers were keeping their eyes directed ahead, or fixed on whatever they were reading. Chris should have been prepared for this. In her mind, she had often rehearsed how she would deal with such a situation — looking the offender square in the eye and uttering two distinct words: *Fuck. You.*

But now when she looked at the boy who had spoken, she could only look away. He made a whooping noise and elbowed his taller friend. "Oh, man, I told you. Didn't I fucking tell you?"

Chris looked out the window, blinking rapidly. She was not a child in a schoolyard. She would not allow them to hurt her. But the feelings of helplessness and rage were flooding into her head on their own. If Farley had come with her, this would not be happening. They wouldn't have dared. This, more than anything, infuriated her, that they expected her to do nothing.

"Hey," the short boy said. "Do you still have your . . . you know. Do you still have it? Or did they like, chop it off?"

His friend let out a bray of laughter.

Chris attempted a forbidding look. The tall boy looked away, reddening, but his friend stared right back at her. His eyes were pale blue; tufts of downy hair on his upper lip and chin. His mouth worked into a mean little smile. Chris broke eye contact and again sought out the faces of her fellow passengers. None so much as glanced at her. She considered pulling the cord to signal the driver to stop, but Farley's apartment was still blocks away. She pictured them following her off the bus, pursuing her through the storm, nipping at her heels like jackals.

"Say something," the short boy said. "Aw, come on! Say something! Is your voice all deep and shit? Man, that would be fucked up!" The boys hooted and slapped hands. The adrenaline roared through her veins. Impulse and action came simultaneously. Suddenly she was up and descending on them — bringing the contents of the purse down, repeatedly, on both of their heads.

"Bastards," she was saying. "You little bastards."

Something solid in the bag struck the short boy's skull. The other passengers were watching now, but still doing nothing. Chris shifted to the tall boy, pummelling him down into the crash position — head on his knees, hands on his head. The bus braked to a halt and the driver hollered back at them. Chris steadied herself, improved her grip on the bag, and continued her assault, focused on the grim, necessary work of retribution. Her arm fell and fell, and she waited for someone to stop her.

HOARY REDPOLL
(*Carduelis hornemanni*)

Even here, among the dead, there is shelter, not in the mausoleums or the chapel, but in the hedges around the grounds: sturdy shrubs repelling the wind and offering pockets of calm, just enough space for it to breathe.

TANIA

TESTING THE LIMITS OF THE VEHICLE in extreme weather conditions was not her favourite thing to do. In her short career, Tania had seen more carnage on the highway than she cared to remember. Even the best drivers were vulnerable to the erratic habits of others: the drunks, the careless, the fatigued — careening through the streets like random bullets. Ambulances crashed too, paramedics attending to other paramedics. It happened more than people realized. But, at the moment, they were in no particular hurry. She feathered the accelerator, trusting her reflexes and her peripheral vision to keep them on the road and in the right lane. Warehouses on one side. The sprawling grounds of the cemetery on the other. The thought of all those bodies under the snow set the hair on her arms to prickling. Since taking on a career as an EMT, death had become the axis that her mind turned upon. She was not preoccupied with mortality, exactly (the idea of death, the obliteration of *her* in any sense that mattered), but with the question of how she would die.

The possibilities were endless. Quick or slow. Natural or unnatural. Intentional or accidental. The most likely immediate scenario involved a vehicle slamming into her door at high speed at some upcoming intersection. With morbid tenacity, she strained to place herself there, on the brink of destruction — meeting the eye of the other driver, both of their faces illuminated with the certainty of what was about to happen. She felt the terror, the shock of overwhelmed pain centres, almost enjoyed the vision of her body being subjected to irrevocable physical damage.

A similar masochism had recently invigorated her sex life. She was not a fan of technology in general, but the internet had provided her with a forum to talk to, and occasionally meet, men who had discovered the kinship between pleasure and pain. They began as anonymous names in chat rooms, became images through photos or (preferably) webcams, acquired voices through bravely exchanged telephone numbers, and were ultimately revealed to her as three-dimensional humans in some mutually agreeable public location. Some were confident online but cowardly in person. Others bore little resemblance to their photos, or none at all. A few were pleasant company, but failed to generate sparks. Some were downright frightening. A very small number had accompanied her home, where the clothes came off, the gear came out, and play began in earnest: the ancient struggle between master and slave unfolding on and around her queen-size bed. So far she had experimented with certain tame forms of S & M, always in the role of submissive, but she had yet to find a partner that she trusted to help her fulfill her primary fantasy. She wanted to be strangled during intercourse. She wanted to climax an instant before unconsciousness. And when she projected a face onto the man who would help her to achieve this, who would bend the poles of sex and death until they met, for one explosive instant, she saw her partner, Miguel Garcia.

At that moment, Miguel sat on the passenger side of the cab, quietly looking out at the snow. The embarrassing state in which they'd found their passenger (now zipped up snugly in the back, like clothes in a duffel bag) had imposed an awkward silence between them. The apartment had been unlocked when they arrived. The man had been in the bedroom, naked, his chest a grey-furred hill, his mouth and eyes open. A candle was burning on the bedside table; beside it, a Zippo lighter and an empty condom wrapper. The condom was still in place on the man. The first thing Tania did was dispose of it, while Miguel shook his head and made small unhappy noises. Whoever had made the call was long gone, but there was no indication that his death had been anything but natural — a massive coronary embolism suffered during strenuous physical activity. The police arrived to confirm this, then lingered in the room, saying things like "Lucky guy," and "It's a hell of a way to go," while Tania and Miguel waited on the opposite side of the room to take the body away. Even if she hadn't been there, she knew that her partner would not have joined in the banter. That was one of the reasons she liked him. In the two years that they had been working together — she as an EMT, he as the more senior paramedic — she had come to regard him as a kind of platonic boyfriend. He had an open, handsome face and was kinder than most of the men she generally dated. In moments of crisis they merged into an efficient unit, anticipating one another's needs, communicating briskly with looks, gestures, and half-articulated requests. In a romantic relationship, theirs would be a union of opposites, a counterbalance of qualities that, in chart form, looked like:

Miguel	Tania
Short	Tall
Introvert	Extrovert
Pessimist	Optimist
Catholic	Atheist
Passive	Aggressive
Conservative	Liberal
Carnivore	Vegetarian
Hispanic	Caucasian

This was only the beginning of a fairly extensive list, but rather than reading hopeless incompatibility into the differences, Tania chose to regard them as perfectly complementary. She had seen what could happen when couples had too much in common. Her parents, for instance, were quiet, reserved souls, who had gradually come to loathe one another because they'd never had a genuine, cathartic fight. And like bred like. Both she and her brother, Martin, had been inward children. As an adult, her brother lived alone, worked with computers, had no friends that she knew of, and called her far too often, expecting her to counsel him through the petty crises of his life. She, however, had gone to great lengths to break the cycle, creating a new identity for herself in college, growing boisterous and social, forging dozens of solid, lasting friendships. She should have been happy. She *was* happy. So where did this nagging sense of dissatisfaction come from? And why this fixation on Miguel?

She glanced over at his hands. Felt the loving pressure on her neck.

For all her stubborn optimism, she was not blind to the obstacles between them. Whenever she referenced sex in any way, or swore ferociously in the middle of a stressful situation, he regarded her with caution. As for the particulars of sex, if she told him what she wanted him to do, he would expect her to regret, atone, do whatever it was that Catholics did, but she did not — would not — feel ashamed of what she saw as a perfectly natural, if somewhat unusual, aspect of her life. Here, she began to feel slightly irritated, as if they were actually together and this was actually an issue.

The radio on the dash burbled and squawked as dispatch called for a vehicle to attend to multiple injuries on a city bus. Tania turned left onto Grousetail and made an introspective noise to show Miguel that she wanted to talk.

"What's up?" he eventually said.

"Hmm? Oh, I was just thinking about our passenger."

"What about him?"

"I don't know. It's a shame that we had to find him like that."

Miguel nodded. "Shameful."

Tania was unsure if he had misheard or was correcting her. She drove on in silence for a few blocks before pulling up at a red light. "You don't really believe that," she said.

"What?"

"That it was shameful."

He looked at her warily. "What do you mean?"

"Well, it's just sex, right?"

"Aren't we assuming that he was with a prostitute?"

"Not necessarily. But, even if he was, would it really be so terrible? People get lonely." Miguel looked uncomfortable, but she did not intend to shy away from the subject. "When you think of all the evil things that people do to each other, doesn't it seem a little silly to condemn someone for having consensual sex, whatever the context?"

"I'm not condemning anyone."

"Of course you are."

"You asked my opinion."

"No, I didn't. I made an observation and you contradicted me."

"Are you angry with me?"

"No. It's just . . . " The light turned green and she eased the vehicle forward. "It's just, what if he lived a good life? What if he was an all-around good person who, as you see it, made a mistake?"

"I don't make the rules."

"Who makes the rules?"

"I don't know. They're just . . . there."

"Well, don't the rules seem awfully strict?"

Miguel looked at her askance. "What good are rules if you're not going to be strict with them?"

Tania laughed and shook her head. She hoped he sensed the fondness in her exasperation. She respected him for having strong opinions, however irrational they might be. Nothing bothered her more than people who refused to take a position on things. Her brother, for instance, was so devoid of opinions that he might as well not even exist. To ask Martin Cullen how he felt about anything was to hear the words "I don't know" spoken back to you without the slightest pause for reflection.

"Okay," she said. "Now, I'm only going by what they taught me in Sunday school, but aren't there degrees of sin?"

"There are degrees of sin," Miguel allowed. "But to die in sin? In the actual act of sinning?"

"So, it's all about luck? Who gets caught and who doesn't?"

"If you want to look at it that way."

"You're telling me that if our friend back there just saved a baby from a burning building. *And* if he just donated his life savings to charity. *And* if he just came back from confession . . . "

Miguel shrugged. "It would be unfortunate."

"Unfortunate? Shouldn't it matter what kind of a person he was?"

"When you start thinking in shoulds, you're thinking in the wrong language."

"So, as far as you're concerned, our friend back there is . . ."

"In hell," he said, without hesitation.

"That's ridiculous," she snapped.

Miguel looked surprised, then abashed. "I didn't mean . . ."

"Forget it"

"It's entirely possible that — "

"You don't have to apologize. It's just that you seem so *certain*. Don't you ever question yourself?"

"Of course."

He fell silent for a moment, perhaps deciding whether or not to confide in her. "I have an aunt," he eventually said. "She's unwell. Mentally. Every time I see her I feel like it diminishes my faith."

"Why?"

"I'm not sure."

"What kinds of things does she say?"

He hesitated. "Well, for one thing, she says I need to get married."

"And you think that's a bad idea." She tried to keep her tone neutral.

"I think . . . I think that some people are destined to spend their lives alone."

"Sounds defeatist to me."

"Maybe it is."

"And you're all right with that?"

"I guess I am."

She thought about this. "What would it take to convince you that you were wrong?"

"I don't know." He passed a hand over his face, suddenly looking very tired. "A miracle." At that same moment a thump resounded from the back of the vehicle.

Tania took her foot off the accelerator and looked at her partner. "Did you hear that?" She could tell from his face that he had. The man had been dead for at least twenty minutes when they found him. He couldn't possibly have recovered. She started to make a joke when another thump came from the back.

She pulled over to the shoulder. They should have been scrambling to see if there was work yet to be done, but neither of them moved. Finally, Miguel unbelted and went back to investigate.

"Well?" she said.

"Just a minute."

Encased in the stifling cab, with snow all around her and wind pounding the vehicle, she would have believed almost anything. "Miguel?"

"It's nothing. Some equipment fell over."

"Are you sure?"

"I'm sure."

"No miracle?" She meant this lightly but her voice was strained.

"No." He returned to the front and buckled himself back in. It was difficult to tell if he was disappointed or relieved. "No miracle."

EUROPEAN STARLING
(*Sturnus vulgaris*)

On the roof behind the marquee, it shelters in a minefield of poison. One grain, if ingested, will send chemicals through its brain, inducing a state that is like madness. Threat will be perceived everywhere. The result will be predictable: calling out in distress, wheeling about in panicked flight, before succumbing to convulsions and, ultimately, death. The instructions on the feedbag against the wall assure that the process is quite painless.

JOE

ONCE MACK WHITE SHOT HIS WAY out of the VC ambush, once he escaped the botched air strike and made his lonely trek through the forest to checkpoint Vertigo, Joe's face would go whirring through the projector and be up there, ten stories tall, for the world to see. The actual premiere had happened in a much larger theatre in Hollywood, but the obscurity of this particular screening lent it grandeur, for Joe was the only cast member present, and so, by default, the most important person in the room. All of his closest friends were there to support him, along with his parents and siblings, and a large contingent from his acting school. Only his girlfriend seemed not to grasp the importance of what was going on, taking in the action onscreen with a faint, supercilious smile. Earlier that evening they'd had one of their epic arguments. Darby had startled him with her entrance: blowing water from her lips as she dragged her bicycle into the apartment. For an instant she seemed a kind of sea hag, her hair plastered to her skull, her eyes preternaturally large. She dropped her backpack to the floor and fixed him with a frightening smile. "I made it!"

Joe had spent the afternoon watching court shows and thinking about how best to end the relationship. He'd grown nostalgic as he waited for her to come home but, in her actual, physical presence, any second thoughts he might have had vanished. "Have you been swimming?" he said dryly.

"Ha-ha." She threw him a small, plastic pyramid.

"What's this?"

"A lucky charm. How much time do I have?"

He threw it back to her. "You know, you don't have to come."

"What do you mean?"

"I mean if you don't want to come, you don't have to come."

"You don't want me to come?"

"Of course I want you to come."

He'd spent the better part of the next hour reassuring her, and by the time they reached an uneasy peace and got ready to go, the storm had been well underway. Darby hadn't seemed the least bit contrite for almost making them late. As the film progressed, she'd made little effort to conceal her disdain for what she was watching, rolling her eyes and laughing at inappropriate moments. In the two years they'd been together, she had become the defender of all things Vietnamese, taking up Joe's cause as if she were a descendant of Hồ Chí Minh himself. She saw racial slights in any mildly rude service from tellers or waiters. She cooked "traditional meals" with which even Joe's uncle, who ran a Vietnamese restaurant, was unfamiliar. Once, she'd ranted for a full two hours about the "flesh-coloured" pencil crayon in her childhood art kit. All this, coming from his very white girlfriend (red-haired, her skin nearly translucent), had been endearing at first but, now that he had lost sight of the qualities that drew him to her in the first place, it was merely irritating.

Onscreen, Mack White uttered a defiant war cry as his embattled company held its position and mowed down an endless stream of enemy soldiers. Joe knew that, given the chance, Darby would have reminded him that in real life, any one of those enemy soldiers could have been his blood relative. To which he would have replied, *It's only a movie.* She didn't understand how difficult it was to make any kind of headway in the industry. As a struggling actor (let alone a struggling *Asian* actor), he could hardly afford to be choosy about his roles. When his agent called to tell him that Hans Berger was casting bit parts in a Vietnam picture that was to be partially shot in Canada, his only question had been when the next bus was leaving for Vancouver.

The audition resulted in a major coup for his portfolio. He would have considered himself lucky to end up alongside twenty bayonet-wielding extras in conical hats, but the speaking role he landed placed him opposite the protagonist, Mack White (aka Taylor Walsh, a genuine celebrity whose face often appeared on the covers of tabloid magazines) for two full minutes of screen time.

With the firefight over, Mack White limped through the eerily silent forest (in reality, a revamped section of Stanley Park) with the dark skinned Cpl. Forrester at his side. A cynical voice in the back of Joe's mind that sounded very much like Darby's observed that Forrester had only been kept alive to this point to cast White in a paternalistic light and to convey a significant piece of exposition. White held up his hand and both men stopped to listen. A droning noise caused them to look up. Planes were approaching, American planes, come to rain flaming napalm down on the Vietcong. "Ho-lee shit!" Forrester said. "Don't they know we're down here?"

"Echo delta niner," White barked into his radio. "Check your coordinates. Repeat, check your coordinates. Damn!" An all-state sprinter in college, White shoved Forrester ahead of him and began to run. Almost immediately, Forrester stumbled and hit the ground.

White bent over him. "Run, goddamnit!"

Forrester clutched at his leg. "I can't!"

"Yes, you can!" He hoisted Forrester into a fireman's carry, the tendons in his neck straining. Then everything went slow motion. White was back at Notre Dame, his eye on the tape at the end of the track. Forrester's mouth was wide open in terror and pain. Behind them, the napalm was taking its time. Just a few . . . more . . . steps.

Out in the audience, Joe was getting caught up in the action in spite of himself. He didn't want Forrester to die, didn't want the explosion to wrench him from White's sure grip and impale him on the broken arm of a tree.

Darby heaved a sigh.

Joe decided that he was going to end things that very night. He was accelerating towards a brighter future, in which she had no place. It wasn't just the movie. She knew him too well. She had seen him at his worst, when the depression left him stranded in bed for days, weeping about nothing. He needed to be observed from a distance, through a worshipful lens that transformed everything he said or did into something glamorous. He would never achieve a thing with her scrutinizing (and commenting dryly on) his every move.

In the wake of the assault, the jungle was hazy with smoke. White lay on his back in the mud — eyes closed, arms splayed in an attitude of crucifixion. He roused himself and crawled over to the dying Forrester, who had grown eerily calm. "Hey, boss," Forrester said. "Looks like I'm on my way out." Coughing up blood, he pulled an envelope from his jacket. "Get this to Harriet for me, will you?"

"Lay off that shit, soldier. You're gonna make it."

"Not this time, boss." Forrester grinned at him. "This time they got me good." And he went still.

"He blinked," Darby whispered.

Joe shot her a poisonous look. But she was right. To get the desired effect, you had to unfocus your eyes, not focus on a point, which was what the actor — Morris something — was clearly doing, his Adam's apple doing a little jump as he swallowed. Playing dead had always been one of Joe's talents. Agonized death, peaceful death, the sudden toppling death of a bullet to the back of the head. Once, he had occupied the state of "death" so fully that he relieved himself in the middle of an acting workshop. It was an exhilarating and frightening moment. As his classmates lined up to embrace him, Joe realized what an arduous career he had chosen. An actor had to be prepared to suffer. Your heart was broken thousands of times. You died thousands of times. Then you dusted yourself off and bowed.

The score struck a sombre note as White closed Forrester's eyes, broke his dog tags, and left him lying in the mud. With his scene approaching, Joe felt oddly restricted in his seat, having to wait out his own entrance along with everyone else. He wanted to race down the aisle and leap onstage to relieve the tension in his stomach.

At the shoot he had tried to make good use of his trailer time, rehearsing his two lines until they issued forth like breath, until he had *become* that border guard. A complex series of emotions passed over his face in the trailer mirror: the half lift of an eyebrow, the hint of a sneer, replaced by narrowed eyes and pursed lips — a grudging respect for the American soldier. Stepping onto the set, he felt as if he had truly arrived. The caterers had laid out a generous spread of cheeses, cold meats, sushi, and coffee. The crew bustled about, engaged in important-looking tasks. The director, wearing a wide-brimmed hat and baggy cargo pants, spotted Joe and came over to shake his hand.

"All set, then? Fantastic! No butterflies? Good, good. This is Terrence. He'll tell you what to do, where to stand and all that. Great to have you on board. It's an important project." He slapped Joe on the back and wandered away. Berger's assistant was more personable, relating a lively anecdote about an exchange that the notoriously abrasive director had apparently had with customs over a small, registered handgun that he kept on his person at all times. Several other crew members confirmed the story and testified to having previously seen the butt of a .38 Special protruding from Berger's waistband (though he had never, as far as they knew, had a reason to draw it on set). As the afternoon wore on and the extras stood around gossiping, Joe noted to the sound engineer that the work of a film actor, like the work of a soldier, seemed to be characterized by long periods of boredom punctuated by bursts of activity. The sound engineer, who wore a military-type vest, approved of the analogy and elaborated on it, attributing ranks to the all the members of the cast and crew (Joe, of course, being a private).

When they were finally ready to begin shooting, Taylor Walsh emerged from his trailer and drew the attention of everyone in the vicinity the way a black hole gathers light. Just to look at the famous actor, and to be looked at by him, was jarring. He had an unquestionable magnetism, a detached, all-knowing look that was like intelligence (though, from interviews, Joe knew him to be incredibly stupid). The director embraced Walsh and ushered him over to the cameras, throwing back his head and saying, "Yes, yes, yes!" to something the actor had said.

Walsh joined the lesser cast members and Joe fixed him with an aggressive look of challenge. The man's career, he'd decided, had a shelf life of ten years maximum, five of which he had already used.

Given the fact that he, Joe, had ability, had *talent*, he saw no such limitations for himself. Walsh began to look uncomfortable under Joe's gaze. Terrence came to his aid, introducing them.

"So, you're from here?" Walsh said, as they shook hands.

"It depends what you mean by here."

"How's that?"

"Well, I'm from Canada."

"Uh-huh. It must be great. Back in L.A. people are totally wrapped up in themselves. Up here everyone seems way more down to earth."

Joe sneered and asked if he was surprised they didn't all live in igloos.

Walsh smiled uncertainly. "Why would I think that?"

Joe was not deceived by the man's public image: the hepatitis awareness campaign, his highly publicized tours of third world countries, his opposition to the war in Iraq. He saw these token displays of decency as manifestations of a profoundly overblown ego. He, for one, would not be fooled. When the cameras were rolling he had no trouble looking Walsh up and down, fiercely. "You no passa here!" he shrieked. "This road-a closed!"

"My name is Mack White," Walsh said, hoarsely. "I'm an American."

Joe shook his head and stood his ground.

"My men are all dead." Walsh said. "I left them back in that hellish inferno of a jungle . . ." He went on to summarize his trials, assuring Joe that his only desire was to return home to his wife and infant son. His duty was accomplished. His killing days were over.

Border Guard Number One, as Joe conceived him, understood little of what White was saying but the mention of a son got through. He had a wife and child of his own. Perhaps they were not so different after all. "Okay, okay," he said. "You go. You go this one time, G.I."

After three takes and backslaps from Berger all around, they wrapped for the day. Walsh mingled with the extras, inviting them out to drinks in a great show of magnanimity, and Joe took the next Greyhound home, confident that he had given Hans Berger some of his best work.

Now, having left Forrester's body behind him in the jungle, Mack White stepped into a clearing filled with bamboo huts. Children came out of the huts and swarmed around him, chattering and vying for his attention. Joe inhaled sharply. His scene came *before* the village scene. For a moment, he held onto the thought that they might have simply reordered the scenes in the editing process, but when White stipped off his bandana and dropped it to the ground (a bandana he'd been wearing when he spoke to Border Guard Number One), the elision became a certainty.

"They cut it," he said.

"What?" Darby whispered.

"My scene. They cut my scene."

"No. Are you sure?"

"Of course I'm sure!"

"Shh," someone behind them whispered.

"How could they do this? How could they not even *notify* me?"

"Shh!"

His friends peered down the aisle at him. His mother and father peered down the aisle at him. Joe suddenly realized what must have happened. Going over the raw footage with Berger in the studio, Walsh would have remembered the uppity Asian in Vancouver and observed to Berger that the film was great, but one thing was bothering him: that border-crossing scene. There was something not quite right about it. They didn't really need it, did they?

He shrank in his seat, thinking about tracking Walsh down and murdering him, or of quietly ending his own life to avoid having to face the several dozen people in this room who knew him. The depression that had spared him for months returned all at once. He felt like curling up on the floor of the theatre and going to sleep. He felt like tearing his seat from the floor and hurling it through the screen.

The film was nearing its conclusion. Hearing friendly helicopters, Mack White turned his face to the sky. Joe could not watch. He felt a firm pressure on his hand, and looked up. Darby had stood and was gently pulling him to his feet. "Come on," she said. "We're going home."

Yellow-bellied sapsucker
(*Spyrapicus varius*)

Tumbling over the motel parking lot, barely keeping aloft in the wind, it swerves and loops and follows a long, sweeping curve that ends, by chance, in the cold tailpipe of a truck. Instinct keeps it still. It knows the comfort of holes, the warm meat in the sides of trees. Before long it has fallen asleep.

Frank

He should have felt different. More than different, he should have felt liberated. But nothing had changed. He was sitting on a motel bed with a towel around his waist and towers of unsold *Woebegone!* boxes stacked beside the door. Juliet was 300 kilometres away, waiting for his nightly phone call. Michael would be asleep in his room across the hall. Cinnamon would be up on the couch by the window, vigilant to neighbourhood threats.

Cinnamon. Like so many details in Frank's life, the name was linked with disappointment. It was his belief that a dog should be named for its personality. As a boy he'd had two dogs: Swift and Radar. Swift had been a runner, Radar a hunter. The Yorkie they'd picked up from the pound two summers before had been a leaper, any bit of stimulation prompting a tireless show of bounding from the animal. The day they brought it home, Frank had conceived the perfect name only to be immediately challenged by his wife.

"You can't call a dog Trampoline," she'd said.

"Why not?"

"It's not a dog's name. It's not any name. It would be like calling him basketball, or tennis racquet."

"Okay, okay. How about Skipper. Here, Skipper!"

The dog jumped about and unleashed a fit of barking at the wall.

"How about Dusty?" Juliet said. "Are you a Dusty?"

The animal gave an identical response, eyes wildly rolling.

"Dusty. I've known ten dogs named Dusty."

"Name one."

"On Pender Avenue. There was a lab named Dusty."

"There was a wolfhound named Buster."

"I don't think so." Frank squatted down and snapped his fingers at the dog. "Anyway, I veto Dusty."

"You veto it? Are you the president all of a sudden?"

In the end they'd settled on Cinnamon, a name neither of them really liked. He could recall countless similar scenes from their marriage. The real miracle was that he hadn't cheated on her sooner. It had been coming since the day of what he thought of as the Original Conflict. She had ambushed him on that one. One week after the proposal, they'd been sitting in the glassed-in patio at Denny's, playing with each other's hands and waiting for their breakfast to come, when he reflected that it was going to be strange, everyone calling her Mrs. Garnett.

"Oh, I'm not taking your name," she said.

Frank began to laugh, but stopped when she pulled her hand away. "What do you mean?"

"We've talked about this. How outmoded it is. You agreed with me."

Did he? He could not recall the conversation, but supposed that he must have been trying to woo her with progressive sentiments at the time. "Wasn't that more of a theoretical discussion?" he said.

"There's no such thing as a theoretical discussion."

"There isn't?"

"Of course not. Besides, would you take my name?"

"No."

"Why not?"

"Because . . . " He looked around the room for help. Burly tradesmen, arms locked around their plates. "Because I like my name."

"Well, so do I. That's kind of the point, isn't it?"

"Okay, let's just think about this." He frowned at the ceiling to show her that he was giving her perspective due consideration. "When men and women get married, women usually take the man's name. Why is that?"

"Because we live in a sexist society?"

"Okay." He made goalposts with his hands to acknowledge the point. "But also, and maybe more importantly, because it's fair. So long as it's one or the other — and for whatever reason, yes, in our society it happens to be men — exactly half the people in the world get to keep their names. Otherwise, whoever had the most power in the relationship would get to decide the family name and *that* isn't fair." He hammered the table with the tip of his finger for emphasis. "*That* isn't democratic."

"Democratic?" she laughed.

"You know what I mean. But this way — "

"You mean your way."

"*This* way, fifty percent of the people getting married get to keep their names. What could be fairer than that?"

Juliet regarded him with an indulgent smile. "Would you agree that I have the same right as you to keep my name?"

"I think it's a little more complicated than that."

"So, you don't agree that I have an equal right to keep my name."

"You have to look at the big picture here."

Juliet took a refill from the waitress and diluted her coffee with four creams. "I don't even know why we're arguing. If we're getting married, I'm keeping my name and that's all there is to it."

In that moment, Frank should have foreseen the years of compromise and concession that lay ahead. He should have walked out of the restaurant and started a new life in a new city with a much more reasonable, much less militant woman. But he was not prepared to leave and forever be branded the chauvinist ex. Nor was he prepared to shed his cloak of sensitivity (he didn't know whether or not he was *actually* sensitive) and make a stand.

"Would you be willing to hyphenate?" he said.

"Would you?"

"Well, if you're going to be silly . . . "

"Who's being silly? Will I hyphenate? Yes. If we both hyphenate."

And so they had kept their own names. Michael's they hyphenated. No doubt he would grow up to marry a hyphenated woman. Their kids would be double-hyphenated. Their kids' kids would be quadruple-hyphenated. That was the drift of the world these days.

Frank lay back on the bed and stared up at the bland seascape over the headboard. He placed two fingers on his wrist and counted off the seconds. 60 bpm. No guilt that he could discern, but nor was there elation. The act had been disjointed and arrhythmic. The girl had been forced to finish him off manually, his climax relieving him like a difficult sneeze. And she was a girl, younger than Juliet by a decade at least.

He had not immediately understood what was happening when she sidled up to him at the casino bar and asked him if he was looking for "a date." Only when he met the eye of a scowling old woman pumping quarters into a VLT across the room had he realized what she meant.

"Well . . ." he said. "I might be."

The girl played with the straw in her drink and gave him an absurdly lewd smile. "Oh, you're definitely looking for a date."

At the time, Frank had believed that she had targeted him, at least in part, out of physical attraction but, logically, the opposite must have been true. Why else would she have been so sure of herself? He lifted the telephone receiver and replaced it, suddenly sure that his wife knew everything. Not consciously, but on that weird, extra-sensory, spousal level — the way she sometimes began to sing a song that had been looping through his head, or how any thought he had about another woman seemed to have a direct and immediate impact on her mood. One disconcerting afternoon, both phenomena had occurred simultaneously. They had been sitting at a red light downtown, waiting for some pedestrians to cross, when she suddenly began singing "Wild Thing."

"Was I just singing that?" Frank said.

"No."

"Humming it?"

"I don't think so. Why?"

"Never mind." A chesty woman in tight jeans stepped into the crosswalk. He did not follow her with his head or his eyes but, rather, took in what he could peripherally, stealing an instant of full-on appreciation as she passed through his focal point.

"She's pretty," Juliet said.

"Who's that?" Frank made a show of looking around. "Her? I didn't notice."

"Didn't you?"

Feeling mentally raped, Frank tried to think of a suitable response.

He sat up on the bed as headlights from the parking lot glanced though a sizable gap in the curtains. Had they been like that the whole time? They must have been. The rooms at the Prairie Dog Inn were all on the ground floor. Anyone within a foot of the window could have seen everything. A private detective, sent by Juliet, could have snapped a montage of his sad rump bobbing up and down. Suspicion on his wife's part would have been justifiable. Every other month a new conference in a new city. *He* would have been suspicious. *He* would have checked up on her by now — not out of jealousy, but out of fear that she had managed to outmanoeuvre him. Now, for the first time in recent memory, he had the advantage, but was unable to enjoy it. The question of surveillance kept pushing into his head. There could be miniature cameras in the light fixtures, recording devices in the headboards. If not a detective, then a hotel manager, dealing in underground pornography. Frank had seen such things on the internet. Hidden cams. Motel love. Yes, he had surfed those sites — perched in the darkness by the computer with Juliet upstairs, semi-comatose on sleeping pills.

One humiliating night the previous winter, he'd had an AVI of close up penetration streaming on RealPlayer and a box of tissues close at hand, when he suddenly realized that his son was standing in the doorway in his Superman pyjamas.

"Jesus!" He killed the monitor with one hand and concealed himself with the other. "What are you — ! How are you doing buddy? Can't sleep?"

"I'm hungry."

"Oh? I, ah . . . I think there's some cookies in the pantry. Go wait for Daddy in the kitchen, okay?"

At four years of age, the boy could not have possibly understood what he had seen, but surely it was lodged somewhere in his consciousness, a dark nugget of trauma for the therapist to pry out in twenty years' time. The very next day Frank had cleaned off his hard drive and resolved to confine his future activities to the uninspiring surroundings of the locked bathroom.

But the sites in question had seemed authentic enough. His picture could be going online already. All it would take to expose him would be an anonymous email with a link to the website and the subject line: *Your husband?*

Feeling under the counters for small microphones and wires, he stopped himself. There were no cameras, no conspiracy. If anything, suspicion would come from the lateness of his call, and the more he put it off, the deeper those seeds of suspicion would go. He returned to his station on the bed and took his pulse. Slightly elevated. Just as he was reaching for the receiver, the phone rang. No one knew he was there. No one but Juliet, and Juliet never called first. Never.

The phone rang a third time, a fourth, then stopped.

Of course it was his wife. Who else would it be? He snatched up the receiver. After a few seconds, the dial tone in his ear cut out and a woman with a reasonable voice asked him to please hang up. A couple passed his room, speaking in another language, their footsteps amplified by the snow. Frank went to the window. It was still storming out there. He yanked the curtains shut, but they fell open again immediately. Something faulty in the way they were hung. He dragged a chair to the window and used it to pin the curtains together. New footsteps resonated outside, seemed to pause at his door, and continued on.

The police? What he had done, after all, was not legal. Not as far along the continuum as armed robbery, but illegal, nonetheless. He'd seen a reality show that was devoted to situations just like this: agents watching their target John on a monitor, before storming the room and reading the Miranda to some poor old guy in saggy underwear, his face a smear of digital boxes. But the girl had come

DEVIN KRUKOFF

onto *him*. That was entrapment, wasn't it? Miranda. Entrapment. Already he was thinking like a criminal.

Frank had always held a deep fear of institutionalized authority. Security guards, police officers, and airport screeners instilled in him an irrational desire to confess. On family vacations down south, the speed of his heart would increase in direct proportion to the decreased distance between himself and American soil. On the last trip (which he vowed would be the *very* last trip), he'd wrung the wheel, frequently checking his rear and side mirrors.

"Just be calm," he said to Juliet. "Don't antagonize them."

She snorted. "So I should *not* tell them about the dope in the glove compartment."

"Not funny."

"Or the bomb in the trunk?"

"Juliet — "

"What's a bomb?" Michael said.

The car inched forward.

"Daddy, what's a bomb?" The car window was open. Juliet was shaking with laughter. She had no conception of the quantity of ill-will circulating in the world, the fact that the unsmiling customs officer ahead had just been *waiting* for an excuse to haul Frank out of the car and subject him to a full, body-cavity search.

No, Frank decided. A thorough check of the room would not be unreasonable. He unscrewed the heat vents with a quarter and felt inside. He checked the seascape, the lamps, and the fire detector. He tried to pry the bathroom mirror loose with his keys. He had no illusions about his privacy. What was it that he had read? You could be alone in a field with no one around for miles and a satellite could snap a picture of you in such detail that they could make out the time on your watch. What was he supposed to do with that kind of information?

~ 172 ~

When he finally emerged from the bathroom, he saw that the gap in the curtains had opened again. He had propped the chair. Firmly. Someone must have crept in and moved it. What kind of sick —

The phone rang and he yelped, then rushed to pick it up. Conscience be damned, he was scared.

"Yes!" he yelled into the receiver.

"Heyyyyy..."

"Hello? Juliet?"

"Heyyyyy...."

"Who is this?"

"I was just in there? And I, like, forgot something."

"Is this..." He lowered his voice. "Is that you?"

"Yeah..." The girl's voice was heavy and slow, dulled by whatever substance she had gone out and purchased with his two hundred dollars. Crack? Blow? He had only a vague notion of what these words meant. The girl linked him to an underworld he had only seen on television, and he wanted to sever that connection as quickly as possible.

"Did you just call a few minutes ago?"

"I just... but no one was home, right?"

"So, you called already."

"I called..."

"This room?"

"My bracelet."

"What's that?"

"I left my bracelet. On the bed."

He threw back the covers and saw it immediately: plastic turquoise beads on a fraying loop of hemp. "No." He picked up the bracelet with two fingers. It was like a small, dead animal. "I don't think so."

"It's blue... It's got, like, blue in it..."

"No, there's nothing here. Sorry. Goodbye."

He hung up and checked his pulse. 90 bpm. Pushing 100. He pulled the curtains shut, propped the chair, and added a telephone book for weight. The phone began to ring again, and stopped. The bracelet had to go. He carried it to the trash, and opted for the toilet. On the third flush it went down. He had to get out of there. Her pimp would be on the way. He had to check out and take a new room in a hotel across town. But what if Juliet *had* called first? He checked his watch. Ten o'clock. Eleven with the time change. The phone was slick in his hand. He punched 9 to call out, then dialled his home number. Juliet picked up just before the machine.

"Hey!" he said. "You sleeping?"

"Mm? No. I was just about to."

"Oh, all right. I'll let you go then."

"No, I'm glad you called. I was getting worried."

"Oh yeah?"

"You're later than usual."

"Am I? What time is it? Holy smokes!" He could not seem to stop yelling. "Yeah, see what happened was, I was watching this movie, this pay-per-view movie, and I totally lost track of — "

Juliet cut him off with a yawn. "What movie?"

"Uh . . . It was a newer movie. That Vietnam movie."

"Who's in it?"

He bit his thumb, leaving a deep indent. "What's his name. Taylor Walsh."

"Isn't that still in the theatres?"

"Is it?"

"I'm pretty sure it is."

"Well, I guess they come out early on these motel machines. So, yeah, it was pretty good. Disturbing. But moving."

"Uh-huh." She yawned again. "So how was the conference?"

"The conference?"

"You keep repeating everything I'm saying."

"Do I? Sorry. The conference was good. Mostly good. There was this crazy girl there who seemed to think that I was killing Vietnamese peasants. Other than that . . . "

"Why would she think that?"

"Because she's crazy? Anyway . . . Hello?"

"I'm here."

"What's the matter?"

"Nothing." She was leaving deliberate silences and he was walking right into them.

"Don't tell me you're mad about me calling late."

"Who said I was mad?"

"It feels like you're mad."

"Should I be mad?"

"Of course not. I just — " He paused. Had something just thumped the door?

"You just what?"

Yes, there it was again. "I just lost track of time. Did you hear that?"

"Hear what?"

"Nothing." Three sharps raps. The doorknob jiggling.

Frank lowered his voice. "I just don't see why you have to make me feel guilty over a little phone call."

"Where is this coming from?"

"I don't know. I'm just saying . . . "

"Maaaaan!"

The girl. Lori, Lisa, whatever the hell her name was.

"You don't hear that?" he asked his wife.

"What is with you tonight?"

"Nothing. I'm just tired, I guess. The neighbours have their TV turned way up."

Now it sounded as if the girl was kicking the door, throwing herself against it. How could Juliet not be hearing this? A shuddering blow sent the chair down and the curtains fell open. The girl's ghoulish face appeared in the crack.

"Maaaaan! Open up!"

"Frank?" Juliet said. "Are you still there?"

SNOW BUNTING
(*Plectrophenax nivalis*)

Ten thousand feet above the ground, it moves in behind the storm, having left the tundra early this season, unsettled by the changing rhythms of weather. Amber lights delineate the city below — brightness ringed by absence — a large quadrant of which suddenly disappears.

LAMBDA

DARKNESS CAME LIKE A BLOW, KILLING everything that survived on electricity alone: the lights, the clocks, the stereo, the fridge; all the comforting murmurs and glows. Lambda's voice trailed away, as if it, too, had been wired into the building.

"Great," Mark said.

Lambda held her breath, afraid to move.

Two hours before, she had raced through the storm to Mark's apartment to tell him everything that had happened that night, everything but the fact that she had fucked their poetry instructor, apparently to death. She had a sudden vision of Adams in the basement of their building — his pale hand in the fuse box.

Someone was moving though the room.

"Mark?" She stood up, then sat back down, not wanting to leave the sofa. Her terror of the dark was something she often joked about, telling people that she slept with a nightlight to keep the monsters in her closet and under her bed, where they belonged. In reality, she was not afraid of what might be lurking in the darkness, but of darkness itself. In a room without light, she became aware of secret undulations in the air, fluid tentacles winding around her and pouring into her mouth. This present darkness seemed an agent of reckoning, as if her lovemaking with Adams had been a binding pact: Hades returning for his doomed Persephone, come to drag her back down to the underworld.

"Mark!" she said. "I need you!"

"It's all right. I'm just over here."

Her eyes had begun to adjust, restoring some order to the room. The truer darkness of the furniture. The pale rectangle of the window, partially eclipsed by Mark's silhouette. "What are you doing?" she said, only slightly less hysterical now that she was not completely blind.

"Checking for lights. Looks like it's out all down the block."

"Well, I could have told you that! It's pitch black in here!"

Mark laughed. "I'll get some candles. Do you have your lighter?"

She checked her front and back pockets, then fumbled for her coat on the couch. "Oh, no."

"What?"

"Oh, no. Oh, god. I think I left it there." She could see exactly where it was: on Adams' night table, beside a lit candle, her initials prominent on the base. Somehow this seemed more incriminating than her fingerprints that must have been all over the apartment. She recalled the nightmarish look of still animation on his face as she stepped from the shower and found him on the bed — eyes open, mouth open, the sheet flung back to reveal his inert, naked body.

Mark moved away from the window. "So?"

"What do you mean, so?"

"I mean you didn't do anything wrong. Besides leaving. And that's not exactly illegal . . . At least I don't think it's illegal."

"You're not helping." She pictured the zombie poet at the bottom of the stairwell, muttering lines from Yeats as he gripped the banister and began his ascent. *The blood dimmed tide is loosed . . .*

"What do want me to say?" Mark said.

"Just find a light."

"I'm looking."

"Don't you have a place for these things?" A creaking came from beyond the apartment door. Adams, staggering down the hall towards Mark's unit. *Moving its slow thighs while all about it reel shadows of the indignant desert birds . . .*

"I'm not seeing it. Damn it!"

"What happened?"

"I bumped my head."

Lambda shrieked as someone knocked, rapidly, on the door.

"Don't get it!" she said.

"Why not?"

What rough beast, its hour come round at last . . .

"Just don't, all right?"

"This is ridiculous." She could hear Mark moving for the door.

"Wait!"

"Someone might be in trouble."

Lambda shrank back as the door opened inwards and soft yellow light broke into the apartment.

"Hey," Mark said.

"Is your power out?" The voice, while male, did not belong to Adams.

Mark laughed. "No, we're just sitting around in the dark for fun."

"Well, I live across the hall and my power's out."

"I was kidding there."

"Oh. LOL! Sorry, this is difficult for me. I have to get back online. It's imperative that I get my computer up and running again."

"I don't think I can help you with that," Mark said.

"Is your telephone working?"

"I don't know."

"Can you check? I have to call the power company."

"You don't have a phone?"

"No, I don't."

"You have the internet, but you don't have a phone?"

"I don't have time to explain."

Lambda had quietly joined Mark, keeping out of sight just behind the door. She jerked his sleeve. He glanced back at her and she shook her head.

"We don't have a light," he said to the man.

"You can use mine."

Mark looked back at her again. She shook her head more firmly and mouthed *no*. He sighed and stepped back from the door. "All right, come on in."

Lambda glared at him and retreated to the sofa.

The man was a bit older than them but appeared harmless — tall and thin with curly red hair and eyeglasses. He swept his flashlight beam around the room. Mark directed him to a second-hand easy chair, before sitting next to Lambda on the sofa. The telephone was working. He paged through the phone book and dialled the power company. The man stared at his lap and fidgeted.

"So, do you work with computers?" Lambda asked him, not the least bit interested in his life.

He gave her an ingratiating (*craven*, she thought) smile. "You might say that."

All knees and elbows, he reminded her of a large, ungainly seabird. She could easily imagine him in his element: stooped before a computer screen, fingers blurring over the keyboard.

"It's ringing," Mark said. "Got a recorded message. Due to the high volume of calls, blah blah blah." He hung up and shrugged. "Sorry."

The man put his head in his hands. "What am I going to do?"

Lambda began to feel uneasy. Whatever the man's problem was, it had nothing to do with them.

"Well," Mark ventured, "you could stay with us until the lights come on." Lambda looked at him in disbelief. He raised his eyebrows. "What?"

"Weren't we kind of in the middle of something?"

The man began to get up. "That's all right. I have to — "

"No," Mark said. "I want you to stay. Can I borrow your flashlight for a second?" He took the light and went off into the kitchen. Lambda remained behind, wondering how he could be so insensitive. She had watched a man die that evening and here he was, entertaining the whole neighbourhood.

She could not see their visitor's features clearly, but felt he was watching her.

"Do you have a webmaster?" he asked softly.

"Excuse me?"

Mark came back with several candles and a box of matches. "I've always loved it when the power goes. It feels like an event, you know?"

"I should go," the man said.

"I don't think I've seen you around before. What's your name?"

"Cameron."

"I'm Mark. This is my friend, Lambda. Hey, you're into computers, right? Maybe you can help me out. My machine's been giving me all kinds of grief."

As Mark attempted to put the man at ease, guilt came spiking through Lambda's resentment. Although they were not technically "together" — had in fact only slept together on one occasion — something in the nature of their friendship hinged on them not seeing other people. Sex with Adams hadn't seemed to count. It had been a game, a lesson in power politics. She had wanted to show him what it felt like to be vulnerable. She had not for a moment taken Mark into consideration.

Cameron seemed to relax somewhat as Mark plied him with questions (though he still sat awkwardly — leaning forward, elbows and knees flared out). Lambda knew that she ought to sympathize with him, but the most she could muster was distant pity, which was more than cancelled out by her desire to have him leave.

"You really think it's a memory problem?" Mark said.

"Well, I don't think you have the space to support the kind of games you're talking about. Extra memory would help. You might want to upgrade your video card, too."

"Mm. You want a beer?"

"I don't think so."

"Do you have somewhere to be?"

"I need to get — "

"Back online, I know. Well, it's not going to happen right now, is it? I'll be right back." Before he could protest, Mark had left the room. Lambda got up and followed him into the kitchen.

"That's nice," she said.

"What's that?"

"What you're doing in there."

He shrugged as if he didn't know what she was talking about, and maybe he didn't. Was it possible to be that selfless?

"Listen," she said. "I have something I need to tell you."

He opened the fridge and called over his shoulder. "All I have is light beer! Is that all right?" Cameron didn't answer.

"Mark, I need to talk to you. About what happened tonight."

He pulled out three bottles and set them down on the counter in a row. "I know what happened tonight."

"You do?"

"I'm not an idiot." He screwed off the caps and threw them, one by one, into the sink. Lambda flinched at each impact.

"It didn't mean anything."

Mark laughed. "Right."

"Well, it meant something. But not in the way that you think. It had nothing to do with you."

"That's good to know."

"That's not what I mean. It's just . . . He *died*, Mark."

"I realize that."

At that moment Lambda knew many things. She knew that Mark was too good for her. She knew that she would end up breaking his heart. And she knew that she was about to do exactly what Adams would have done in her position. She took the poem from her back pocket and held it out to him.

"What's this?" he said.

She stepped forward and kissed him, insistently, until she felt him yield and begin to kiss her back.

When she opened her eyes, the lights were back on, the clock on the microwave flashing 12:00. They looked around, blinked at one another, and laughed. He began to say something, but she kissed him again, pressed the poem into his hand, and left him alone in the kitchen. Out in the living room, the overhead lights made the candles seem dim and redundant. The front door was ajar, and Lambda realized with some relief that Cameron had gone.

Blue-fronted Amazon
(*Amazona aestiva*)

Two hours of pressure from beak and talon and the door swings wide. It emerges tentatively and circles the darkened apartment. The window above the sink is propped open. A regular rhythm, pounding from below. Perched on the sill, it looks out at the swirling world. Raised voices. Pretty red and blue lights. It inches forward and finds itself sucked out in the alien air. Stunned by the cold and the ungentle wind, it batters the windowpane, searching for those few inches of space that will lead it home.

Sawatski

They should have just rolled on by, given him a free pass on account of the weather. The guy hadn't done anything, besides breaking into a run when they pulled up and gave him a friendly hello with the siren, but Wade had been itching for something to do. Well, he found it. He had his door open and his feet on the ground before the car had even stopped moving. The foot chase was over in seconds. Wade took the guy down in the parking lot outside the Grinder, tussled with him for a second, and got a knee into his back.

"Easy, Wade," Sawatski muttered.

He stuck his chewing gum on the visor and hauled himself out of the cruiser. Snow roiled around him. The wind seemed to come from ten different directions at once. With a familiar pressure starting up in his chest, he jogged over to his partner, who had the guy in handcuffs, his face jammed into the snow. "Hit me, will you, motherfucker?" he was shouting.

Sawatski pulled him off and the guy rolled over, gasping, his face smeared with blood and snow. Wade made as if to walk away, then came back and kicked him in the ribs. He'd always had trouble adapting to a situation that had been contained. One of these days a video was going to surface on the internet and people would start asking hard questions. Questions like, *Officer Sawatski, why are you just standing there, watching Officer Nichols kick a handcuffed man?*

"Hey!" Sawatski gripped Wade again, harder this time, by both arms. "Are you all right?"

Wade touched his split lip and looked at his hand. "Look at this asshole." He spat blood in the guy's general direction. "He was going for something in his pants."

Sawatski didn't bother to ask how the guy could have been going for anything with his hands cuffed behind his back. "All right, I'll deal with him. Go call it in."

Wade stared at the guy for a second, as if he wasn't quite through with him.

"Wade."

He glanced at Sawatski, then headed back to the car. He had to get his domestic situation in hand. He'd been working himself up all night, griping about his son, who'd apparently gotten into some trouble at the city zoo that afternoon. "He just doesn't *listen*," he kept saying. With his own kids grown and out of the house, the only honest thing Sawatski could have told his partner was that in the next six to ten years it was only going to get worse. As for his wife, if she was as heartless and conniving as he claimed (throwing out an old family heirloom, for instance — a certain bronze horse — because it didn't go with the furniture) he had no idea what he was doing with her in the first place.

Sawatski helped the guy up and led him over to the shelter of the nearest building. Already his hands and face were numb, and the ache in his chest wasn't going away. The doctor had warned him about this kind of thing. Avoid stressful situations, he'd said. And how in the hell was he supposed to do that? He checked the guy's pockets and came up with a wallet and some keys.

"Is that all you've got? Why'd you run, chief?" The guy gave him a look like this was the dumbest question he'd ever heard. Sawatski chuckled. Fair enough. "What's your name?"

The guy hesitated before seeming to realize that there was no point lying with the cop holding his wallet. "Gene."

"Well, that was really dumb, Gene. You can't just go around hitting police officers. We're going to have to bring you in now. You know that, right?"

"Fucker hit me first," he said.

"Oh, I don't doubt it." Sawatski peered across the parking lot. Wade was still on the radio. People were coming out of the Grinder now, gathering under a broad, red awning to watch. The blizzard had been pounding the city for hours but the yahoos were out as usual, half of them in short sleeves. Sawatski was thinking about how best to motivate them back inside when the wind suddenly intensified, washing everything out. He grabbed Gene with both hands, for support as much as to keep him in place. A kind of wind tunnel had formed around them, a pillar of calm in the snow. He met Gene's eye and something passed between them. Confusion. Terror. The world had disappeared. Then, just as abruptly, everything surged back into focus. The people under the awning had scattered and were trying to orient themselves to the building. Wade was out of the cruiser and heading towards them — leaning into the wind, his hand on the butt of his revolver.

Sawatski had no time to wonder why his partner would advance on an unarmed crowd with the apparent intention to fire. He tried to call him back, but it felt as if a tennis ball had lodged in his throat. Gene squirmed in his hands. Finally, Sawatski found his voice. "Wade!"

Wade looked over. At that same moment, Gene broke loose and ran — leading with his head, hands still cuffed behind his back. Sawatski watched him go, almost wishing him luck, but with no arms for balance, he kept slipping, and Wade caught him up easily, using his momentum to send him, face first, into the wall of the closed pharmacy next door.

"Police brutality!" someone shouted from the crowd. Had Sawatski been in civilian clothes, he would have been inclined to agree.

Then why aren't you doing something, Officer Sawatski?

Control the crowd, he decided; that was priority number one. He propped himself against the wall with one hand and extended the other, palm-out, as if he was on traffic duty, keeping a line of cars at bay.

"Just . . . stay calm . . . "

A huge man in a football helmet stepped out of the Grinder and stood for a moment under the red awning, like some insane general surveying a battlefield. Across the parking lot, Wade had Gene in a bear hug. He sat him down, then pinned him, and flipped him over like a fish he intended to gut.

Revised priority number one: control your partner.

He got his feet moving, shutting out the pain in his chest. He had almost reached Wade when the crowd let out a cheer. He turned to find the 'general' bearing down on him. He had played enough football in his life to know how much what was about to happen was going to hurt. But, at the last second, the general slipped and hit him off centre. Sawatski caught him and fell back onto his partner, who fell back onto Gene, all of them toppling like dominoes. Wade grappled with the general and got him into an elbow-wrenching arm lock. Gene tried to squirm away and Sawatski jumped on him. For a few seconds, they all lay there, breathing. More people were coming out of the Grinder now, inching up to that line of invisible police tape.

And what, Officer Sawatski, is Officer Nichols doing now?

Well, Wade was doing two things. He was keeping the general still, which was good. And he was twisting his own body to more easily get at his sidearm with his free hand, which was bad. Which, in a few seconds, was going to be very bad. To draw on them would be one thing. To unload on them would be something very different. He put his hand on his own weapon and tried to gauge where a shot would do his partner the least damage. But then two more cruisers came screaming up and everything changed. Doors opened and slammed. Familiar faces appeared. The crowd backed away.

The cavalry consisted of two men and one woman, who helped Wade first, then came over to see if Sawatski was all right. His heart still hadn't quieted down but the pain in his chest had eased up. "I'm good," he said, making a show of sitting on the little guy. "Just getting to know my new best friend here."

As they loaded the guys into separate vehicles, the wind began to ebb away, and soon the snow was coming down thick and peaceful. Bass thumped through the closed door of the Grinder. Most of the crowd had lost interest and gone back inside. Sawatski was standing around joking with the few that remained, even getting a laugh or two, when the manager of the club came out and informed him that the general was the lead singer of a band that had been playing that night.

"Are they any good?" Sawatski asked him.

The manager seemed taken off guard by the question. "I . . . really don't know. Listen, I'm not going to be liable for any of this, am I?"

"Oh, probably." He spotted his partner over by one of the cars, talking to Lyle Greene, and headed over. "Whoo!" He clapped Wade on the shoulder. "That's my cardio for the day! What do you say? Time to get the fuck out of Dodge?"

Wade gave him a spooky look, and Lyle moved in between them, hands in his pockets. "Wade's going to ride with me for awhile," In the back of the car, the general was rocking back and forth, like a kid trying to capsize a boat.

Sawatski looked Lyle up and down. "Oh, yeah?"

"Yeah," Lyle said. "We've got some things to talk about."

Sawatski turned to his partner for confirmation. Wade shrugged and nodded. Sawatski watched him closely. "You're all right, then?"

"Yeah, I'm all right."

"You going to the restaurant later?"

Lyle grinned at him. "Sure. We'll be there."

It was rumoured that Lyle liked to drive detainees out of town and leave them to walk home after confiscating their shoes, a breach of protocol (and basic decency) that would not have surprised Sawatski. He'd always had this sneaky look about him, like he was trying to negotiate your wallet into his pocket, or your wife into his bed.

Sawatski stone-faced him for a second, then shrugged. "Whatever." He made a gun of his hand and tipped it at them. "You girls have fun now."

Back in his own car, he fired up the engine, turned the heat on high, and adjusted the rear-view to have a look at Gene in the backseat. He was resting his head on the window, staring out at the snow. Sawatski considered saying something to him, but nothing came to mind.

GREATER FLAMINGO
(*Phoenicopterus rubber*)

Far from any city, in a lagoon where snow never falls, it bends
its head to the water to feed. This window into paradise a
kind of purgatory. Time and again it will raise its foot, stamp
the muddy bottom, and strain the swirling particles that rise
to meet it. Immortalized on the screen at the foot of the bed.

QUINN

"WILL YOU TURN THAT OFF?" HE said.

Antoine stopped pacing and looked at him. "What?"

"The TV. You're not even watching it."

"I'm watching it."

"Bullshit. Turn it off."

Antoine opened his mouth, then shrugged and turned off the
television. Quinn returned his attention to the pile of magazines
on the writing table. He smoothed out page twenty-seven of the
most recent issue of *Star* magazine, made a deft incision around
the F in "facelift" with an X-Acto knife, and teased out the glossy
square. He would have found the work calming if Antoine hadn't
been pacing the room, talking incessantly. His partner had been
wound up tight ever since the police showed up earlier in the
night. They'd been watching soft-core porn on HBO and eating
Vietnamese takeout from paper boxes when they heard the siren:

distant at first over the roar of the storm, but rapidly swelling until it stopped right outside the building. Quinn turned off the lights and peered out through the curtains.

"What is it?" Antoine said. He was sitting on his bed in his underwear, eyes wide, grease around his mouth, chopsticks in his hand. A dismantled shotgun lay in the gym bag at his feet in a nest of folded shirts and towels. "Quinn?"

"I don't know." Quinn pulled on his shoes. "There's only one car out there."

"One car? One *cop car*? Jesus Christ. What do we do?"

Quinn told him to stay put and went out alone with an empty ice pail. Snow had blown in over the landing, making stealth impossible, so he walked straight down to where the cruiser was parked in front of an open door at the far end of the motel. He took in the room with a passing glance: a man in a towel sitting on a bed, a woman in a miniskirt standing and yelling at him, two cops between them, one trying to calm the woman down while the other bowed his head, clearly trying not to laugh. Quinn circled around the building, filled the bucket with ice, and returned to his room.

Antoine hadn't moved. "Well?" he said.

Quinn shook his head. "Nothing to do with us."

If the cops had come for them, Antoine would have been less than useless. He would have raced out, squealing, with his hands in the air, and Quinn would have taken him down himself — one shot, right between the shoulders — before striding out to meet his fate. Part of him had been wanting to do it, if only to shut him up, since they first met in the oil fields of northern Alberta.

Between lines of cocaine in the bunkhouse and twelve-hour shifts in near-complete darkness, they'd found that they had certain things in common. Antoine had a master's degree in Political Science and had served two years in minimum security for defrauding the federal government of ninety-eight thousand dollars, while Quinn had discovered politics in the Kingston Penitentiary library, where he'd served eight much more arduous years for second-degree murder. Working the pipeline together, they'd plotted hundreds of assassinations: politicians, stockbrokers and CEOs (Antoine had known such people and evoked them well — gazing through plate-glass windows at the Toronto skyline like feudal lords). They agreed about the need for social upheaval, admired the simplicity and singularity of the Middle Eastern paradigm, outlined what such a campaign would look like on Western soil: the recruitment of disaffected youth, their use as knowing or unknowing propagators of terror; a campaign of single-minded, unwavering brutality that no one would be able to ignore.

Antoine would have kept talking forever if Quinn hadn't nudged him into action, browbeating him, flattering him, telling him they were destined for greatness, like Castro and Che. At the end of the summer, they quit their jobs and relocated to a city where no one knew them, researching explosives in internet cafés, and scouring activist gatherings for likely candidates. On the one occasion that Antoine showed a trace of a spine and talked about leaving, Quinn had calmly put the shotgun in his face and informed him that he was looking at the only way off that particular ride.

Antoine rubbed his nose and walked the length of the room, turned and walked back again. The bureau was coated with powder. He'd done three lines in the last hour. "You know what it's like?" he said. "Collages. You remember collages? From school? Cutting out pictures based on different themes?"

Quinn liberated an R and two Es from the magazine, smudged them with glue, abutted them with the F, and smoothed them flat on the computer paper with a surgical-gloved finger. He was looking for text half an inch high, in bold, white type. Consistency was important. The more varied in size and colour the letters, the more insane they would look.

"Well, it's like that," Antoine said. "What with all the hunting and cutting. Like a dead-serious collage."

Quinn stretched out his neck. "What time is it?"

"Around eleven."

"I didn't ask you what time it was around."

Antoine sighed and looked at his watch. "Eleven oh-four." He sat down on the bed, then stood up again almost immediately. "Jesus. It's happening, isn't it? It's really happening. You're trucking along, talking and planning and whatnot, and then all of a sudden, boom! Everything changes. Year One starts tonight. September 22. That's like, double nine-eleven. You'd almost think we planned it that way. It's like . . . synchronicity or something." He came over and straddled the chair next to Quinn. "You know what the funny thing is? I think that he knows. On some level, I think he knows exactly what he's doing, which is kind of beautiful when you think about it."

"Yeah?"

"Oh, yeah." Antoine tapped out an erratic rhythm on the back of his chair. "No question in my mind. He knows."

Quinn sliced out an uppercase D and set it beside the double E, wondering just how much Antoine had let on at the café that afternoon. His instructions had been to earn Jared's trust, not to convert him to the cause. That the kid couldn't be spared was unfortunate, but the event wouldn't have been enough on its own. A sacrifice was what would give the event power.

"And the Middle East connection?" Antoine was saying. "How lucky was that? The fact that he's Lebanese — "

"Half-Lebanese."

"Whatever. They'll be off hunting the Muslim hordes, and we'll be working on number two right under their noses."

"Let's just focus on number one, all right?" Quinn switched magazines and paged through the latest issue of *Vanity Fair*. In his mind's eye, he conjured the moment of detonation and experienced a pleasurable sensation of release. The device was small and crude, but it carried a blast radius of some thirty feet, barring obstacles, and would do a significant amount of damage.

After acquiring all the necessary materials from home improvement stores, and transforming the innocuous parts into a deadly whole, they'd tested a prototype in a field outside of town. Quinn had been impressed with the results — a rough circle opening in the wheat as they watched from the distant road. It was impossible to say how many people would be caught in the blast. Half a dozen. Maybe more. One they could be certain of, and that was all they needed, really. It was the gesture that mattered. The threat as much as the blow.

In his prison psych evaluations, Quinn had been diagnosed with "sociopathic tendencies", which, as far as he was concerned, was not a bad thing. The architecture of his brain allowed him to operate coolly and decisively, divorcing action from emotion. Antoine was not so fortunate. His doubts about the campaign were clear, given how often he talked about having none. Now, as he hovered beside Quinn, drumming the back of his chair, he made a lateral shift from the events of the evening to one of his favourite subjects: the conspiracy between big oil and the United States government to precipitate the attack on the World Trade Center.

"It was a beautiful thing, the way it all came together. They take out both towers *and* building seven with controlled demolition? Talk about ballsy. When did they rig it? That's what I want to know."

Quinn traced the knife along the O in "Oprah" (shown beside the article, her head thrown back in laughter). "You remembered to set the alarm, right?"

"What?"

Quinn's hand stopped moving. "The alarm. On the bomb. Did you set it?"

"Yeah, I . . . " Antoine trailed off, frowning. "Holy shit. For a second I was thinking did I set it for AM or PM."

"So which was it?" Quinn said, keeping his voice even.

"What?"

"Which was it? AM or PM?"

"PM."

The knife in Quinn's hand jagged off, through the O, beheading the billionaire talk show host. He looked at Antoine.

"AM!" Antoine said. "PM's noon, AM's midnight. Jesus, I wouldn't forget a thing like that. AM. Definitely AM. I'm all over it."

Quinn considered the blade in his hand and the proximity of Antoine's throat. As if reading his mind, Antoine paced over to the kitchenette to put on another pot of coffee, still jabbering on about how certain he was.

Quinn knew that he should have set the clock himself, but he'd been wary of handling the device. It was vital that he remain alive to orchestrate things. People like Jared were weapons, and while people like Antoine might help acquire those weapons, Quinn was the one who would ultimately put them to use. He knew exactly what he was doing, why he was doing it, and what the inevitable consequences of those actions would be. They were engaging with an enemy that they could not possibly defeat. The only question was how long they were going to last.

The coffee machine rattled awake and Antoine peered out the window. "Snow's still coming down out there. It's like a sign, isn't it? That something major's about to happen. Like even God's on board."

Quinn stared at him.

"What?" Antoine said.

"You're sure."

"About what?"

"The clock."

"I'm sure, I'm sure!"

"Is there a possibility you set it for the wrong time?"

"What?"

"Is there a possibility — "

"Fuck, no! Relax, buddy. I thought about it and I remembered. I am ninety-nine point nine — no, I'm a hundred percent certain that I set it for the right time. Twelve AM. Midnight. All right?" He poured out two cups of coffee, his hands visibly shaking. "Now this weather is another story. It could seriously fuck with our plans."

"Denny's never closes," Quinn said.

"What if he can't get there?"

"He'll get there."

"But what if he can't?"

Quinn found another O and carefully excised it. If the kid couldn't get there, the bomb would go off wherever it happened to be, hopefully with him in range. He might not know their real names but he knew their faces. If they drove past Denny's in an hour and nothing had happened, they would have to get out of the city fast. Or rather, he would have to get out of the city fast. What he was going to do with Antoine, he wasn't yet sure.

He set the O beside the D.

Antoine carried both cups of coffee over to the table and put them down. "I just suddenly have a very bad feeling about everything. I mean, what if there are kids there?"

"We've talked about this," Quinn said.

"I know, I know. It's late at night. But what if some idiot brings a kid anyway? Stranger things have happened."

"What are you asking me?"

"I don't know."

"Sit down."

"What?"

Quinn unhooded his eyes and showed Antoine what lay behind them, the details of his future: arms bound, legs bound, duct tape around the mouth, a knife in the belly. Antoine sat on the bed.

"Good. Now turn on the TV."

"That's all right."

"I know it's all right. Turn on the TV."

He waited for Antoine to obey before returning his attention to the writing table. As his partner sat staring at an aerial perspective of migrating flamingos, Quinn found an M and snugged it up to the O, finishing the last word in the manifesto: FREEDOM.

Chimney swift
(*Chaetura pelagica*)

Like a mass of drowsy bees, they are calmer in numbers,
bolstered against the nightmare of snow. For months the
chimney has been cool and quiet. They are unprepared for
this sudden, new persecution that comes from below: the
flue banging open, an arm of heat forcing them back out,
streaming into the night.

Albert

"I have your king, Albert."

    "What are you talking about? He's safe."

    "I have him in eight moves. I'm coming for him."

    "Keep talking."

    "The end is in sight, my friend."

    "Uh-huh. Where's Paula?"

    "Upstairs resting. The weather has given her a migraine."

    "Snow gives your wife migraines?"

    "Sudden changes in air pressure give my wife migraines."

    "I don't know that I've ever had a migraine. What's the difference
between a headache and a migraine?"

    "Intensity mostly. It's like the difference between "feeling blue"
and clinical depression. If you suffered from chronic migraines,
you would know it. So, this boy you were talking about."

"Well, the little idiot almost jumped into the bear pit."

"And what did you do?"

"I stopped him. Eight moves, you say."

"You saw him earlier in the day?"

"Yeah, sort of wandering around by himself. But I'd never have thought . . . Your queen's open."

"And what happened next?"

"Why the hell are you sacrificing your queen?"

"What did you do with the boy? After you stopped him."

"Hmm? I called his parents. Turns out his class had left without him. You think they'd do a head count."

"Did you meet the boy's parents?"

"Why so many questions?"

"I'm simply curious about his motives. People always have motives for their actions, you know, however obscure. In that respect, we're not so different from our animal cousins."

"I don't know about that. I've seen some pretty random human behaviour in my time. The other day I'm out shopping when this old man comes up to me on the street and says, 'Taylor Walsh.' You know, the actor? That's all he says. 'Taylor Walsh.' But it's not what he says, it's the *way* he says it. Like it's the most important thing in the world. He stares at me for a couple of seconds, then he turns around and walks away."

"Well, to him, I'm sure it was important. To him, that name — Taylor Walsh — could very well represent the meaning of life. If you believed you knew the meaning of life, wouldn't you feel compelled to share it with someone? You see, there is no such thing as entirely random behaviour."

"No?"

"Absolutely not."

"What if I hauled off and hit you right now? Wouldn't that seem a little random?"

"You would be proving a point."

"But if we weren't having this conversation."

"You would be enraged by my imminent victory. Or by some irritating personal habit of mine. Or by nothing conscious at all. A single action is a determined by the countless events that precede it. To fully understand why you struck me, we would first have to travel back in time, to where you were perhaps having an argument with your wife over dinner. Then we would go back further, to the incident with the boy. Then years back, decades back, all the way to your childhood, beyond childhood, to sensory input in the womb."

"And your job is to follow the trail back to the beginning."

"As nearly as I can. It's your move, my friend."

"I just took your queen."

"Yes."

"In exchange for a pawn."

"Yes."

"And you're going to sit there and tell me that I have six moves left."

"I'm afraid the game ended the moment you advanced your queen's bishop. In a way it's analogous to the scenario we were just discussing. If you were to strike me now, it would certainly be shocking, but it would not be without motivation. The moves preceding that move would simply be invisible to me. And possibly to yourself."

"There must be a way out of this."

"I'm afraid not."

"What if I open my king up? Give him to you sooner?"

"Let me amend that. You have, at the *most*, six moves. Had the game started with the premature advance of your queen's bishop, six moves would be a kind of victory, representing the absolute best you could do."

"And what if I just knocked all the pieces off the board?"

"There's no need to get angry, my friend. I'm only teasing."

"I'm not angry. I'm speaking to your point."

"Well, in that case, in our rudimentary model, the sweeping hand could actually be an appropriate metaphor. The future is not only controlled by the familiar, established patterns of the past. One is always vulnerable to outside influence, to intervention; a sweeping hand, as it were, to clear the board."

"And you're the hand."

"Professionally speaking? Yes, you might say that. I am the hand. Should we see what my son has to say about it? Jared, if I am the hand, what does that make you? The finger? Or the wrist? Are you going out? Jared?"

"Yeah?"

"Are you going out?"

"Yeah."

"Are you taking the car?"

"Yeah.

"Have the roads been cleared? Jared? Have — "

"They're fine!"

"When should I expect your return? Jared? Goodbye, Jared! Quite a verbose son I have."

"He's at that age."

"He's beginning to overstay his welcome at that age."

"How's he doing in school?"

"It seems that my son has decided not to follow in his father's illustrious footsteps after all. I suppose it's just as well. I never thought he was suited to the field to begin with."

"What's he doing now?"

"Finding himself. Can't you tell?"

"Ah, he's a good kid."

"He would be an even better kid if he was employed. And married."

"He's still young."

"Paula and I married at nineteen. Two years later, we had Jared. It helps one grow, to have responsibilities at a young age. Nowadays, there's no incentive to grow up. We're ruining our children. We think we're doing the best thing by sheltering them but, in reality, the opposite is the case. I suppose I shouldn't complain. Psychologists have never been in such high demand."

"But you want them to have a chance to be kids first, don't you? Look at Sam. What kind of prospects does a pregnant sixteen-year-old have?"

"I'm sorry, Bert. I wasn't thinking about Samantha."

"Wel,l I can tell you, there's nothing good about it at all. You know, I've been thinking about accidents lately."

"The boy."

"Sure. He could have jumped right in there with the bears and gotten himself killed when no one was looking. Everyone would just have assumed it was an accident. "Boy falls into bear pit," the headline would read, not "boy jumps into bear pit," and there's one hell of a big difference as far as who's at fault and — I'll be damned if it doesn't look from this board like I'm winning. But you see what I'm saying. How some things we call accidents aren't really accidents at all."

"I think so."

"As far as Sam goes, I don't know. Maureen calls it an accident. Like she just *fell* pregnant. Like it wasn't anyone's fault. But it seems to me that an accident's a totally random thing. You go off the road because the roads are icy — that's an accident. You go off the road because you're drunk, it's something else. Can you really call something an accident just because you didn't mean for it to happen?"

"I really don't know, Bert. But do you think it matters in the end?"

"Of course it matters. It's like you said, about kids taking responsibility. Do you know that she hasn't even told us who did it yet? Who the father is."

"And that's important."

"Of course it's important. The most important thing is obviously that she's healthy and all. But how would you feel if you were in my position, not knowing something like that? You start suspecting everyone. It could be the kid that delivers my paper. Or the guy that bags my groceries. It could be Jared, for god's sake."

"Now, come on, Bert. I'm all for a good analogy, but don't you think you're taking this a little far?"

"You're right . . . I'm sorry."

"Perhaps we should save the game for another night."

"No, let's finish it. After all, I only have, what . . . "

"Four moves."

"Ha! Four moves left. You've got to give me a chance to fight my way out of this. And, to be honest, I don't think I'm ready to go back home just yet. If that's all right with you."

"Of course, my friend."

"Maybe it's this weather. It plays with your mind, doesn't it? I know the animals felt it coming. They were skittish all day. And this whole thing with Sam, it's just so . . . "

"How is she doing?"

"Sam? Well, this afternoon she snuck out of the house without saying anything and had Maureen all in a panic. But she seems all right. It looks like she's finally settled on a name. It's going to be a boy, I told you that, right? Anyway, she says she wants to call him Doug. Why Doug? Who knows. Maybe it's a good sign. Maybe it means she's ready."

"And you? Are you ready?"

"Sure. Not really. Not at all, actually. You know, I envy you. The kind of insight you have into people's motivations must have really helped with raising Jared. I have no idea why Sam does half the things she does."

"We all have our difficulties."

"Yeah, but things must not take you by surprise as much. I mean, what's the worst thing Jared's ever done? Sorry, you don't have to answer that."

"It's all right."

"I still don't know what I was — "

"It's fine."

"Yeah? So where are we at here? Three moves. That's what you've been telling me, right? That I've been doomed from the — Jesus."

"What's wrong?"

"I see it."

"Yes?"

"I'm done. Three moves."

"Yes."

"Remind me why I come over here again."

"Because you live across the street."

"Is that the only reason?"

"Are you asking me to analyze you?"

"Maybe."

"That, my friend, would cost you."

"I'll bet it would. So what now? Should we play it through to the end?"

"Of course."

Dark-eyed junco
(*Junco hyemalis*)

Nestled in the attic, it dreams in song: individual notes threaded into complex ropes of communication. A stuttering achromatic trill — a rest — a drawn out glissando — the explosive accented close. The song is charged with a meaning known only to its kin, a language honed in sleep. A nocturnal rehearsal blazing through the head tucked into the wing.

Tang

He had been working the grill since noon. His back was on fire, his feet were sore, his lungs were raw from too many cigarette breaks, and, still, he had to put on a cheery face for the officers who were too lazy to walk around the building from the parking lot. He had to let them use the back door and tramp through his kitchen whenever they wanted. He had to smile when they treated him like some kind of mascot. He had to pretend he didn't mind the air of proprietorship they brought with them into his restaurant. Well, this evening Tang minded very much. Not just the police, but the stupid dishwasher who was always dropping plates, his wife who was continually mad at him, his daughter who had cultivated a western teenager's disrespect for her parents, and, more immediately, the tremendous headache growing behind his eyes.

"Hot water!" he called to the dishwasher who responded with a blank, questioning face. "In a bucket! Quick! Quick!" The urgency in his voice failed to motivate the dishwasher to move faster. He was about to give up and fetch the water himself when the bell dinged out front and his wife came back into the kitchen to tell him that his nephew had arrived with his girlfriend.

"Do they want to eat?" Tang said.

She shrugged. Knowing better than to press her, Tang turned the burners down and went out into the dining area himself. The two officers that had come in minutes before lowered their voices when he passed their table, as if he cared what they had to say. Joe and Darby had taken their usual booth, under one of the red, paper globes that helped to give the room its mood. As he got closer, Tang saw that his nephew's eyes were bloodshot and swollen.

"Everything okay?" he asked, warily. His nephew was more emotional than most of the women he knew, lacking any sense of decorum or restraint. Tang resisted the notion that Joe had an "artistic temperament", or that acting qualified as artistry. Any child or mentally deranged person was capable of playacting. It embarrassed him to think that Joe considered it his vocation.

Darby smiled a brave smile. "Oh, we're fine."

Tang disapproved of the girl's presumption of speaking for Joe, but said nothing. He noticed that she was holding a small plastic pyramid and jerked his head at it. "What's that?"

Darby looked embarrassed. "Someone gave it to me today."

"Huh. So how was the show?" Tang did not feel guilty for failing to attend his nephew's premiere. He could hardly have been expected to shut down the restaurant for something so frivolous.

"Terrible," Darby said.

"Big surprise." Tang's eyes went over to his nephew, who still hadn't spoken. "Hey, movie star. You want food?"

Joe deigned to shake his head.

"We'll just have tea," Darby said.

"All right. I'll come talk later."

Again, the officers went quiet as he walked by their table and, this time, Tang found it slightly unnerving. Back in the kitchen, the dishwasher had not filled a bucket with hot water and was slowly loading the big machine. Tang's wife was sweeping out the deep freeze, and his daughter was perched on a stool by the pass-through, reading a fashion magazine. Tang got the water, put in a bag of frozen dumplings to thaw, then lit a cigarette and leaned against the grill. He wondered if the police had found out about his citizenship issues and, if they had, why they would care. And, if they cared, why he should care. Was his life so perfect that he would fight to stay in the country if they told him to leave? Before he could reach a conclusion about any of this, three more officers came in the back door, dragging clumps of snow into the kitchen.

Tang roused himself and raised his hands in celebration. "Howdy, boys!"

"That's a health violation there, boss," the fat one said, indicating the cigarette he had just lit. This was a running joke between Tang and Constable Sawatski, who had assured him years ago that, as far as the police department was concerned, he could smoke wherever he liked, just as long as he didn't tap his ashes into their food.

"Cold out there, huh?" Tang said.

"One bitch of a night," Sawatski agreed. He stopped to grab a carrot off the cutting board as his friends passed through into the restaurant. "Wade here?"

"Been here maybe . . . twenty minutes?"

"Is he acting funny?"

"Ah . . . I'm not sure what you mean."

Sawatski laughed. "All right. I'll see you later, boss." He left the kitchen, gnawing on his carrot. As Tang set about preparing their usual meals, his head throbbed in an irregular rhythm. The dishwasher let one of the big plates slip and shatter and Tang flinched dramatically.

"Sorry," the dishwasher said.

Were it not for the headache, Tang would have yelled at him to clean it up. Instead, he cast a beleaguered look at his daughter, who rolled her eyes and went to fetch the broom. The front bell dinged again and Tang's back flared, the muscles bunching all the way up to his neck. He peered out front to see how many new customers he would be dealing with. An old native man stood swaying by the front door, with snow on his jacket and in his hair. The police officers were all twisted around and leaning back to look at him. "You've got to be kidding me," the old man said. He shook his head and backed out of the restaurant.

"Bingo hall's down the street, chief!" Sawatski called after him. His friends all laughed. From his corner booth, Joe was looking over at them with open hostility. Tang caught his eye, gave a small but firm shake of the head, and went back to tend to the piles of meat and vegetables on the grill. The dishwasher was staring at a stack of pots that needed scrubbing, his arms at his sides. His daughter had swept up the broken plate and was back on her stool, dozing lightly. Only his wife seemed to have any energy, albeit grim energy — clearing away the officers' wet footprints with violent strokes of the mop. It hurt Tang to see how his customers treated her: pantomiming their demands, speaking loudly and slowly (she had never developed more than a rudimentary knowledge of English), or ignoring her altogether. Perhaps deportation would be the best thing for them both. He doubted that it would mean any more work for him personally and, overseas, their Canadian dollars would go far. Of course, his daughter — a year from her high school diploma and already looking at universities — knew nothing of Vietnam. It would be unfair to uproot her and unthinkable to leave her behind. Tang felt as if he had a foot on each continent, holding them all in stasis.

He checked the sticky rice, determined that it could use five more minutes in the steamer, and was contemplating lighting another cigarette when raised voices came from the dining area. He hurried out to see what was wrong, and found his nephew on his feet, facing the police, who formed a small, dangerous unit at their table. "Bingo hall?" Joe was saying. "Chief? You go and say something like that as if we're not even sitting here?" He had become a character from one of his plays, a tough-talking American detective. Tang was mesmerized by the transformation: his nephew — not his nephew — spewing invectives. "You want to call me something now?" he said. "Dink? Gook? What?"

"All right," one of the officers said. "Remember who you're talking to now."

"Fuck you," Joe said.

Before anything else could happen, Tang strode across the room, and slapped his nephew in the face. He slapped him as he would have slapped a son of his own. A spoiled and foolish son. No one said anything. Joe sat down and pressed a hand to his cheek. Darby looked horrified. The officers seemed embarrassed and unsure of themselves. Tang walked past them all — past the officers, past his wife and daughter who had come into the room, past the dishwasher who was hovering behind them — back to the kitchen, to the grill, where the vegetables were now burning.

Turkey vulture
(Cathartes aura)

Massive wings splayed in the snow, the terrible head, skinned and ferocious. As if in homage to a fallen emperor, scavengers arrive to claim the body piecemeal: rats and coyotes, insects swarming up from the cold earth.

Bill

The old man was snoring in the next room, as only old men can snore, as if there were no more difficult job in the world than breathing. His house must have been a hundred years old, but most of the appliances inside looked brand new and seemed to have never been used. It was like a showroom set up in the woods. A microwave on a tree stump, a television on the ground.

Bill hadn't given much thought to how they'd managed to stumble upon the only inhabited building in the area when the blizzard hit. They had been lucky, that was all. The door had been unlocked and they went in without knocking — shivering, the bag of geese clamped in Leah's hand. The old man had looked at them calmly, as if he'd been sitting there in his kitchen, waiting for them for years. A pair of mangy cats under the stove gave the more expected response and dashed from the room. Leah clutched at Bill, sobbing hysterically. He felt as if the wind was still caught in his head, banging his thoughts around.

"Telephone," he said. The old man shook his head and touched his ear. Bill raised his voice. "Telephone!"

The old man understood and pointed to a device with oversized buttons that looked more like a child's toy than a phone. Bill picked up the receiver and put it back down. He had no idea who to call. The old man rose with some difficulty, hobbled into a back room, and returned with some blankets. He gave them to Leah, who, still sobbing, tried to explain what had happened. The old man nodded vaguely and went over to the stove.

Bill strode back to the door.

"No!" Leah said. She tried to hold him back, but he shook himself free and headed out into the storm. After twenty paces, he was lost, unable to orient himself back to the house even. He chose an arbitrary direction and walked for what seemed like miles. Finally, he came upon another building from behind. Hugging the wall, he made his way around to the front. His sister was waiting in the doorway. Disoriented and shuddering, he allowed her to pull him back inside.

It pained him to remember how he'd stood with his arms at his sides as Leah embraced him and berated him for his stupidity. She shifted beside him now, inches away in the narrow guestbed.

"Bill?"

"Hm."

"Are you awake?"

"Yeah, I'm awake."

"What are you thinking about?"

"Nothing."

He wondered why women always asked that question. As if knowing another person's mind was desirable, or even possible. The old man seemed to know the value of silence. The second time Bill had come in he'd been putting a kettle on the lit cast iron stove (which was standing, for some strange reason, beside a modern electrical stove). He moved slowly, but with purpose, sway-backed and stooped over almost ninety degrees. Leah sat Bill down at the kitchen table, and the old man set two cups before them, along with a ceramic creamer and a bowl of sugar. After a minute, he brought over the steeping teapot, filled both of their cups, and settled in a chair on the far side of the room. Leah thanked him and he nodded distractedly. She began to tell him what had happened to them in the marsh and he listened for awhile, then closed his eyes and seemed to fall asleep. After some discussion, Leah called the police, who told her what Bill had known already, that nothing could be done until morning. Then she called their mother and left a message on her machine.

As Bill lay staring at the ceiling in the guestroom, he wondered if Leah could hear the click of his eyes opening and closing.

"Bill?" she said.

"Mm."

"Why didn't you want to talk to Ian?"

He yawned deliberately. "No point talking twice. You got all the information we needed."

In the two hours that they had believed their brother was dead or dying (curled in a drift somewhere, alone and hypothermic) they'd hardly talked. The old man insisted that they change their clothes, so they took turns in the bathroom — a shock in itself: an IKEA showroom attached to a barn, professionally tiled and outfitted with pink hand towels and shell-shaped soaps. Bill stripped off his wet hunting clothes and put on a flannel shirt and a pair of the old man's trousers. The material was soft from countless washes and wearings, but the fit was nearly perfect. He looked at himself in the mirror, unsettled by the sight of himself in another man's clothes. Leah changed next, into an ankle-length dress with frill at the wrists and throat. She came out of the bathroom and smiled at them wearily.

"How do I look?"

"Very nice," the old man said. "Get you something to eat, then." He began to get up, but Leah insisted that he stay where he was and set about preparing a meal out of what she could find in the cupboards and fridge: dark rye bread, sliced sausage, mustard, and pickles. Bill and the old man watched her work. At any other time, Bill knew, she would have been horrified to see herself dressed as a country wife, making sandwiches for the men. They ate by the window, watching the storm and listening for signs of it abating, as the old man's cats prowled around their legs.

When the telephone rang, Leah and Bill both jumped. The old man indicated that they should answer it, and Leah picked up. On hearing her mother's voice, she broke down sobbing. Bill cleared his throat and coughed into his fist. Clearly embarrassed, the old man left them alone in the room.

"What?" Leah said. "Oh, my god! Thank god!" She could hardly speak for the relief, and Bill realized that, somehow, Ian had survived. "Someone picked him up," she told him, then passed him the phone and covered her face with her hands. Bill talked to his mother, briefly, learning the specifics of what had happened and keeping the conversation otherwise focused on the more practical matter of getting home. After passing the phone back to his sister, he went and sat by the television, which had been on since they arrived — the sound off, the picture warped. He toyed with the colour and contrast, while his sister got the number of the hospital in the city where Ian was being treated for frostbite. He turned to the Weather Channel, where they were showing a satellite image of a massive spiral-shaped cloud formation passing over the central provinces and states.

"Bill," Leah said. "He wants to talk to you."

He sighed and passed a hand over his face. "Tell him . . . Just tell him to get his ass out here and pick us up."

Why hadn't he wanted to talk to his brother? How the hell should he know? He wished that Leah would stop putting these difficult questions to him. She shifted again in the bed, and he tensed at the approach of another emotional curveball.

"Bill?"

"Yeah?"

"How long until we get home?"

He relaxed, more comfortable with this line of questioning. "Well, it'll take them a while to clear the roads. Most of the day, probably. We'll have to get a lift back to the truck, dig it out, maybe get a jump. I'm thinking we'll be lucky to get back by dark." He propped his hands behind his head and chuckled.

"What's so funny?"

"Nothing."

"What?"

"I didn't even see you held onto your birds until we got to the house. Two black eyes and a bag full of birds."

"Hilarious."

He was unsure about teasing her, but could hear in her voice that she was smiling. "So, what do you think of the old guy?" he said. "What's with this place? He's got DirecTV and the roof's about to fall down."

"Shh."

"What?"

"He'll hear you."

"Are you kidding? He's deaf as a sledgehammer. And probably half crazy, living out here by himself. Did you notice how he wasn't even surprised to see us today? Two strangers show up at his door in full camo in the middle of a snowstorm and he doesn't want to know what happened."

"It was pretty obvious."

"Yeah, but he didn't want to know the details." He smiled as he listened to the old man snoring in the next room. The more he thought about him, the more he liked him.

"Bill?" Leah said after awhile.

"Hm?"

"Is this what it was like hunting with Dad?"

"Well, not exactly. It wasn't so . . . " He searched for a word she might use. "Eventful."

She laughed. "I mean before the storm."

"Yeah. Well, I guess it was more or less the same."

He stared at the ceiling, trying to conjure his father's face and failing.

"Bill?"

"Hm."

"Do you miss him?"

"Let's just try and get some sleep, all right?"

He could feel Leah turn over on her side to face him. "It's strange," she said. "I don't feel like I miss him. I'm sad that he's gone but, in some ways, it's like there's nothing for me to miss. He was more of an idea to me. An abstraction."

"Uh-huh."

"Does that make sense?"

"Sure."

They lay together in silence for a minute. "Bill?"

"Hn?"

"Thanks."

"For what?"

"For coming back for me."

He glanced over at her and nodded. "Yeah, okay."

Cedar waxwing
(*Bombycilla cedrorum*)

Unsettled by the absent sky and the windless air, it flies the length of the corridor and comes back through the lobby, nudging walls and windows, before looping over the front desk and the duty officer's flailing broom to alight on a high windowsill, just out of reach.

Gene

They weren't letting him see a doctor because they wanted him to suffer. His nose was broken, he was pretty fucking sure of that. His left arm too. He couldn't even lift it without pain ripping through the socket. It felt bad. It felt permanent. It was going to heal all wrong and he was going to end up a crippled gimp for the rest of his life. Assholes. Motherfucking *assholes*. He gripped one of the bars with his good hand and called down the hall. "Hey! My arm's fucking broken in here!"

Nothing. Just a couple of guys in the other holding cells telling him to shut it. He tried yelling again, but the effort hurt too much. Fuck. Tomorrow he'd get himself a lawyer to take some pictures. A big, fat, white lawyer. Gene saw himself up there on the stand in a suit and tie, pointing the cop out for the courtroom, explaining what had happened. Fucker kicks him when he's already down and cuffed. Steel toe jamming into his ribs, doing all kinds of damage inside. One second he's walking down the street, minding his own business, the next all he can see is blue, blue, blue. The cops hit the lights, you run. He wasn't about to let them take him to the edge of town and leave him to walk back in the snow, like they did that time with his cousin Tommy. At least he'd given them a good run. Got the one fucker in the mouth with a solid right. If he hadn't hit the ice on his cheap runners, they wouldn't have caught him at all.

"Hey!" he called again, and again got no response. He sat down on the cot and hammered it with his shoe. "Hey! Hey! Hey!" How fucking typical was this? Throwing him in a cell like he'd raped and killed ten women. Always the way. But this time it had almost been worth it, seeing everyone come together like that, pushing things to a place where something big might actually happen. And how about that crazy fucking Tommy? Running in with his helmet on, looking like a true warrior. Then everyone was down. Tommy squawking when the one cop did something to his arm, Gene pinned under the other cop, looking out into the crowd to see Raymond Solway reaching into his pocket where he kept his .32, seriously considering. On his stomach, face burning in the snow, Gene looked him in the eye and thought, *do it.* He saw it happen like a scene in a movie about revolution. One shot from Ray's gun triggering something huge. The cop with the moustache holding his chest and looking down in surprise, the fat cop fumbling for his gun as the crowd took him down. Then Gene would have been up there at the front, shouting orders, and they would have all started walking down the street, heading south, over the Grousetail, to the rich end of town. People coming out of their houses with bats and sticks and Gene leading the way with the fat cop's gun in his waistband. How sweet would that have been? A few more seconds and it could have happened. But then two more cop cars pulled up, Ray's hand came out of his pocket, and that was that. Gene got shoved into one car, Tommy into another.

Wait a second. Where the fuck was Tommy? Gene limped over to the bars.

"Tommy?"

He hadn't seen his cousin since the parking lot. When they ran him through, the only other people in the room had been a drag queen with his makeup all smeared, and a hooker screaming at a bald dude with glasses.

"Tommy!"

If Tommy was there, he'd be hearing him, the place wasn't that big. And if Tommy was hearing him, he'd sure as fuck be calling back. "Tommy!" Maybe the fuckers took him on another Starlight Tour. Maybe this time when he got back, they'd have to saw off his fucking feet. He could see the cops wanting to break him. He was a strong fucker. At the house the other night he hadn't connected all the way, but he still laid Gene out pretty good. "I pulled it!" he shouted over the music, helping Gene up and smiling into his face, before heading off through the crowd doing that weird dance of his. Same dance he'd done when they were kids — the adults all standing around like giants, laughing to see Tommy drunk on nothing. Suddenly, Gene was scared. "Hey, Tommy! Tommy Cochrane!"

The guys in the other cells were starting to get worked up, but Gene kept yelling until a bald old fucker with a handlebar moustache and a cup of coffee walked up, looking bored and pissed off.

"What are you doing?" the guy said.

Gene tried to shut out the pain in his arm, his face, his chest — it would have been easier to list the places he didn't hurt. "Hey, man. Can you do me a huge favour? Can you check and see if my cousin's here? His name's Tommy Cochrane."

The fucker sighed and shook his head. "If you have a request you're going to have to wait until morning."

"Come on, man. Just check the book or whatever . . ."

But the fucker was already walking away. Wouldn't hear him out for two seconds. They slap on the cuffs and think they fucking own you. Well, not this time. This time they'd listen. This time he'd *make* them listen. He took off his shoe again and started slapping it against the bars, getting a good rhythm going. "Tom-mee! Tom-mee! Tom-mee!" Other guys were yelling too, saying they were going to kill him, but Gene kept it up until the old fucker came back, this time without the coffee. The guard shouted everyone else down, but Gene kept chanting.

"What are you doing?" the guard said.

"Okay, look." Gene tried to put on a reasonable face. "In case you can't tell, I've been having myself one shitty night. First your boys jump me for no reason, then they beat the shit out of me for no reason. Then they leave me sitting in here with a broken arm, not getting to see a doctor or anything, but I'll tell you what. I'll be quiet about the whole thing and not get myself a big-time lawyer tomorrow like I was planning if you do me this one favour."

The guard moved up closer to the cell. "Here's what's going to happen. You're going to lie down on that cot and you're going to shut your mouth and you're going to keep it shut until morning."

"Just — "

"I'm not going to tell you again."

Always the fucking way. Why did he even try? He started slapping his shoe against the bars again, looking right at the old fucker and chanting Tommy's name. The guard shook his head and walked away. Fuck his arm hurt. He dropped the shoe and paced the cell, looking for something bigger, but everything was bolted down. Fuck it. He unzipped, pulled out his dick, and sent a long arc of piss through the bars. Guys were yelling again, but some were laughing and cheering too. Now two different cops came down the hall. All right. This is where it was going to start, with a peaceful protest. Just like fucking Gandhi.

"Tom-mee! Tom-mee!"

They weren't wearing riot gear or anything, just great big fuckers with billy clubs and mace. He finished pissing and waved his dick at them before tucking it back into his pants. A hard energy was running through him, his arm hardly hurting at all.

"Here comes the KKK!" he shouted. "Time to play beat on the Indian, huh? Brave fuckers."

The rest of the holding cells were quiet, everyone listening to how this was going to play out.

"Just cool out, okay?" the first cop said.

"We come in there," the second one said, "you are not going to like what we bring with us."

He couldn't wait, the fucker. Just dying to use that billy club. Bap, bap. Rodney King, down on the ground. It was too fucking much. No more. He wasn't going to take their shit for one more second.

He ripped off his shirt and stomped around the cell. "Bunch of chickenshit motherfuckers! Wake up! Let's bring this place down!"

He was seeing another movie now, a movie about a prison riot — the other inmates taking up the call, pounding the walls, lighting things on fire. He stopped, breathing hard. The second cop cleared his throat.

"You about done?"

Gene balled up his shirt and whipped it through the bars, hitting him square in the chest. The cop staggered back like he'd been hit with a rock. There it was: bright hate, right on the surface. Gene smiled at him, showed him his middle finger, and started up his chant again.

"Tom-mee! Tom-mee!"

The first cop nodded down the hall and the door unlocked with a heavy clank. The second cop tapped his hand with his billy club to let Gene know what was coming. Gene backed up to the wall, spread his arms as wide as he could with his wrecked shoulder, and sent their hate right back at them. They wanted what he had. They wanted it so bad they'd kill him to get it.

American robin
(Turdus migratorius)

One hundred bodies clotting for warmth in the arms of the poplar. They are one organism, thinking stillness, a tuning fork shivering itself calm. All along the avenue similar songs are being sung in the trees. The worst of the storm has passed. They have only to wait until morning.

Patrick

He'd been matching the Brit and the German drink for drink for hours. They drank to the Canadian prairies. They drank to each other. They drank to the unattractive Dutch girls across the room — salt on the tongue, a shot of tequila, grinning with limes in their mouths.

"I like the chubby one," the German said, earnestly. He had a narrow face with close-set features and blond hair to his shoulders. "I've always had some liking for chubby women."

Patrick laughed at this, until he leaned over, believing he was going to vomit.

The Brit was the undeclared leader of their group — stocky and prematurely bald, with an endless repertoire of tasteless jokes and a voice that dominated the room. "You all right, Pat?" he said, watching Patrick with amusement.

"I'm great," Patrick said, truthfully, chagrined that he could remember neither of their names. He rummaged in the box at his feet and pulled out three more bottles.

The Brit took one and clapped him on the arm. "You Canadians are great people."

"I keep telling you, I'm an American."

"And I keep forgetting, don't I? Let me see that bird again."

Patrick rolled up his sleeve to show him the eagle, the globe, the flag.

"Lovely tattoo, mate. It's a bold statement. Like I've always said, an American's just a Canadian with a spine."

"My friend," the German said, looking around the hostel lounge, "are you trying to get us killed? There are some very large men with no spines in this place."

This set Patrick off again, laughing and rocking. It was like something out of a movie — the drinking, the banter. Back home, he wasn't even legal. The fact that they would ship him off to war but wouldn't let him drink was as good an illustration of what was wrong with his country as any.

Just days after his eighteenth birthday, he and his best friend Dwight had decided to enlist after seeing a recruitment ad in a movie theatre that pushed every adolescent button in their heads: capable-looking, young soldiers shimmying under razor wire and jumping out of airplanes; patriotic music and a gravelly voiceover compelling them to "live the adventure". It was like a trailer for the movie that could be the rest of their lives. Later, Dwight changed his mind, opting to fight the war on terror in his own way — by shooting digital enemies on a Sony PlayStation in his grandmother's basement — but Patrick had followed through on the pact. In the reserves, he suddenly found his life very much simplified. He stepped where they told him to step, did what they told him to do, and proved to actually have decent soldiering skills.

When they activated him for duty in Iraq, he was thrilled to be going somewhere, anywhere, to be finally getting out of North Dakota. The war movies he rented on the weekends did not deter him or even worry him, for the simple reason that he was the protagonist of this particular film.

The week before he was due to climb onto a transport plane, he had been downloading as much pornography as his laptop would hold when his search engine picked up a file he hadn't been looking for: HARDCORE IRAQ BEHEADING. He played his cursor over the bold type, thinking that it couldn't possibly be real, just floating out there on the internet for anyone to see. He double clicked on the link. The video came in like any other, and began to play.

A row of men in black balaclavas appeared on the screen; two clutching automatic rifles, three apparently unarmed. In front of them, a blindfolded man knelt on a concrete floor. He raised his head and identified himself as William Nightingale, a truck driver for an American contractor operating in the Middle East. He denounced his company. He denounced his government. He denounced his president. Then he bowed his head and waited. One of the unarmed men began reading something from a sheet of paper in a foreign language. He read in a monotonous yell. A series of stills — scanned photos his captors must have found on him — passed across the screen. Nightingale with his arm around a woman at the base of a redwood. Nightingale in an armchair with an infant on his lap. Nightingale mugging with his friends beside a company truck. The video returned to the original room, half a dozen men arranged like a choir, all very still.

Then one of the masked men, without warning, drew a machete from his shirt and, very unceremoniously, began to saw William Nightingale's head off, front to back. The blindfold slipped to reveal a stunned expression on Nightingale's face. The head separated from the body and dropped to the ground, eyes frozen in an upward-directed position, mouth half open. The executioner picked up the head by the hair and held it out to the camera. He placed the head on a red pillow in the middle of the room and the men chanted something in unison. Finally, what appeared to be credits tracked down the screen, along with festive Arabic music, and the screen went black.

Less than five minutes had passed. The ordinary sounds of the neighbourhood continued around Patrick: children shouting in the park, the drone of an airplane passing over the house, his mother humming to herself in the kitchen. He sat with his head in his hands, gripping his own face so hard that the next morning he would discover bruises.

He had, of course, heard of the beheadings. He had even seen the pleading statements of the captives broadcast throughout the world. But this was a different kind of knowledge, watching one man transform another man from a living thing to a dead thing with the camera not once cutting away. Three days later, he slipped out of his mother's house at two AM with a duffel bag and thumbed his way to the Greyhound station. By the time the sun came up, he was eating pancakes at a truck stop flying a Canadian flag.

There were many convenient rationalizations for the decision. The government was corrupt. The troops had been lied to. The war was unjust. But the truth was, he was deserting out of fear, and that stung. At the same time, he felt complicit in Nightingale's murder, as if by watching it, he had somehow consented to it. As he rode the Greyhound from town to town, he wrote Nightingale's widow a long letter explaining who he was and how he had come to his current situation. But when he finally worked up the nerve to mail it, he'd proved himself a coward all over again. The security cameras in the post office made him uneasy. An exchange with a nosy clerk led to a near-scuffle in line with another customer, and he left the building in a hurry, leaving his unstamped letter behind. Now he assumed that it would sit in a bin of lost mail until someone destroyed it, and he doubted that he would have the heart to sit down and write it again.

He'd revealed none of this to the companionable Brit and German who had befriended him on his return to the hostel, but the information was much closer to the surface than it should have been as they touched their bottles together and tipped them back. Looking into their lively, shining faces, he was on the verge of telling them everything, certain that he would find them a sympathetic audience, when the conversation turned to the Middle East on its own. The Brit said that his brother was stationed in Basra on the U.K. side of the coalition. The German took an airily dismissive stance towards the war.

"I'm not sure I'm following you," the Brit said. "Are you saying that the world would be better off with Saddam still in power?"

"No. I think the world would be better off if it was not being ruled by a cowboy." The German's English was good, but certain pronunciations were beyond him ("think", for instance, became "sink"), and Patrick, who could not fully disassociate him from parodies of German intellectuals he'd seen on television, found himself fighting off inappropriate laughter.

"So, you're *for* dictatorships," the Brit said.

"There is lots of dictatorships in the world. What is so special about this one?"

As the debate continued, it seemed to Patrick that his companions were well-trained parrots, squawking at one other. He knew that he should change the subject, or at least refrain from saying anything, but could not help interjecting with an abrupt non-sequitur. "How would you feel if he deserted?"

"What's that?" the Brit said.

"Your brother. How would you feel if he deserted?"

"What kind of question is that? He wouldn't."

"But if he did."

"He fucking wouldn't."

"Yeah, but — "

"Well, then he'd be a coward and traitor, wouldn't he?" He was directing all this to the German, who shrugged and looked away. The Brit set his bottle down on the table and looked at Patrick. "Why do you ask, mate?"

"I don't know. Forget it."

For a moment, Patrick was less certain that either of these men were who they claimed to be. Then the German began to antagonize the Brit again, and the argument took on a nationalistic edge. They exchanged sarcastic references to the Nazis and the Royal Family, disparaged one another's celebrities, soccer teams, and brands of beer. Patrick decided that it was time to leave. He stood up and headed for the door.

"Hey!" The Brit said. "Where are you going?"

Unsteady on his feet, more drunk than he'd realized, Patrick weaved through the lounge and pushed out into the street. A single set of tracks had been left in the snow, and he followed them away from the hostel. His companions came out behind him, apparently forgetting their altercation. "What are you doing?" the Brit shouted. "What the fuck's he doing?"

Patrick began to walk faster, then to trot, then to full out sprint, until his legs gave out and he vomited a mess of barbecue sauce and half-digested bird parts into the snow. Office towers swayed around him. The sound of a large machine scraping asphalt came from somewhere nearby. He experienced an eerie sense of déjà vu, before realizing that he was not recalling an actual event, but the first-person shooter games that he'd been raised on — a terrible noise off-screen foreshadowing the arrival of an as-yet-unseen enemy of unfathomable dimensions. He started walking again and caught sight of a lit Denny's sign up ahead, slowly revolving on a whitewashed pole. He followed the sign as he would have followed the porch light of his own home.

The restaurant had the identical layout of every other Denny's he had ever dined in, with more patrons than he would have expected at that time of night sitting alone or in groups, fried food heaped on plates before them. The hostess led Patrick to a booth opposite a long, Formica counter. Through a gap in the wall, he could see the cooks at work.

His waitress was the waitress of a thousand movies, in a pink, starched dress with a pin informing him that her name was Amanda. She could not have been older than twenty, but acted as if she'd been working the night shift for decades. He accepted a cup of coffee from her, and this action, the filling of his cup, was so simple, and yet, so *necessary* that he found himself blinking back tears of gratitude. "Thank you," he said, and repeated himself. "Thank you."

She fixed him with a weary look. "Are you ready to order?"

"I . . ." He hid behind his menu. "I need a few more minutes."

She sighed and moved on to the next table.

Patrick felt as if a drill sergeant had just screamed him down and left him withered and quaking. His goodwill transformed into sheer loathing. He watched her cross the restaurant, cruelly lingering on what he now perceived as flaws. She was flat-chested and wide-hipped, with too much makeup and bovine eyes. When she laughed at something a table of beefy farm boys said, it looked like she was missing teeth. Across the aisle and down several booths, a man around Patrick's age — darker complexioned, possibly Middle Eastern — was sitting alone with a box wrapped in brown paper on his table. Patrick warmed his hands on his cup and watched him. The man kept checking his watch and looking over at the door. Finally, he seemed to come to a decision. He stripped the paper from the box, opened the top flaps with a bread knife, and peered inside. His body stiffened, and he looked around, clearly terrified. He stood up and took several steps towards Patrick (who, certain he had been recognized, gave him a pleading look), then stopped, went back to collect his box, and walked quickly from the restaurant. Patrick's heart was racing. A strange energy lingered behind the man, as if something significant had just occurred that only he and Patrick had been aware of. This city, this whole country, was slightly off kilter, menace lurking behind a veneer of politeness. The customers around him were small-eyed and mean, throwing brutal looks around the room as they hunched over their plates. Towards the back of the restaurant, a man with a long, bony face was peering down at an open newspaper. He looked exactly like William Nightingale.

"Decided?"

Patrick jumped and looked up at the waitress who had returned to take his order. Genuine concern passed over her face.

"Hey, are you all right?"

"I'm fine. I'm sorry . . . " He withdrew a twenty-dollar bill from his wallet and placed it on the table. "I have to leave."

"All right. I'll make you some change."

"That's okay, keep it."

"That's a twenty."

He blinked at her, not connecting the words to the money on the table. *That's a twenty.* Was it some kind of a code?

"Hey." She touched his shoulder. It took all he had not to grab her hand. "Are you sure you're all right?"

"Yeah." Emotion frogged his voice, and he shook his head. "I'm sorry. I have to get out of here. I need to get home."

Western kingbird
(*Tyrannus verticalis*)

The sky, newly clear, a map of burning points. Strings of gravity holding the body on course. A new light alters the pattern, not fixed but swelling: a gathering point of longing, tyrannical and hypnotic. The television tower is invisible. The wires spanning down to the ground are invisible. There is only the light — a warning; the opposite of a warning.

Eileen

She had read somewhere that the state of a marriage could be assessed by how often the television was on. Theirs was never off. They had five sets in the house: one in the den, one in the basement, one in Cameron's old room, one in the kitchen, and one in the cabinet at the foot of the bed (which she and her husband were currently staring at, hands folded on top of the bedspread, the sheet tight around their legs). From outside, their window would be blink-blink-blinking, just like thousands of other windows in the city. Eileen wondered if it linked them in some way, made them less alone. She wanted the television to seduce her, guide her mind elsewhere, but her eyes kept sliding over to Cameron's convocation portrait on the wall.

"Do you think he's okay?" she said.

"Hmm?"

"Cameron. Do you think he's all right?"

George patted her leg without taking his eyes off the screen. "Try not to think about it."

How could she possibly not think about it? She had been waiting for that phone call for almost a year. Then to hear the remoteness in his voice. His strange jargon. His cryptic promises. Something about bodies, something about a resurrection. When he hung up, her first impulse had been to call the police, her second, to climb in the car and go looking for him. George had talked her down, insisting there was nothing to do but wait. It chilled her to think what could have happened in the hours since she last heard Cameron's voice, what could be happening at that very moment.

Any chance that her husband was merely pointing his eyes at the screen, thinking terrible thoughts like hers, evaporated when he chuckled at something one of the characters said.

"What do you think he meant by online?" she said

George sighed and shook his head. "Nothing. It meant nothing at all."

"It must have meant something."

He stared at the television, blue light reflected on his moist corneas. Eileen found him repellent. Cameron's rambling telephone call had stirred up memories that she had not so much repressed as deliberately set aside. He'd repeatedly said he forgave her. Why her? What had she ever done to forgive?

"Can you please turn to the news?" she said.

George was silent for a moment, an ancient computer processing information.

"Why?" he finally said.

"To see if something's happened."

"To who?"

"To *Cameron*."

"Nothing's happened to Cameron."

"How do you know?"

A character on the screen tripped and fell over. The studio audience laughed. George laughed. The sheet kept Eileen pinned to the bed. All the dead things around her pulsed with light. She was relieved to hear Marionette's bell jingling as the cat came down the hall and sat on the threshold of the room. She held out her hand. "Come here, sweetheart. Come here, girl."

The cat ignored her, preoccupied with cleaning itself.

"Marionette." Eileen snapped her fingers and made kissing noises. "Come."

"Hey, kitty," George said. The cat perked up and began to jog towards him. Eileen said her name more firmly and she hesitated. Two of the characters on television were trading one-liners. A smattering of laughter followed each quip. At the ultimate quip, the audience cheered and applauded.

"Ma-ry," George said. "Mary-Mary-Mary . . ." The cat tensed to jump up on his side of the bed.

"No!" Eileen sent a throw pillow spinning at the cat, who yowled and dashed from the room.

"What the hell are you doing?" George said.

She looked at her husband. "Hit me."

"What?"

"Hit me!"

"Jesus, Eileen! Have you gone insane?"

Her eyes clouded over with tears. "I want you to hit me."

"No! For god's sake, Eileen! Why would I hit you?"

Had he moved to embrace her, to touch her even, she would have struck him, but he simply looked at her. She wiped her eyes savagely. On the television, two characters were chasing each other around a sofa. Chandler and Joey. Why did she know that? Why did she know their names?

"Eileen? I need you to get a grip, all right?"

"Something terrible is happening."

"He's just being stupid. He'll be back."

"No, he won't," she said, quietly.

They lay there for some time, not touching, staring at the screen.

"What I don't understand," she finally said, "what I never understood, was why you never beat *me*."

The word she'd never dared to speak before lay between them like a dead bird. For an instant, George almost looked relieved. But then another look came into his face, a look of grim determination that she had not seen in some time. He picked up the remote and began flicking through channels. She watched him for a full minute, waiting for him to give her a reason not to hate him. Then she moved to the edge of the mattress, as far from her husband as she could get without leaving the bed, and closed her eyes.

Burrowing owl
(Speotyto cunicularia)

A peripheral blur; a rustle of motion. Silently, it drops from its perch and grazes the earth, the instant of capture leaving a dent in the new snow. The arc of its descent carries it back up over the highway. Then it's subterranean, thrashing down a throat of feathers and leaves to its nest, before heaving itself up once more at the stars.

Martin

He met his own eyes in the rear-view mirror and shook his head. Night visions. Brought on by too much stress and too little sleep. As if he didn't have enough problems, now he was *hallucinating*.

Was he?

Yes, he was. And he had no one to blame but himself. Somewhere along the line, he had become the unofficial troubleshooting tech for the entire agency, allowing people like Doug Foster to blithely take advantage of his inability to say no. Late that afternoon, he'd been finishing his own work for the day when a typical email from Doug appeared in his inbox:

URGENT: What's wrong with this picture?

He warily double-clicked on the subject line and Doug's message swelled into the screen.

Hey Kimosabe,

Big fuckup with the photo people. Check out the sightline.
Has to be moved down five degrees. Urgent we get this by
tomorrow AM.

D.

The attached photo was for the *Woebegone!* line, and like most
ad photos, it had nothing to do with the product being sold, in
this case an herbal antidepressant. In the foreground, an older
gentleman in cream pants was standing on a golf course, club over
his shoulder in a classic follow-through, his expression confident
and serene. In the background, a young redhead in a golf cart was
looking at something outside the frame, her mouth open in a wide
smile. Martin worked the mouse and strung out a temporary line
of vision. Doug was right. Five-and-a-half-degrees would bring her
gaze down from the gentleman's chest to the gentleman's crotch.
Hunkered down at his desk, he lost himself in the reconstruction.

The winter landscape that met him as he rolled out of the
parking garage, several hours late, came like a three-month leap
in time. He took the change personally, as a pointed act of cosmic
mockery, designed to draw his attention to how completely his job
dominated his life. Other than the few city workers out ploughing
the streets and a suspicious-looking man trudging down the
sidewalk with a green duffel bag, the whole city had been home in
bed, as it should have been. As he should have been. At least the
roads had been cleared. The off-ramp to the highway had been
treacherous with black ice, but he'd had no problems since leaving
the city.

No problems.

That's right.

Did hallucinating not qualify as a problem?

He shook his head and turned his attention to the radio,
comforted by the bright, logical console: heat, defrost, cigarette

lighter, am/fm band. "Don't let that white stuff get you down, folks," the DJ on Kit 103 advised him. "Tomorrow they're calling for sun, sun, sun with a high of twenty-one!"

The clock on the dashboard said 3:00 AM. He, of course, had agreed to work on Saturday, so in four hours time he would find himself driving right back into the city — caffeine in his veins, the sun low and poisonous on the horizon. He wondered where all the other traffic was, all the big trucks that should have been booming through the night with their mysterious cargos. He hadn't seen one other vehicle since leaving the city, just that endless stutter of yellow dashes rushing towards him, and a cover of luminescent snow on either side of the road.

And something *in* that snow.

Shut up.

He spun the knob and tuned to the college station. Whistles, clicks, and the occasional ominous groan came through his speakers. He tapped the steering wheel and tried to find the rhythm, believing an appreciation of contemporary music might be useful if he ever worked up the nerve to go to one of the singles bars his sister had advised him to visit.

Something in the ditch, maybe twenty feet from the road.

It could have been a million things. A log. A rock.

"A mannequin," he said out loud, and chuckled. "A mannequin that fell off the mannequin truck."

A person.

No.

Why not?

Because it didn't make sense. He could think of no plausible reason for someone to be out on foot, twenty kilometres from the city, at three in the morning. There had been no broken-down vehicle that he could recall, no flashing hazards on the side of the road.

This was all Doug's fault. With his chummy smile and novelty ties, Doug Foster was the closest thing Martin had to a nemesis. All the men at Contrail loved him. At least two of the women had slept with him. He left early every day, and seemed to do literally nothing of value around the office: organizing betting pools, flirting with the secretaries, holding forth on the genius of a twenty-year Nike campaign. *Just do it. How brilliant is that? They've got millions of kids running around with "just hump" on their T-shirts.*

Someone in the ditch, down on all fours.

A deer?

No.

He turned back to the radio, scanning deeper into the static.

"Next up on the late-night free for all with Johnny Zee, we have . . . is this right? Nutweb?"

"Netweb."

"Uh-huh. What can I do you for, Nutweb?"

"This is a glorious day. The users have commenced their simultaneous upload."

"Oh, boy. Dennis, have you stopped screening my calls entirely?"

"My own passage will be broadcast via live web cam at — "

"All right, all right. Just calm down there, Nutweb."

Martin snapped off the radio. Weirdos. The heater fan rattled away. He thumped the dashboard and the rattle became a tortured whine.

A man.

Yes.

A man on his hands and knees, crawling in the ditch.

It might not have made sense but that was exactly what he had seen, less than five minutes ago.

And what was he supposed to do about it?

Go back.

He watched himself whip the car around, speed back to the scene and make his way, purposefully, down the embankment to what was indeed a body. He would help the man — carry him — back to the car and race to the General Hospital where they would treat him for exposure. Before they could get his name, he would go home, turn off the alarm, take the phone off the hook and sleep for ten blessed hours. The next afternoon, as he was sipping his coffee in front of the television, a news anchor would relate the deeds of an unidentified "mystery hero" on Highway 22 the night before, and he would smile to himself — satisfied, but not self-satisfied — and leave the phone off the hook all day, letting them muddle along at work without him. In his absence they would recognize both his worth and Doug Foster's ineptitude, and agree to his reasonable request for less hours and a modest pay hike. On his days off, he would go to the singles bar, where he would impress a hip, intelligent woman by dropping the band names he had gleaned from the college station. *The Blue Fuses. The Generous Beavers.* He would note that such bands seemed to find their names by flipping through the dictionary and pairing adjectives and nouns at random. She would find this both insightful and hilarious, touching his leg and promising with her eyes to do things to him that had, until then, seemed hopelessly unattainable. Everything could change overnight. All he had to do was stop the car.

His foot maintained its steady pressure on the gas pedal.

This was not his responsibility.

Whose responsibility was it, then?

Someone other than him. Ten cars must have passed by that exact spot by now.

What cars?

"Shut up," he said, and winced.

Yes, this was all Doug Foster's fault. Or was it the photographer's fault? How could they have overlooked something so obvious? A cursory look through the viewfinder should have alerted them to the error.

A large man without shoes, looking into the headlights and mouthing the word "help".

Now he was inventing. There hadn't been enough time to take in all that.

But subconsciously? He knew better than most how much the mind absorbed on its own. It was his job to slip things in there without people knowing it: digitally altering the wave pattern in a glass of whiskey to suggest labial folds, streamlining an ice cream cone in a woman's hand to make it more phallic.

He strained back, willing the man's face to come.

There was no point agonizing over the details. He was not getting out of the car. He was not letting a stranger into the car. This was not him. This was not Martin Cullen. Martin Cullen worked in a bright, climate-controlled office without windows. Martin Cullen leased a space in an underground parking garage with prominent security cameras and commuted to an outlying suburb where no one slept in your bushes and every suspicious vehicle in the neighbourhood was reported to the police. Martin Cullen did *not* go nosing into other people's business. Martin Cullen did *not* go throwing himself into unpredictable situations in unpopulated areas, in the middle of an extremely creepy night.

Then stay in the car. Just go back and have a look. He might feel like a fool and a coward, but at least he would be doing something.

And then? What if someone was actually out there?

The way he saw it, there were four possible scenarios.

One: The man was harmless and in need of no help (which was unlikely).

Two: The man was harmless and in dire need of help (Martin preferred not to think about this scenario).

Three: The man was dead (which would be tragic and sad, but there would be nothing Martin could do for him at that point anyway).

Four: The man was *playing* dead to lure him into stopping.

The more he thought about it, the more probable this last scenario became. The moment he stopped, the man would pull out a gun and order him out of the car, forcing him to hand over his wallet and his keys, or worse.

"No, thank you, bud," he said.

All right. Then don't go back. But at least call someone.

His eyes went to the glove box where he kept his cellular phone. Why hadn't he thought of using it until now?

Because it was stupid. Who was he going to call? 911? *Hi, I think I just drove past a body on the side of the highway. You might want to send someone to check that out. Did I stop? Well, not exactly . . .*

The call would not be anonymous. They would trace the number and his sister would just happen to be driving the ambulance they sent out to the scene. Word of his cowardice would spread. His coworkers would find out. His parents would find out. And it would all be for nothing, because there was nothing back there.

The beacon of a weigh station appeared up ahead and he drew strength and conviction from it. One could not underestimate the power of suggestion. A shadow suggests a human figure on hands and knees. The mind fills in the details.

The world brightened around him: streetlights planted at regular intervals, his exit fast approaching. His house was situated in the basin of a coulee and, as the elevation began to drop, wisps of fog passed over the road.

A shadow, a rock, a tree. He would be a fool to worry about it.

His exit came up and he took it, mist sweeping over the car as he rode down into the canyon.

SWAINSON'S HAWK
(*Buteo swainsoni*)

Perched on a fencepost by the highway, motionless, watchful in the dawn. Almost totemic, as if hewn from the wood. The long eye owns the horizon, scanning for small animals drawn from their burrows by the thaw — the twitch and the mad scurry, the things that will give them away.

JULIET

HER RAGE HAD MAINTAINED A CONSTANT pitch for the whole of the three-hour bus trip, left at a low boil to thicken and set into a toxic yearning for vengeance. This was the most impulsive thing she had ever done. An hour after losing her husband on the phone and failing to reconnect with him or anyone else at the hotel, she had contacted the police in the area. The constable on duty chuckled. He sounded as if he was eating something.

"Yeah, he's here. It's a weird one. The girl turned him in. Which, under the circumstances, was basically like turning herself in. Said he stole her bracelet or something."

"Girl?" she said.

Outwardly calm and mechanical, she'd hung up, roused her son, packed a suitcase, collected the dog, and called a taxi. She hated mass transit, but felt an imperative to be in the same city as her husband, in the same room, to confront him with the consequences of what he had done. She tried not to think about how frightened Cinnamon must have been just then — stowed under the bus with the luggage — keeping her mind focused on her husband. Her soon-to-be ex-husband. That she hadn't taken Frank's name when they married seemed a kind of foresight now. There was no question that she was leaving him, and nothing he could say or do would change her mind. She harboured no ill feelings towards the girl. As a volunteer at the shelter, she knew what drove girls like her to allow men to use their bodies — bodies they had come to regard with horrifying detachment. To think that her husband was one of those men. How many others? That would be her first question. How long has it been going on? She wanted to hit him. To hit his face. She wanted Michael to be there to see him in his disgrace. Frank, the travelling salesman, peddling his sugar pills. Frank the professional liar.

Her son was curled up on the seat beside her with his feet in the aisle, his eyebrows knit, his mouth puckered, as if sleeping was an act that required great concentration. He was growing much faster than she would have liked, more independent and more wilful by the day. In the past, Frank had resisted the idea of home-schooling, but his opinion had depreciated significantly in the last few hours. As the wronged wife she would have the advantage in any custodial battle, and she intended to be ruthless.

The realities trailing behind this thought made her waver. In many ways, Frank was the adult in their marriage. He did the taxes, paid the bills, attended to the yard work and much of the housework when he was home. When the plumbing went, he fixed it. When the roof leaked, he reshingled it. In the future, she could employ people to do these things for her, or learn to do them herself, but why should she have to? Why should she suffer for Frank's mistake? And then there was the father-son bond to consider. Michael loved Frank. So much so, that she worried that he favoured him. In the event of a divorce, Michael would not understand what was happening, and Frank — the bastard — would not hesitate to cast himself in the role of victim. She could hear him now. *I don't know why Mommy made me leave the house. I'd like to see you all the time, but your mommy won't let me.* Her anger was mounting again but, in her present, calculating frame of mind, it drove her towards a different conclusion. What would be the worse punishment? To subject Frank to a brief confrontation and set him free, or to make him stay and atone for his actions?

As the bus broke the city limits, other passengers began to stir around them. All the familiar signs of modern civilization were appearing outside the windows, the big box franchises Juliet referred to collectively as Mc-Wal-Bucks. She found them oddly comforting now — the way one city was increasingly like every other city, and so, in a sense, home. She shook her son gently. "Michael."

He stirred, looked at her blankly, and closed his eyes.

"Michael, you've got to get up now, honey. We're almost there."

With some effort she managed to sit him up. He rubbed his eyes, a dour expression set on his face.

"I want to go home," he said.

"We can't go home just yet."

"Why not?"

"Because we're on a trip, silly."

"Is Daddy going to be there?"

She smiled at him and fussed with his hair. The night before, the only way she could get him moving without a scene was to tell him that they were going to surprise his father. He was obviously under the impression that it was going to be a pleasant surprise. Now, in daylight and among strangers, she was uncertain what it was going to be.

The bus pulled into the depot and she began helping Michael with his shoes and jacket.

"I can do it," he said.

"I know, sweetie, I'm just helping."

"I can *do* it." He shook her off and began slowly buttoning his jacket. He was his father's son, all right. But that could change if she approached the situation correctly. A confrontation was just what Frank would expect. Instead, she would be entirely calm and reasonable, explain what this meant, what was going to change between them. Michael got up and trudged down the aisle, the buttons of his jacket misaligned, one shoelace flapping. Outside, the air was warmer than she had expected, the sky pale and painfully bright. She wondered if she looked as worn out as the other passengers wandering around with their mouths stretched in unattractive yawns.

The driver helped her collect her luggage from under the bus, and she crouched before Cinnamon's carrier. "It's okay, we're here now, Cinnabun."

She poked her fingers through the grate and the dog retreated to the back of the carrier, trembling. She had forgotten to bring his leash. She did not trust him for a second off-leash. The instant she opened the grate, he would slip through her hands and bolt: a small, tan blur in the field behind the bus station. A hawk would mistake him for a rabbit and snap him up, his heart-shaped nametag jingling as he was carried away. Juliet suddenly felt very close to tears. She was in a strange city with no leash for the dog, a full, aching bladder, and there was snow on the ground. Snow, for god's sake. Aware of a significant absence, she looked around for her son and spotted him on a bench talking to a young man with short hair and a large, green duffel bag. She shuffled over as quickly as she could, suitcase in one hand, dog carrier in the other. "Michael! Quit bothering that man."

"It's okay," the man said. "I don't mind."

"Michael. Come over here."

He stayed where he was, swinging his feet and pouting. "I want to go home."

"Michael — "

"I want to go home!" Cinnamon began whining in his carrier. Juliet's bladder throbbed in sympathy. Standing up and walking around had exacerbated her need to use the toilet, which was growing urgent.

"Everything all right?" the young man asked.

"Yes. No. I . . . " His sleeves were rolled up, revealing a tattoo of an eagle on his forearm, but he appeared normal enough. "I'm sorry, can you do me a huge favour? Can you watch my son for a minute? I have to use the washroom."

He shrugged. "Sure."

"Thank you." She set her bag beside the carrier. "Michael? Stay here. Right here on this bench. I'll be back in a minute." He wagged his head from side to side and ignored her.

The terminal washroom was vacant. For the few minutes she was on the toilet, her mind cleared. Food would be next. Then shelter. Once they found a motel, she would have a nap and decide what to do next. She washed her hands and face and fixed her hair in the mirror. Feeling moderately more in control, she stopped at a small café that was just opening and bought two sandwiches, a coffee, and an orange juice for Michael. She carried the food out of the terminal and looked around.

The bench was empty. The bus they had come in on was gone.

"Michael?" She turned in circles, scanning the parking lot. The moment she had dreaded for so long had come. She was forever losing important items — keys, credit cards, identification. This was just the next logical step. She would have to report the disappearance at the police station that was holding Frank. His transgression was laughable compared to this. She saw them at the press conference — a broken unit at a bank of microphones, airing their incompetence to the world. "Michael!"

Then she noticed something confusing. The man had left his bag beside the bench (along with her own bag, and Cinnamon's carrier, now empty). Clinging to her coffee and her paper bag, she rounded the building and saw the man a way off in a field. He had Cinnamon on a leash, and Michael was beside him, kicking through the snow.

She charged over. "What do you think you're doing?"

Seeing her approach, Cinnamon set his legs and began to bark, as if at an intruder. The man looked sheepish. "I thought your dog might need to go to the bathroom. I had some rope."

Cinnamon was not properly leashed, after all, but tethered to his hand with a length of twine. Unsure who to be angry with, Juliet called Michael over, and turned back to the young man. "I'm sorry. It's been a long night."

"No," the man said. "My fault. It was stupid."

They made eye contact and an unexpected charge ran through her, their attempts to reassure one another creating a sudden intimacy. "Would you mind bringing the dog back?" she said.

"Sure."

Michael joined them, oblivious to the drama sparked by his absence and, as they walked back to the terminal, Juliet realized that she was not thinking about Frank at all. She put Cinnamon back in his carrier and tried to return the man's rope, but he insisted that she keep it. Cheerier now that he had fully woken, Michael sat down on the bench and began to unwrap his sandwich. Juliet and the man stood at a distance from one another in the parking lot, staring off at the horizon.

"Snow," she said.

He nodded. "Yeah."

"It's melting already."

"Uh-huh."

"Where do you suppose the birds go? When it snows."

He shrugged. "South, I guess."

"But the ones that don't make it." She turned to face him, arms crossed. "The ones that can't get out in time."

Another bus rounded the corner and pulled into the parking lot and the man appeared relieved.

"Is that you?" she said.

"Yeah, that's me." He hoisted his bag. "Listen, I'm sorry I scared you."

"No. I'm . . ."

He gave a small nod, then shouldered his duffel bag and strode off to catch his bus. Juliet went over to her son on the bench. She touched the back of his head and he smiled up at her. "Are we having an adventure?"

Red-winged blackbird
(Agelaius phoeniceus)

Flaring out its wings, it marks its territory in bold swoops and passes over the wakening neighbourhood. The symbols are universal, circumventing language to directly address the primordial eye. Twin crimson patches like epaulettes. The colour of blood, strength, and dominion.

Dalton

It was a small round marble from his daddy that was smooth in his mouth and under his tongue and in his cheek but that his mommy had taken away — you will choke on this — and when a thing went away it always went somewhere new so he looked and he looked and he looked under his bed in his closet in his drawers but he did not find it anywhere and on the table the clock said 822 so he took off his peejays and his undies and he remembered to put on new undies and socks and his red pants and his blue Batman shirt that was a present from his daddy and the sun in the window was warm and yellow and it filled his head with a peaceful humming so he rocked himself on his bed until the clock said 844 and then he went out to find that his mommy was not watching TV or browning his bread or making his scramble in the kitchen and he opened her door and he saw her feet and her scraggle-hair on the bed and he cheeped at her but she was dead and the rememberings that came into his head made him feel dizzy and sick so he pushed them away and he flapped over to the front door to look inside the pockets of coats and in the shoes on the floor but a new pair of shoes made him stop — his Auntie Dawn's shoes — and when he turned around he almost peed to see her there on the sofa with her eyes closed and her mouth pulling air into her big smooth face and he cheeped at her but she did not say hello birdie because she was dead and could not laugh or smile or tickle him and now the rememberings came back and he could not stop them — his mommy screaming the phone ringing the clock saying 432 his Auntie Dawn and his mommy talking and crying saying Tommy Tommy Tommy his wings over his ears his mommy in his room saying it's all right you don't have to be scared and hugging him through his blankets his hiding self trying to sing her away the phone ringing his Auntie Dawn saying identify the body bail for Gene his mommy saying it's okay you don't have to come out if you don't want to I love you honey and then going away — which made him want to pee so he went past his Auntie Dawn's dead self and into the bathroom where he sat down to pee and remembered to flush and he flushed three times and his mommy did not tell him to stop so he flushed three more times and then fluttered back out into the kitchen where the fridge made the buzzing noise that scared him and he made himself brave by buzzing back and then looked in the drawers and opened the cupboards and felt inside the boxes where he sometimes found prizes but they only had cereal so he perched on a chair by the table to wait for his mommy to brown his toast and make his scramble and he remembered the empty bottle on the table from his Daddy's house — the one that made him walk funny and his eyes leak — and beside it sat two glasses and he sniffed at one glass but did not taste it because his mommy was snoring so loud in her room and the sun came through the windows and lived in all the pots and pans all the taps and handles and when the marble started calling again it was coming from outside so he remembered to put on his shoes at the back door and he went out into the yard where the snow was sticky and new and the birds were talking in the trees and the cold air moved through his head and into his chest and lifted him across the yard to the fence where the snow melted over his fingers and on his tongue and when the old man next door banged out of his house coughing and moaning he crouched by the fence and watched him smoke a whole cigarette on his porch and scratch himself and go back inside and he looked back at the tracks that followed him through the snow to where he was standing and a dog started barking close by who sounded like his friend Mange so he hopped around the house to have a look making new tracks follow him in the snow but when he got to the front his friend Mange had stopped barking and a black bird dropped from a tree and the sun flashed off its wings so he hopped from the house to the gate and went through to the empty street where the snow was melting and running to the end of the block and the cold water moved around his fingers and a candy wrapper came floating along and bumped into his hand and sailed away so he followed the wrapper to a metal grate where the water rushed around it and pulled it down into its belly and then the marble started calling again so he flapped his arms and he went off to find it.

Sandhill crane
(Grus canadensis)

Flight is nearly effortless, a gift of buoyancy delivered by the rising morning thermals. The long neck, the impossibly broad wings, the intricate system of feathers moulding to the wind. That something so large could remain aloft with so little effort astounds the sky.

∽∽∽∽

Farley

HE HAD BEEN COASTING ON THE fringe of oblivion all night, only to resurface in a panic, with his eyes anchored to his lover. The angle of her limbs, the drapery of the sheet, the quality of the light; all these things altered the composition of what he saw, but most of all the light. Farley was grateful for the fraction of the world it revealed to him, and mindful of the fact that his view was limited, that he was only seeing the illuminated surface. When photographing anything — a plum, a sparrow, his lover — he felt that he was attempting the work of philosophy: probing the surface to reveal the obscure essence of a thing. Light was his main tool in that process, manipulated in the studio with flashes, screens, and filters, or adapted to in the field through the setting of the lens, but this surreptitious study of Chris was more of a passive enterprise. He was simply watching her — turned away from him on the bed, her long back holding the morning light. For a moment, her failure to sense his restlessness, to wake up and relieve him of it, seemed deliberate, almost callous. He considered getting up and starting his workday, but doubted that he would have the clarity to achieve anything worthwhile. Even the most basic shot required a great deal of care and attention.

Chris, whether she realized it or not, was engaged in a similarly creative act, altering her body to more accurately reflect her mind. He had tried to remain objective in the ongoing series of portraits that they had undertaken, but his feelings — tenderness, desire, revulsion — crept in at the borders of each frame. When she was away, he would line the negatives on the light box in chronological order and note the gradual effects of the treatment — the chest swelling, the diminished penis, the layering of fatty tissue around hip and thigh. If there was a unifying element in the photos, it resided in the eyes. Only when they were open did he have a hope of capturing her. She rolled over onto her back, revealing a strong, almost classical profile. It hurt him to know that she would never fully achieve the transition she was attempting, that her physical gender would always be detectable.

He closed his eyes and tried to weary his brain with mathematics — simple counting and, when that failed, exponential calculations — but his thoughts kept drifting back into their familiar restless grooves. Money was prominent in his concerns. He'd resorted to commercial work lately, and had lost a contract with an ad firm after deliberately misshooting a ridiculous piece of subliminal advertising. It had been foolish of him to stand on principle over something so trivial, but he was far from financial ruin. More troubling were the events of the previous evening. He had never suspected that Chris was capable of such violence. When she called from the police station, he had responded like a parent:

first concerned, then, after he'd learned that she was all right, sternly disapproving. The boys on the bus hadn't touched her. With a double charge of assault, she could conceivably (though he knew it was unlikely) be facing a prison term. He'd held her hand on the way out of the station, but could not help lecturing her on the drive home. The fact that she felt bullied and threatened did not excuse the attack. What if nations operated that way? Did she think that the kinds of preemptive wars being waged by the United States were the best course of action?

"Don't be an ass," she'd said. Farley regarded her with surprise, unaccustomed to her abrupt, almost derisive tone. She touched his hand and apologized. "I didn't mean that. It's just a strange analogy. Listen, can we stop by my apartment?"

"You're not coming over?"

"I'll come over. I just want to check on Jangles first."

Annoyed by what he considered an unnecessary detour, he'd chauffeured her home and parked in a tow zone outside her building.

"I'll run up," he said.

"Why?"

"Because I want to."

"I'm perfectly capable."

"I realize that."

She looked over at the building. "The elevator's broken."

"The exercise will do me good."

Before she could protest any further, he was out and high-stepping through the snow to the front stoop. In the lobby he tried the elevator, waited a minute, tried it again, then climbed the stairs to her floor, where he let himself into her apartment. The birdcage was empty, its door ajar. He caught a chill and closed the kitchen window before making a cursory sweep of the apartment and going back down to the car.

"He's fine," he told Chris, and buckled himself in.

She stared straight ahead, through the windshield. "I saw you."

"What?"

"Through the door. I saw you try the elevator."

"Chris — "

"I told you it wasn't working."

"Yes, well — "

"Why did you try the elevator when I told you it wasn't working?"

"Chris." He looked at her closely. "I don't know what this is about, but you're really not yourself right now."

That night their lovemaking had been urgent and physical. Afterwards, she had quickly fallen asleep, abandoning him to his thoughts.

Farley opened his eyes, unable to find a comfortable position to lie in. The light in the room had intensified from a soft yellow to a deep gold. Chris had turned towards him, still asleep, her mouth slightly open, her skin fairly glowing. When he turned sixty, she would still be in her thirties. How much use would he be to her then? His concerns about the incident on the bus, he suddenly realized, had nothing to do with morality and everything to do with autonomy. He was terrified that she no longer needed him. From the day they first slept together, it had not once occurred to him that she could leave. He wondered now at his arrogance. Of course she could leave. More than that, she *would* leave, had all but left already, and all he would have to remember her by were the hundreds of photographs he'd taken, none of them adequate. He saw them lining the wall of a gallery, the audience passing their judgment with folded arms. He saw Chris silhouetted in a doorway of light, a bag in one hand, a birdcage in the other. As he watched her sleeping face — barely a foot from his own — he felt like weeping for the loss of her.

But then, as if he had spoken her name, she stirred and opened her eyes. He smiled, embarrassed at being caught observing her at her most defenceless. Her response was immediate — a soft, genuine smile in return. Such a banal and miraculous thing.

"I couldn't sleep," he said.

She made a sympathetic sound of dismay, put her open hand on the pillow between them, and he took it.

Domestic chicken
(Gallus gallus)

Under the constant light of the shed, it sits with clipped wings and trimmed beak, too large for its bones. The doors open, and men with gloves wade in. One snatches it by the legs and forces it into a crate. The crate is loaded onto a truck and transported to a building that smells of blood and fear. The body is removed from the crate, hung by its feet, and moved along — shocked, slit, scalded, plucked, eviscerated, and finally taken by refrigerated van to the grocer. There, bundled in cellophane, it waits on a cold shelf, reborn.

Cadenza

"I can heal you," she said, and snapped her fingers. "Like that. I could heal you until you didn't have an ache or pain to worry you and you'd be left scratching your head, thinking, now where'd all that pain go? That's the power of the blue fire. And the blue fire's burning in these hands." Cadenza showed them her hands, let them feel the power. She had attracted a small crowd outside the Pennywise Supermarket: two tourists, a smirking young man with a beard, an obese woman with wide, shocked eyes, and a dull-looking boy in a Batman shirt with a blunt forehead and a gaping mouth. She stopped pacing and pointed to a man across the street who was trying to walk with crutches and talk on a cellular phone at the same time.

"See him? I could heal his leg in two seconds. Bam. Wouldn't take hardly any effort at all." As he struggled through the revolving doors of Sears, she turned back to her audience. "I know what you're thinking. You're thinking, here's a crazy old woman telling stories. Well, I could tell you stories. I could tell you twenty-two lifetimes worth of stories. I could tell you about the time I was called Appolonia and they burned me alive! I could tell you about the time I was called Joan of Arc and they burned me again! I could tell you about the men at Salem who trussed me up to a big pile of tinder and set the whole thing ablaze! Oh, I could tell you stories!" She began pacing again, letting the words come. "I could tell you the story of Mr. Jesus H. Christ. He's the one who let me burn. No, I can't say I have much cause to be sitting down with mister J.C. these days. Or his old man neither. I'm sorry if that shocks you, but it's how I feel."

No one in her audience appeared shocked. The tourists snapped a picture and wandered away.

"Now, I can tell that you're wondering how I came to all this knowledge about my twenty-two past lives. Well, I'll tell you. It came to me . . ." She passed her eyes over the crowd. "In a vision."

The bearded man snickered and rubbed his mouth.

"I tell you, it came to me in a vision!" She delivered him a weighty look of challenge. "I was standing in the shower when it hit me, like an unholy baptism filling me up with truth. All my twenty-two lives came rushing back, and at first I couldn't take it! I ran straight out into the street, naked and dripping wet and on fire! My hands flashed out! *Bang* went the blue flames! *Pow!* Shazam! It was so powerful it knocked folks off their feet! It was so powerful they locked me up and tried to shock it away!" She shook her head, remembering. "It took time. To gather everything up and make sense of it all. How long I've been walking the earth. It got me to thinking about what I was doing with this particular life.

Working as a housekeeper for not six-fifty an hour. Feeling sorry for myself. Killing myself with rum. Then one day I'm walking down the street, minding my own business, when I pass a garbage can and hear this sound." She hunched over and her eyes darted to one side. "This fluttery, thumping sound. And when I stop to have a look inside, what do I see but this fat, old crow! Well, it starts flopping harder now that it sees me, and I can tell that its poor wing is broke. Now, I can't say if it flew in there by itself or if someone just picked it up and threw it out like any old trash, but it's caught in there and it's surely going to die and everyone is just walking on by, and I'll tell you . . . "

The bearded man wandered away, saying, "Yeah, yeah, yeah." The obese woman followed after him. Now only the dull boy remained, gazing at Cadenza expectantly. She sensed his passivity and poured her words into him.

"I'll tell you I could *feel* that bird's pain. I wasn't just imagining it. I could feel the pain like it was my own. And you know what else? I knew that I could make that pain go away! So I reached right in and pulled that bird out. I let the blue fire do its business. Then I opened my hands . . . " She made as if throwing piles of confetti. "And that damn crow flew right away!"

The boy's eyes widened. A man with unkempt hair and wild eyes stopped beside him, rocking gently and looking at his feet. Cadenza included him into her audience with a broad sweep of the arm.

"You see that's what the blue fire can do. It's a healing fire. And I've been carrying it around for what seems like forever. The men keep burning me, and I keep burning them right back. It's a terrible curse, knowing there's no end to things. Like a story that just keeps on going. No 'the end'. No 'happily ever after'. Would you like a story like that?" The dull boy shook his head. The wild-eyed man was sidling closer and closer to Cadenza. "How about you?" she asked him.

The man froze, as if caught in the glare of a searchlight. His mouth quivered. "Mel Gibson," he said.

Cadenza laughed and slapped her thigh. "That's right. Nobody likes a story like that. Especially when you don't know who the hero is. Who the good guys are, who the bad guys are. You can't go around healing any old body, can you? There's rapists and murderers out there. There's politicians out there. Lots of people that deserve more trouble than they've got."

The wild-eyed man seemed excited. He was nodding and waiting for an opportunity to speak. "Brad Pitt," he said.

"Him too," Cadenza agreed. "You see, nobody gave me x-ray vision. Nobody gave me the power to see into people's minds. I can't tell if somebody's good or bad just by looking at them. Or by how messy their house is. And what good's a thing if you don't know when to use it? What good's a — "

"George Clooney," the wild-eyed man said.

" — a bucket and a mop if you're too blind to see a dirty floor? Why give that blind lady a bucket and a mop in the first place? It doesn't make sense. And that's how I knew that Mr. G-O-D had nothing to do with it."

"Tom Cruise!" the man said.

Cadenza raised her hands. "Amen! So I stayed inside and wrestled. Wrestled with what to do. Clean everybody's floors? Or just let them all get dirtier and dirtier? Use the blue fire?" She reached out to the dull boy, who took a step towards her. "Or keep it all inside." She drew her arm back and his face fell. "For months and months I wrestled with it. Because if it wasn't a gift from Mr. G-O-D, then maybe it came from someplace else. Maybe they were right to burn me all those times. Maybe the best thing to do was to burn myself."

The man shook his head, tears in his eyes. "Ben Affleck, Matt Damon, Leonardo DiCaprio."

"Oh, they were dark times. But then, last night, the storm came and brought with it a howling wind of change. All night long I listened to it banging away outside the window, with nothing but candles to see by, because the men had taken my juice away. No TV to bring me bad news. No rum to mess with my head. And just as I was falling to sleep, you know what happened? All the lights came back on. My boy had brought them to me."

"Johnny Depp," the man muttered. He seemed to be losing interest in Cadenza.

"My boy that's been gone ten years now was standing in the middle of the room, real as anything, and I was lying in bed shaking hard like with a fever. I asked him what he wanted, and he just looked at me and smiled. Then I asked *where* he was because I knew he was out there somewhere living in a new body, but he shook his head and said he didn't know. He said he was coming at me out of a dream. Then he said, 'Momma, you've got to listen to me now. The world is sick, and you've got to do what you can to make things better. You've got to start using the blue fire.' And I said, 'but how do I know if people deserve it?' And he said, 'you've got to make them promise to be good.' And I said, 'but how do I know if they're lying?' And then he said something to me that I'll never forget. He said, 'Momma, sometimes you've just got to trust people.'" Cadenza stared at the ground, in a kind of trance. When she returned to herself, the wild-eyed man was gone, but the boy was still looking at her.

"Carlos?" she said. "Is that you, Carlos?"

The boy didn't say anything.

"Carlos, baby?" Cadenza covered her mouth. "It is you! Do you remember me? Do you remember your mama?"

The boy nodded.

"Oh, baby! I'm sorry! I'm sorry I couldn't make things better. I couldn't heal you back then, because I didn't know about the blue fire. It didn't hurt too much, did it?"

The boy smiled and shook his head.

"That's good. I've missed you so much, baby. You don't know how much I've missed you. Miguel tries. He checks up on me, but it's not the same. What are your new folks like? They love you?"

The boy, still smiling, nodded.

"They make you happy?"

He nodded again.

"That's good, Carlos. Because I can't take you back, you understand? When we pass into our new lives we've got to leave the old ones behind. Those are the rules. But I'm here now and I can help you, baby." She extended one wavering arm to her boy. He understood and shuffled towards her, making a happy, moaning sound. Pedestrians passing by cast sidelong looks at them. She took him into her arms, feeling pockets of hurt all over his body — his stomach, his limbs, his head. Blue fire poured out of her, and she willed it out, giving it to him. Her and her boy, burning together in the sun.

Mourning dove
(Zenaida macroura)

The promise of light makes it strain to break free. Light the way plants know it, as a force to grope at blind. The egg tooth pips the shell, crazing the surface. Its efforts grow more urgent as the imperative takes hold. Fissures expand around the pink skull, and all the elements are gradually revealed to its blind eyes. The nest. The branch. The tree. The sky.

Louis

STRUCK FROM BEHIND BY A TREMENDOUS, concussive blow, he fell to the ground. Black wheels rolled past his face. The sun crashed off everything metal. He tried to get to his feet and failed. Tried to find his rifle and failed. Who hit him? What Kraut sonofabitch shot him? He rolled onto his back to find dozens of flaming white birds descending upon him. French civilians were standing around, gaping at where the bomb fell. Trash everywhere, on fire. Far above, a hexagonal sign, stamped against the sky. A name in red script.

Where the hell was he?

He had been having coffee with Benjamin. Not Benjamin from the war, but an older, slower version of Benjamin, a Benjamin with dark glasses and a metal walker that his daughter had folded and left by the door. They sat at their usual table and he made forays into Benjamin's fog — found him, lost him, found him again. When conversation had grown difficult, he'd read the paper aloud to his friend, all the sections, cover to cover, until his daughter came to take him home. Then he'd stepped out of the restaurant and something had happened. Something to do with the smoking dumpster where people were running around, pointing and yelling without sound. He got his elbows under him and lifted his head, but a surge of dizziness pinned him back down. Down on that stony beach with the world exploding around him. Someone kneeling at his side. A medic? He tried to sit up but a second wave laid him out on the cold cement. He closed his eyes and the cement became a table, scattered with grains of sugar. Benjamin sitting across from him, talking about the storm that hit the night before, grappling with the words.

Bad things always come that way. Like a lion, like an atomic wind.

Louis nodded. He understood. How close disaster was, waiting to take you off guard. A headless body in the mud at his feet. His wife on the kitchen floor, no longer breathing. All the rooms in the house where she used to be.

Benjamin looked at the thing in his hand.

What's this?

That's cream, Bennie.

Benjamin smiled, suddenly seeing him. *Louis.*

That's right.

Lucky Louis.

That's right, Bennie.

The cop bent over him, moving his lips. He looked at the cop's watch: both hands pointing to the twelve. Noon or midnight? Everything surged around him strangely. His body was unharmed but something enormous was happening inside. Spinning tires. Melted snow in the gutter. A city bus with its ladder of windows, a face in each rung. The twenty-eight. That was his bus. He was going to miss his bus.

Benjamin put a hand on the paper. *American boys.*

That's right.

Deserters.

That's right, Bennie.

Good for them.

Louis did not disagree with his friend, but the sentiment made him uneasy. Sometimes, you had to fight. Sometimes you had to grapple in the mud, murderous and terrified.

Was that true?

A spray of blood on the ice. His son on skates, punishing the face of another boy on skates. Louis rising to his feet with the rest of the crowd, rage in his throat.

He jerked awake, grabbed a scrawny soldier by the arm and told him to move on over that ridge or he'd shoot him himself. The ambulance walls swayed around him and he let the paramedic go. A waitress in a pink uniform walked past the stretcher with a pot of coffee. The paramedic held a mask over his mouth, breathing for him. He pushed it away and called for his son, heaving up to a sitting position. Strong hands forced him back down and held him there. Torturers approaching with their instruments. Then he was slamming out of the ambulance on a gurney, rolling past a blue-haired girl in a wheelchair. The girl was holding her huge belly and crying. He met her eye for an instant, then looked up at the sky — the sun and moon, both pale, both visible — and went under.

Voices bleeding through the darkness. Calling out coordinates. The radio operator dead. Flares splashing over the trees.

"He can see us?"

"What you're seeing are his autonomic functions."

"What does that mean?"

"His body. You're seeing his body."

Fuzzed out. He almost knew where he was but needed something to hold onto.

A cup of coffee. A newspaper. A dark ring on the page.

What's this?

That's cream, Bennie.

Benjamin, sitting on a rock near Rouen, looking at his hands, and talking about the strangeness of guns. And what about airplanes? A giant steel bird bringing them home to their wives. Imagine that.

His wife looked him in the face. *Did you kill anyone?*

I don't know.

How could you not know?

It's like that.

Her hand on his shoulder. *What was the worst thing?*

I don't know.

Death was not the worst. The worst was the realization that he had come to a place without reason and that nothing said or did could keep them from trying to destroy him.

Or was the worst coming home? Standing in the grocery store, weeping at the sight of rows of eggs in their cartons. His wife's innocent mouth. His hand stinging from the blow that sent her reeling across the room. Charlie bent over his homework in his room, seeming so fragile and far away.

Pressure on his hand, or something like pressure on something like his hand.

"Dad? I'm here, Dad."

It was coming from somewhere else in the house, they needed to speak up, to turn on some lights. He was not afraid, but the voices hurt and left him wanting quiet. The door opened, and a crazy woman's voice came in from the street. The newspaper. Hundreds of black dots forming pictures. Advertisements. What looked like a cock and balls but was really a bottle of wine resting between bunches of grapes. Movies. Benjamin put his finger on the page.

What's that?

I don't know. Some kind of war movie.

Hollywood bullshit.

It was true. There was nothing brave about it. You head straight into enemy fire because there's nowhere else to go. Smooth stones underfoot, stumbling you, the ocean behind. The emptiness he felt walking down from the memorial years later, past bathers on towels, stooping to pick up one of those same stones and turn it over in his hand. Back at the hotel, making love to his wife for the last time. The last everything and you don't know it.

Like a lion, like an atomic wind.

Thanksgiving. Sliding extra leaves into the table to accommodate the grandkids. A bird in the centre. A knife in his hand. His son in the kitchen, yelling for him to come. The coffee. The paper. So many unhappy stories. A dead poet. A suicide pact. A body in the snow. Classifieds. Are you a manic, moody, anxious, overdriven, overstressed, time-obsessed, workaholic? No, he was not. He was building the foundation for a house. He was looking up at the skeleton. Struts and beams, thousands of nails holding it all together. How it was the opposite of a bomb falling through a roof. The spray of shrapnel. The booming of church bells. His bride in the aisle. The organ lifting him from his pew to mingle voices with the congregation. His mother in a red dress, his father without his hat, his brothers and sisters, all of them singing. The room leaning. Woody Guthrie on the turntable. An empty glass in one hand, a gun in the other.

"You're going to have to make a decision."

"I know. But I can't . . . "

Can't. The word caught in Louis, both meaningless and pure meaning. He grasped at it as a point of light in the darkness and the voices grew louder. He drew himself towards them, pulling on a rope of light. Brightness and noise swelled around him. An oblong smear, strange with depth. Something familiar in it. He wanted to pass something to this apparition. He knew the sense of it and burrowed into the two wet holes in its middle, straining to hold himself there. The voice gave him one last word, a word that he understood, and he released the rope and tumbled back into the windy darkness, exalted. The light receded to a pinpoint. The voices faded, soft and unlanguaged. For a time he was dragged along, bumping against the surface of things. Then the rope was cut, and his end came all at once, like the starburst of creation, like millions of birds exploding from one tree into flight.

Acknowledgments

I would like to thank my family, as always, for their support, especially my wife Rebecca. Thanks also to Bill Gaston, Lorna Jackson, Peter Liddell, Stephen Ross, Sarah Feldman and my editor Sean Virgo. I am greatly indebted to the Saskatchewan Arts Board and the Colleen Bailey Memorial Fund for their generous assistance.

DEVIN KRUKOFF won the 2005 McClelland & Stewart Journey Prize for his story "The Last Spark". He is a current member of *The Malahat Review*'s editorial board and has been published in literary journals and magazines across Canada. His first book, *Compensation*, was published by Thistledown Press in 2006.

DATE DUE
